THE CHELTENHAM TORSO

JACQUELINE BEARD

By Jacqueline Beard

Constance Maxwell Dreamwalker Mysteries

The Cornish Widow
The Croydon Enigma
The Poisoned Partridge
The Cheltenham Torso

Vinci Books

vinci-books.com

Published by Vinci Books Ltd in 2026

1

Copyright © Jacqueline Beard 2024

The EU GPSR authorised representative is Logos Europe, 9 rue Nicolas
Poussion, 17000 La Rochelle, France
contact@logoseurope.eu

Chapter One

NEVER FORGOTTEN

May 1938

I BRUSH loose earth from my face and wonder how best to explain the grass-coloured graze on my chin. The flowers Elys bound in a ribbon, which I carefully carried from Pebble Cottage, lie bruised and broken in a heap on the ground. I quickly gaze behind me to see if anyone has witnessed my clumsy fall. Jory waits patiently beyond the gate, sitting to attention in the second-hand car he purchased to replace his horse and trap. He is too busy fiddling around with some interior mechanism to have paid any attention to me. My mishap has gone unseen.

Time has forged on since Drake Mallard tried to poison me. My health returned to normal, though my life did not. It took months to assimilate the consequences of Crossley's wickedness and the betrayal of his acolytes, most notably Dolly. My recovery was slow, as was my willingness to accept that Roxy Templeton was my protector, not a foe. I still can't abide her, and I am sure the feeling is mutual. But we are on the same side, so I plaster a smile on my face and hide my dislike whenever our paths cross. It is the least I can do after she saved my life.

A wet nose snuffles against my legs, and I lean forward to tickle Teddy behind his ears to signal my forgiveness. The little spaniel caused my latest tumble. I foolishly let him loose in the churchyard, and he darted before me, sending me off balance. But Teddy is quieter now, his muzzle gently greying with age. He has exceeded me in dog years, though at the ripe old age of thirty-three, I am now a spinster of the parish and metaphorically covered in dust on the highest shelf. Even Cora has admirers, and she is rapidly heading towards her sixties. But Cora has something I don't – sex appeal in spades. Cora is the mistress of flirtation. I wouldn't know how to flirt if someone gave me an instruction manual.

I feel a draught and examine my stockings to find a large rip where I knocked my knee on the gravestone as I fell. I have inadvertently smeared a trickle of blood down my leg, and that, together with my muddy, grazed chin, has made me look a fright. Thank goodness the churchyard is empty; unsurprisingly, as I have picked a day during what must be the wettest May in memory to pay my respects at the little church in St Mawgan in Pydar where Mrs Ponsonby now rests.

Vera Ponsonby passed away almost a year to the day after first revealing her illness. I was the last to know she was unwell. Mrs Ponsonby protected me to the end, only revealing her secret when she knew there could be no cure for the cancer ravaging her body. But at least I got to spend time with her. I will be forever grateful for the chance to show my appreciation while she was well enough to understand. I had taken Mrs Ponsonby for granted, treated her unkindly, and misunderstood the depth of her devotion to me. And when I held her hand on her deathbed and told her I loved her, I truly meant it. She heard me and died knowing I cared.

I gather the handful of bruised violets, her favourite flower, and place the forlorn bundle in a glass vase on her grave. Then, ignoring the sodden ground, I sit by the side, take a brush from my bag, and begin cleaning moss spores from her gravestone. I trace my fingers along the simple inscription and the words I chose to remember her by – 'a good heart, well loved'. Tears fill my eyes as a vision of the past springs to mind. It is summer, and we are walking from Pebble Cottage to the bus stop about to go shopping in Newquay. I am sullen, reluctant to be seen with my guardian, though glad to be allowed out for once. She is excited, pleased to be with me, and looking forward to our day together. Why must I always remember my ingratitude? Why didn't I realise she was my protector, not my captor? The unwanted thoughts sting like jellyfish, and I use the techniques Oliver Fox taught me to slam metal gates down, blocking them out of sight and mind. It works. The image of Mrs Ponsonby changes. She is now in bed, and I am bringing her a cup of tea and reading articles aloud from *Country Life*. She catches my eye and smiles gratefully.

"I thought I'd find you here," says a familiar voice, snapping me out of my reverie. The memories of Vera vanish in a heartbeat, and I gaze at Peter with thinly veiled irritation.

"How did you know I'd be here?" I ask.

He makes a great show of examining his watch. "Where else would you be on Vera's birthday?" he says.

"Fair point," I say, using my stick to get to my feet. Peter looks me up and down, his gaze settling on my chin.

"Well, you've been in the wars. What happened?"

"I fell. Blame Teddy."

"Of course," says Peter, pulling a leaf from my hair. "You're always covered in bruises these days."

"So, I'm clumsier than most. It's not a crime."

"That wasn't what I meant."

"It doesn't matter. I don't care what people think of me."

"Then it's just as well they like you, by and large," Peter says, reaching for my hand. "Finding it tough?" he asks gently. I nod.

"I thought you might. I hoped I'd get to Pebble Cottage before you left, but you know what Mr Whitstable is like – a stickler for time."

"I'm glad you're here," I say. "Really, I am. I thought I'd like to be alone with my thoughts, but they are of the intrusive variety, and I don't much care for them."

"Vera loved you, Connie. And more importantly, she understood you. There were no grudges, I promise, quite the contrary. Vera sang your praises to my mother at every opportunity. She said she couldn't have coped without you."

I choke back a sob. "Don't be kind," I plead.

Peter puts an arm around me and draws me closer, which is enough to open the floodgates. I cry on his shoulder, fat tears dripping down his macintosh. I try to stop, but my shoulders shudder harder as the lump in my throat expands.

"There, there," he says.

I wait for the sobs to subside and try to explain myself. "Mrs Ponsonby left us five years ago, but my heart still hurts."

"I know," says Peter. "But time heals all wounds, eventually."

I hold back a waspy remark. Peter always says this, and it only irritates me, even though he means well. If five years

4

isn't enough to take the edge off my grief, I don't know what will be. I draw a deep breath and change the subject.

"How is your mother?"

"Very well," he says. "And still busy on all things WI. You should join. There's always something to do."

"Me," I exclaim, appalled.

Peter steps backwards in mock horror. "It's a good way to fill your time."

"But they are all old."

"Don't let Mum hear you say that. She's just recruited Sally Howard."

"Sally? I don't believe it. She's a good-time girl in her twenties."

"And also very fond of knitting and local history. Age is no barrier to enjoying time with other people."

"It is for me, so that's a big no thank you."

"You should find a hobby, Connie. Vera would hate to see you cut off from the world like this. I can't remember the last time you visited the hotel, and as for your little cave..." Peter looks sadly towards me, but his words are like a red rag to a bull.

"I don't use the hotel library, as I can't move without bumping into Roxy bloody Templeton. I know I should be beholden to her, but she's arrogant and full of herself. I can't bear her at any cost. And as for my lovely cave, it's bad enough that Drake poisoned me there. But knowing that Dolly conducted her horrid rituals inside is worse. They have spoiled it forever."

"Or you could stop being a victim and make it yours again."

"I thought you were here to cheer me up?"

"I am Connie. I don't mean to hurt you. But I hate to see you like this. Perhaps you should speak to your doctor?"

I narrow my eyes at Peter, and he stares quizzically back. I have never revealed my crush on Kit Maltravers to Peter, and I've no right to expect him to know. But his careless words feel like he is goading me, nevertheless. "He's too busy," I say.

"Too busy to see a patient? I doubt it. But I understand why you might not want to talk to a family friend about your feelings."

"That's exactly it," I say disingenuously. "Anyway, Kit has better things to think about than me."

"Doesn't he just," says Peter wryly.

My mind drifts to Charlotte Napier, who had agreed to wait for Kit to return from the Scottish Islands, where he was working as a locum for his sick uncle. His six-month stint turned into two years, and despite their engagement and her many promises to stay faithful, Charlotte succumbed to the dubious charms of Edgar Sutton. A broken-hearted Kit returned to patch things up but left just as quickly when he realised Charlotte was with child. A hastily arranged marriage soon followed, and Charlotte is now a mother of three. If the housemaid's gossip is true, it is not a happy home. Mrs Ponsonby disliked village gossip, and I try to avoid it in her memory. But that does not extend to Charlotte Napier, who once called me a little crip-ple. Tittle-tattle is fair game where she is concerned, and I actively seek it.

"I'm surprised Kit came back at all. It can't have been easy," says Peter.

"I know. You could have knocked me down with a feather. But his uncle died."

"Did he now? That explains it."

"Partly," I say. "I'd have found somewhere else to live if

it were me. Who wants to bump into a traitorous best friend and a faithless ex-fiancée? He should have gone to London."

Peter grimaces. "There are worse residents there."

He is thinking of Felix Crossley. I am, too. These long years of inactivity feel like the lull before the storm. Crossley threw down the gauntlet in 1933, and we prepared ourselves for chaos. But he quietly vanished. The manifestations slowed, then stopped. Calicum Aureum retreated. Our intelligence was scant, and with nothing more to glean, life returned to something approaching normal. But it left us with a sense of nervousness, on edge and with unfinished business.

I pull my collar higher as the drizzle turns into fat droplets of rain.

"We'd better go," I say. "Jory is waiting."

"No, he isn't. I sent him away. I'll run you home."

"Why?"

"So we have more time to chat and prepare for the meeting."

"It's routine though, isn't it?" I ask, thinking of the twice-yearly get-togethers at the hotel. It is my only remaining contact with the members of the Shining Path. We travelled to London in the earlier years, provided Crossley was away. But things are so quiet that they've risked coming here while Crossley is absent from our lives and focused on other things. Besides, with Roxy in charge, the hotel is well-shielded. Her hotel staff are not as they first appear, with some skilled in psychic defence.

"Yes. Nothing untoward, but we must attend."

I force a smile. "I suppose we must," I say.

Chapter Two

A WARNING

PETER DROPS me at Pebble Cottage, parks the car, and follows me up the pathway. I am not in the mood for visitors, but he presumptively crosses the threshold without an invitation and waltzes into the kitchen as if he owns the place. By the time I reach the end of the hallway, he is chatting with Elys.

"Sit down, Connie. I'll make you a nice cup of tea," she says before waddling towards the kettle. Elys is heavily pregnant with her second child, but the sizeable bump in her belly does not stop her extraordinarily active lifestyle. When she is not helping me at Pebble Cottage, she strides around Porth Tregoryan and often walks over the cliffs to Mawgan Porth. Elys is unstoppable and brings up her young daughter in her indomitable style. Lowenna is only three years old but climbs the hilly village like a mountain goat, following her mother from work to home.

"Where is Lowena?" I ask, noting the orderly kitchen.

"At home with Mum," says Elys. "I needed some peace and quiet today. As much as I love her, Lowenna is going through the 'why' phase, and I'm losing patience. She keeps demanding to know how the baby got inside me and, more importantly, how it's getting out. I'm running out of ways to tell her without revealing things she doesn't need to know."

"Oh dear. She's a little too young for that," says Peter, trying not to focus on the bump.

"That's what Jory says."

"I think Lowenna's bright," I say.

"That's as maybe, but she needs to know when to speak and when to stay quiet."

"The poor little thing is only three," I say protectively. We sometimes play when Lowenna comes over, and she listens to my stories with rapt attention. She is not mine, but I would bite a tiger to keep her safe.

Elys disregards my words. "That little madam is preco-cious. I dread to think how Lowenna will feel when she realises she must share my attention with this one." Elys nods towards her belly, and my thoughts drift selfishly to how I will cope alone while Elys gives birth. She only spent a week away from Pebble Cottage after having Lowenna, which was time enough to create frustrating changes in my life. I didn't mind fending for myself while Elys was away, but Peter and his mother started turning up at odd hours, and after two days, Cora came to stay. I couldn't get a moment alone. Cora still visits almost every weekend, keeping a careful eye on me despite the lack of activity from Calicum Aureum.

I sit at the old kitchen table and stow my stick beneath my chair, accidentally poking it into Mr Moggins, who yowls plaintively.

"Sorry, old boy," I say as he stalks towards me, flashing a disappointed stare. Moggins still proudly bears a tattered left ear, a triumphant scar from youthful fighting, but age has crept up on him now. He is more a pampered house cat than an outdoor warrior these days, and the fur around his face is greying. We are all getting older, yet little has changed. It's as if we are waiting for something to happen, like pupae in a cocoon.

"Drink this," says Elys, handing me a cup of tea. She follows it up with a chunk of Hevva cake.

"I really shouldn't," I say, patting the annoying beginnings of a second belly above my first. I am not overweight, but too much of Elys's cooking has left me needing to lose a few pounds.

"You'll offend me," she warns.

"Hand it over," says Peter. He has already wolfed down his slice and is daintily dabbing crumbs from the plate with his fingertips.

"Eat it," demands Elys. "Peter, you can have another piece."

I nibble a corner with good intentions not to finish the slice. But Hevva cake is one of Elys's specialities, coming as she does, from a long line of fisherfolk. Casting caution to the wind, I take a large bite and another until all that remains are a few crumbs.

Elys beams. She has made it her mission to feed me well and takes her self-imposed job seriously. We fell out a few years ago when I finally told her how much I loathe stargazy pie. Elys took revenge by putting me on an invalid diet of unseasoned chicken, vegetable broth, and tapioca. They were miserable weeks. But Elys is too good a cook to be satisfied with producing a bland diet day after day. She couldn't keep it up, and my expressions of gratitude when she finally relented bordered on toadying.

Elys draws up a chair and joins us, sighing as she crosses her legs and leans back. I can see she is tired, but that won't stop her. In a moment, she will be back at the stove putting together something tasty for my evening meal. She takes a well-earned mouthful of tea and speaks.

"You'll never believe who I saw in Newquay this morning," she says.

Peter shrugs, and I follow suit, neither of us in the mood for guessing games.

"Only Dolly Gray!"

"I start at her mention of my former friend, and Peter frowns. "Are you sure?" he asks.

"Of course. I would know Dolly anywhere."

"Did you speak?" Peter continues, giving Elys the third degree.

"No. I thought I'd better keep quiet, or I would give her a piece of my mind, make no mistake," says Elys, anger flashing from her eyes. Elys is nothing if not loyal, and Dolly's duplicity would have hurt her almost as much as it hurt me.

"How was she?" I ask, torn between hostility and concern.

"Thin," says Elys. "And she didn't look healthy. She'd been sleeping on the streets, if you ask me."

"Surely not." I can hardly bear to think of it. Dolly was always meticulous about her appearance.

"It serves her right," says Elys. "She's one of them."

"By accident, not design," I say.

"That's more like wishful thinking," protests Peter. "Dolly was a traitor from the start."

"She didn't want to be, though. It just happened to her."

"Nonsense," says Peter sternly. "Dolly knew exactly what she was doing."

"It's not that simple," I say, warming to my theme. "Years ago, Dolly told me she wanted to leave but had no choice but to stay in the hotel. I didn't understand what she meant back then, but of course it turned out that they'd installed her as a spy. Still, I always felt she was there under duress. Dolly was kind to me for a very long time."

"Only because she wanted to keep you on her side," says Peter, making no effort to spare my feelings.

"But she was frightened and genuinely hurt by Roxy's evident dislike."

"Think what you wish," says Elys. "Dolly looked a fright."

"We'll have to report it," says Peter. "She's with Calicum Aureum, after all."

"But is she though? Wouldn't they be better off looking after Dolly than letting her roam the streets? And who should we tell? Stella McGregor?"

Peter considers my question. "I don't know," he says. "But if it were up to me, I'd grill Dolly for information. She shouldn't be here. Our friends in the Shining Path have already chased her from Cornwall once."

"Away from her friends and her work. How did the poor thing manage for money?"

Peter looks incredulous. "One wrong word from Dolly and Crossley could have found you. How can you be sympathetic to her? This is not good news, Connie. I don't like it one bit."

"Please don't fuss," I say, feeling a rising panic in my chest. Though I now understand why she did it, I still remember the restrictions Mrs Ponsonby imposed during my earlier years. She kept me cocooned inside, with no access to newspapers and a limited ability to interact with the world. Dolly risked her job to help me break free several times, and I owe her. And if Peter starts worrying, he will want to monitor me. I can't go through that again – not that anyone could ever make me.

"He's not fussing," says Elys, exchanging glances with Peter. My skin crawls. I've seen those sneaky little looks before from people deciding my fate without my participation, and I won't allow it again. I am thirty-three years old and an independent woman, regardless of my inability to walk more than a few hundred yards. I will be the one that decides my future, whatever it may be.

"Don't tell anyone," I plead. "What can Dolly do if she is as down on her luck as you say?"

"Desperation is a terrible thing," says Elys. "God only knows what mayhem she could cause. You can't ignore this, Connie."

I place my head in my hands and consider my options. If I were younger and more impulsive, I would run away and think it through from a distance. But my home is in Porth Tregoryan, and I will stay and fight my corner.

"Then tell them if you must," I say, and, pausing only to collect my stick, I stomp upstairs.

Chapter Three

MEMORIES

NOW THOROUGHLY FED UP, I reject my bedroom in favour of Mrs Ponsonby's. This isn't always an option because of Cora Pennington's frequent visits. I don't mind her using Vera's room. After all, they were great friends long before I was born, but it's nice when I can relax in Mrs Ponsonby's old quarters and commune with her most treasured possessions, most of which are still there in the large closet at the end of her room. I remember the days when I couldn't get inside. If I had a shilling for the many times I tried and failed to break in, I could make a substantial investment. It is too easy now, but no less satisfying. Vera left a large collection of postcards, and other paper ephemera, all of which I find fascinating without knowing why.

I hear a soft thud. Mr Moggins follows me and scrabbles onto the bed with arthritic legs. He rolls over with his belly in the air, inviting a tickle. I do not fall for it. Moggins is partial to an ear scratch and generally well-behaved during delivery. But that does not extend to the foolhardy individual who risks a tummy rub. When Moggins sees a hand moving into his vicinity, he seizes it, claws unsheathed, scratching, clawing, and shredding. Mr Moggins is the Jekyll and Hyde of the cat world.

I rub his nose with my finger and make my way to the closet, settling on the floor near Mrs Ponsonby's box of treasures. She kept all her personal items in a large, carved trunk with a padlock through the hasp, mainly to keep me out. But the key is now mine, and I wear it around my neck at all times, for Mrs Ponsonby still harbours some secrets that I hope to decipher one day.

I know little about the series of photographs stored in an album at the bottom of the trunk. Some are happy family shots, others crowds of evident strangers. I can't identify them, but I'd like to. And then, there's her postcard album full of interesting pictures – an office in London, a drawing penned in childish scrawl signed Daisy, and a colour-tinted card of a Greek monastery with an x in the corner. They must have meant something to Vera. I wish she'd explained it to me.

But she did leave me something more valuable than any amount of money. Mrs Ponsonby handed me the key to her box a few days before she died. I didn't use it until after her funeral. Then, one day, when my grief was so raw that I cried from dawn to dusk, I remembered the key and found my way to her room. I unlocked the box and opened the lid with trepidation. And there, on top of all her treasures, I found a blue envelope addressed to me.

I bite my lip, trying to decide whether I can cope with the flood of emotions that reading the letter always brings. Time has not muted my reactions, probably because I can't think of Mrs Ponsonby without a stomach-churning surge of guilt. A malign thought intrudes in my head, involving a box of matches and the fireplace, but I dismiss it out of hand. I would never burn the letter and worry that my mind could conjure up this appalling scenario. I snatch the letter in defiance and pull it from the envelope. Then I open it and run my fingers along a watermark at the bottom of the page, wondering if it is a flaw in the paper or the tracks of Vera Ponsonby's tears. I take a deep breath and start reading.

Dearest Connie

By the time you see this, I shall be gone. I have lived a fulfilling life with no regrets, and now, as my time approaches, it is only right to tell you more about your childhood. I hope you will understand that I can't reveal everything, but enough time has passed for me to right some wrongs and tell you as much as I dare.

Firstly, I beg your forgiveness for lying while trying to protect you from harm, especially for saying I did not know your parents. It was easier to pretend so you wouldn't ask awkward questions. But I deceived you. I knew them well and lived briefly at Netherwood House with you and your mother in 1909. Sadly, she died the following year.

I expect you would like to know something about her, my dear, so I will draw on my memories with the caveat that there is still much I cannot say. Your mother, Aurora, grew up in the south of England and travelled to London and from there to Suffolk, where she met and married Michael Farrow. She came to work for him, and although there was an age difference, they quickly fell in love. Your mother, Aurora, was petite with olive skin, dark hair, and bottomless brown eyes. Though meek by disposition, she was also courageous. You were her world, and she loved you deeply. But Aurora had secrets. She had unwisely joined an esoteric organisation and entered Felix Crossley's ambit. And I can say no more than that. But though I didn't know it then, Aurora had unique and special powers that she passed on to you.

I realise in hindsight that my failure to acknowledge your particular gift caused more harm than good. And though I am sorrier than I can say, I was never entirely sure whether you possessed the ability to leave your body, and I took the stance that it was best not mentioned. Astral travel is a rare and unique gift. Being under the tutelage of Stella McGregor and her adepts might make your skill appear commonplace. But if I tell you that there are only a tiny number of practitioners worldwide, you may understand how special you are. Cora and I tried our hand at dreamwalking, hoping we could guide you should the need arise. But like thousands of others who studied the path and failed, we could not progress in any meaningful way. Unlike you, we did not have it in our genes. And that, more than anything else, helped our decision to stay quiet and never mention it.

You were five years old when you came to me, my dear, but not from abandonment – quite the contrary. A more loved and wanted little child, I never knew. But evil was afoot, and the only way to keep you safe was through an unconnected third party. Though I had worked for your family, it was under an assumed name, and no one could easily trace me. Your mother and I hatched a plan to pretend I was an old family friend, and I entered the household anonymously. It was an ideal arrangement while it lasted, but things soon changed. An insidious danger put your life in peril while I was staying in the Cotswolds. Cora was engaged to be married, and the time was right to move on. We closed our detective agency, Cora married Andrew Pennington, and I moved to Cornwall to care for you. We couldn't trust anyone, so Cora and I parted ways permanently. We did not speak for several decades, as you know.

That, my dear, is as much as I can say except for one thing. My father was a stern Victorian gentleman who believed children should be seen and not heard. I have grown up in his shadow, always keeping my feelings to myself. But that does not mean I lack them. I regret not having the capacity to show you how much I cared for you. No child should grow up uncertain of their place in the world, and my inability to express myself has left you with childhood wounds that I wish I could go back and mend. I have never regretted leaving London behind. You have grown from a nervous child into a beautiful, accomplished young woman who has never let her injury hold her back. I am truly proud of you, Connie. It has been my privilege and pleasure to watch you grow. And I know you will play a vital part in the fight against Calicum Aureum.

Be brave as always and remember me sometimes.

Your ever-loving guardian,
Vera Ponsonby.

It is no good. I am pulling ugly faces and sobbing like a banshee by the time I reach the bottom of the page. I should not have re-read the letter. It hurts too much. I wish I could go back in time and see Mrs Ponsonby once more and tell her how much I care. And that thought suddenly creates another. Is it possible to see Vera again? I have astral travelled backwards in time before. It was tricky and fraught with uncertainty, but I ought to be able to do it in theory.

I place my hands over my face, feeling like a naughty schoolgirl as I mull the idea over. I have not walked through walls alone in years. Not even accidentally. The last time was about six months after I left the convalescent home after Drake Mallard tried to poison me, and nobody knew I had tried. Mrs Ponsonby had made me promise not to attempt dreamwalking unless supervised by Stella or one of her allies. I agreed and trained with Stella in London before the meetings moved to Cornwall. Over time, our sessions petered out, and I was not sorry. It was a dreary time of drills and rotes, mainly theoretical, with the occasional opportunity to practice. But it was not like running over the Cornish cliffs, uninhibited and free as a bird. How I miss those days.

And suddenly, I am struck with the fear that I might have forgotten how to astral travel. I remember how often I would fall into an unintended dreamwalk. I could not help myself. Perhaps it does not happen now because my powers have gone. The thought chills me. Anxiety stokes my heart, sending flutters of tension through my soul. For a moment, a black cloud of despair weighs me down. I agreed to their plans to keep me safe and promised not to test Crossley by stepping onto the astral plane. But I never considered losing my powers forever. I cannot. I would rather die. How strange that it has taken me four years to realise I am not whole anymore. Without the freedom to move outside my body, I am not me. I must make a change.

I rise from the floor and settle on Vera's bed. Hers lacks the sea view, and the tall mirror on her dressing table obscures the window. But the large oval glass gives me a useful focal point as I do not have a candle to hand. Ignoring all my promises, I narrow my eyes and concentrate. Nothing happens. I try again. Moggins stirs and settles beside me, disturbing my thoughts. Three times a charm. Staring until my eyes cross, I finally feel a sense of weightlessness. I glance at my hand but cannot tell if it is on or in the mattress. One more try, and for a second, I am falling. But then the bedroom door flies open. Teddy launches onto the bed, and Mr Moggins yowls, arching his back as he makes a porcupine impression. I never find out if I was heading for the astral plane. Urgent pet management is the order of the day, and as I separate the warring animals, my concentration vanishes into the ether. I give it up as a bad job and head downstairs.

Chapter Four

AN ORDERLY MEETING

I AM NOT in the mood for a meeting when Peter arrives at Pebble Cottage to collect me. Not even catching up with old friends makes me relish the Shining Path members' twice-yearly get-together. Peter and I had initially arranged to meet at the hotel, which Stella may have influenced to ensure I went. My recent participation has been half-hearted at best, which is one of the many reasons we now meet in Cornwall instead of the capital.

"Come on then," says Peter, eyeing his watch.

"Wait a moment. I'll need my stick."

"Where is it? I'll fetch it for you."

"No need," I say, grabbing the banister and hauling myself upstairs. The devil is in me this morning. I have several sticks, one in the living room and the other in the coat stand, directly in front of Peter's eyes. But I won't let him hurry me and elect to take the fetching silver-topped version gathering dust in the corner of my wardrobe instead. I keep this stick for high days and holidays, but as I never go anywhere, it spends most of the time in the dark.

The tips of Peter's ears are pink by the time I return, and he is shuffling from foot to foot as if that will speed me up. "Do shake a leg, Connie. We are already late."

I gaze pointedly at my built-up shoe.

"Sorry. I didn't mean that," he mutters.

I leisurely fasten my jacket and grab Peter's arm. "Off we go then," I say.

The relief on his face is palpable as we slowly stroll towards the hotel. I have stopped playing up and pick up my pace now we are outside. We are close to the entrance when we hear a car horn. Peter remains calm, but I jump like a startled cat. Clutching my chest, I turn around to see Cora take the corner on three wheels while distractedly waving to us. I cover my eyes with my hands and peek through my fingers. Cora's driving is a terrifying thing to behold. She has no sense of danger for herself, her passengers, or the innocent public at large. She screeches into the hotel car park, leaps from her soft-top car and strides towards us.

"Connie, Peter, how lovely to see you. Two weeks is too long."

"Nice car," says Peter admiringly.

"Isn't it? It's fresh from the factory, too."

Peter smiles. "Can I take a look?"

"Drive it if you like," offers Cora, dangling the keys.

"I'll take you up on that another time." Peter abandons me and walks towards the vehicle, peering inside as if it were the most precious object in the world.

"Will you look at that leather," he says appreciatively. "What is it, Cora? I've never seen anything like it."

"You wouldn't," she replies. "It's a Flying Eight and one of only half a dozen in this design. But it passed quality checking and will soon go into production."

"Then how have you managed to get your hands on one?"

Cora winks. "Friends in high places," she says.

I wrinkle my nose. "New car smell. Disgusting. Sorry, but I can't get excited about a lump of metal. Edgar's fascination for fast cars put me off."

"Nasty little man," says Cora. "I can't bear him."

"I don't know anyone who can," agrees Peter, tearing his gaze from the car. "Certainly not Charlotte's poor parents."

I spare a second to think of Colonel and Mrs Napier, whom I have known for years. They are much nicer than their daughter and deserve better, although a sneaky part of me can't help blaming them for spoiling her as a child.

Cora glances at her watch, and I note the sparkling jewels around the dial. She smiles serenely. "Chop, chop," she says. We are late, but Cora speaks calmly, and a sphinx-like smile never leaves her face. Smart cars, expensive jewellery, signs of contentment – something has happened to Cora, and I bet it involves a man.

I slowly approach the hotel, remembering all the times I have passed through the doors on my way to the library, my former sanctuary. Those days of passing Mrs Ponsonby's copies of *Country Life* to Dora and curling up with a good book by the fire are long gone. I didn't appreciate what I had back then, those innocent days of youth.

"Come on, Connie," says Peter.

"Go ahead. Let them know we're here." Cora gestures him onward and hooks her arm through mine. "Tough week?" she asks perceptively.

"Yes, a little."

"Still missing Vera?"

I bite my lip. "Always."

"We'll go for a drive later. Pick up a nice bottle of wine and cheer ourselves up."

"If you like." I sound apathetic because I am. I am not a great drinker, and alcohol is not a cure-all. Nor even a cure any. I don't mind a glass with dinner, but that's my limit. Still, I don't articulate this. It makes me sound dull and is doubtless one of the reasons I am still alone.

"Look. There's Roxanne," says Cora, waving ahead.

My heart sinks as I realise I must be nice. I plaster on my best smile and follow Cora.

"Roxy," I say warmly. "How are you?"

"About to lose my patience," she curtly replies. "How hard must it be to get two dozen people to arrive on time? Really. This is intolerable."

"Who are you waiting for?" asks Coralie breezily, as if we are not the best part of ten minutes late ourselves.

"Marjorie Morgan and Roderick Grove, amongst others."

"Ah. VIPs," says Cora.

Roxy frowns. "I don't like these new-fangled acronyms."

I smile sympathetically. I don't like them either. But Cora spends much of her time in London fraternising with bright young things. I sometimes think she is too trendy for Cornwall, and then I remember she has been very good to me, and I must not judge her. Life is too short.

"Ah, I take it back. There they are." Roxy's face lightens as she powers towards the hotel door.

"Let's go inside and sit down," says Cora.

"Dining room?"

"I suppose so. They haven't said otherwise."

We make our way through double doors and into the room where I once danced with Kit Harrington. I can almost smell his cologne as I remember how good he made me feel until the moment his horrible girlfriend humiliated me. The short-lived warm feeling evaporates at the thought of that night, and I examine my surroundings as a distraction.

Stella McGregor is sitting behind a covered table at the top of the room with two empty spaces either side. Everyone else has taken positions around a clutch of circular tables in front. But there are markedly fewer people than last year, and Oliver Fox is nowhere in sight.

I sit and am stowing my stick under the chair when I hear the clack of metal-toed boots on the wooden floor. Three uniformed officers head towards Stella. She greets them and points to a table close to hers. Cora and I exchange glances. Peter looks perplexed.

I peer at the officers, two slightly built, fair-haired men, sharp-suited and distinguished, the other a burly, florid-faced chap whose uniform has bunched over his fulsome torso. He reminds me of someone.

Roxy enters and claps her hands. "Quiet now," she says as if she has caught us in some act of childish disobedience. I refrain from mentioning that nobody was actually talking until she came in.

"Over to you," Roxy says, pointing at Stella before sitting with her back to me.

Stella gets to her feet and coughs. She starts speaking, but I am not listening. The penny has dropped, and I have just realised I am standing in the presence of a face from the past, albeit one that is vastly different. The shambolic, burly officer is none other than Hilda Grady.

Chapter Five

THE PSYCHIC DEFENCE UNIT

PETER PRODS ME. He has been watching me with my mouth hanging open like a starving guppy.

"What's wrong?" he asks.

"It's Hilda." I tilt my head towards her.

Now Peter's eyes start. "What's he doing here?" he whispers.

Cora puts her finger to her mouth and narrows her eyes. We listen.

"Thank you for coming today," says Stella McGregor, her loud, proud voice projecting across the room. I gaze admiringly. Stella is a strong, confident woman who could wrestle a tiger and still draft a dissertation on the finer points of psychic defence before supper time. "You will notice we are much depleted in number."

I nod. I had noticed, and judging by the similar responses across the room, I was not alone.

"We have let things drift. When Crossley went to ground., we relied on our intelligence and spent less time and resources on defence. I do not regret that decision. It was right at the time. But things have moved on."

I sit up and pay more attention. This meeting is shaping up differently than those in the past. Stella is prickly, her eyes darting this way and that as if eager to get on with it. She has given no jocular introduction, no positively framed roundup of our yearly activity. She stands, her mouth firmly set as if holding in the words that will put us on a different path. What is going on? Has something changed?

Stella reacts as if she has read my thoughts.

"May I introduce you to Brigadier Gus Hetherington-Shipley of the psychic division, Captain Clive Parker and Lieutenant Harold Grady, both of Number 1 Special Defence Unit. Gentlemen, kindly deliver your briefing."

Silence falls over the room. We barely breathe. The Brigadier and Harold advance to the top table. Harold leans over and picks up a large, framed photograph, which he places where everyone can see it. I involuntarily gasp at the sight of Felix Crossley, bald, bad, and dangerous to know. He lurks before us in long, flowing robes, wearing a malign expression. Harold says nothing. His face remains impassive. He reaches down again for another picture, this time smaller, and inserts it directly in front of the original. It is Crossley again, but a dapper-looking version in a well-cut beige suit and matching fedora. He looks ordinary, like any other man going about his daily business. I wonder what point they are making, but all becomes clear when Brigadier Hetherington-Shipley takes the stand.

"This is Felix Crossley," he says, brandishing a telescopic pointer. "I expect you will find this picture more familiar. He jabs the pointer too firmly at the larger picture, and the frame wobbles precariously. The brigadier pauses, waiting to see whether it will fall, but it does not. "Crossley is a chameleon. He is a complex man, fixated on self-indulgent esoteric matters and base carnal desires. But that is not all. Crossley is quick-thinking and well connected. He is charming, manipulative, and convincing – a perfect purveyor of intelligence.

Furthermore, Crossley mixes with the great and good." The brigadier stands, hands on hips, waiting for a reaction. Stella shakes her head. "Please elaborate," she says coldly.

"Might I?" asks Harold, noting Stella's evident impatience.

The brigadier nods, and I wait with bated breath, trying not to visualise Harold's alter ego, Hilda, shuffling around the Worple Road kitchen, making dinner. He catches my eye across the room and smiles. Rumbled.

"As the brigadier was saying, Crossley has a remarkable ability to ingratiate himself. He is eloquent and able to mix at the highest levels. This might make him dangerous, but harnessed in the right way, some have found him useful."

"For what?" asks an insipid young man I don't recognise.

"We are on the brink of war," says Harold. "And Crossley is in the thick of it."

SILENCE FALLS ACROSS THE ROOM. Peter shuffles uncomfortably. Half the audience examine the floor, and the other half stares uncomfortably through the window out to sea. Anything to distract themselves from what we all know, but everyone ignores. The spectre of war is moving towards us like a ghost ship of smugglers' past. We are all doomed, but only if we admit the unthinkable. It might pass us by if we go about our business and nobody mentions it.

Nobody moves, nobody speaks. Harold reads the mood and coughs into his hand.

"The prospect of war is nipping at our heels," he says. "Sadly, it is inevitable."

"What's that to do with Crossley?" snaps Jory, who has arrived with Elys and stands quietly at the back of the room as if positioned to make a quick escape. Elys has always been party to our discussions. She knew too much about my nocturnal wanderings for Mrs Ponsonby to leave her out. But Jory is a more recent participant. He followed Elys one night, thinking she was up to no good when she left their house with little explanation. His relief at finding her with us did not temper his concern at the danger she might face should she cross paths with Crossley. Nor did he accept the notion of astral travel. But Jory is loyal and robust. Though on the periphery, we know we can call on him if times get tough. He will fight to the bitter end regardless of his beliefs.

"A good question," mumbles Harold. "Let me tell you with the usual caveat. This information is classified and must not leave this room."

"Whatever you say," drawls Jory, placing a protective arm around Elys, who is as white as a sheet. We have recently spoken about the prospect of war. Or rather, she has. I cut the conversation dead and changed the subject. There is time enough to worry if it happens. I prefer to take an optimistic approach.

"I'll take that as a yes," says Harold, loosening his tie. "As I said, Crossley has many character traits which make him suitable for certain operations. The brigadier raises an eyebrow and shoots him a warning glance, but Harold continues. You all know the Nazis are manoeuvring in Germany, agitating for political change, and targeting certain racial groups. They mean to rule by terror, control by force, and defend their foul beliefs through fear. But you may not know that esoteric forces guide certain influential leaders among them. Heinrich Himmler is in thrall to satanism and has indulged in black magic rites. Rudolf Hess makes his judgements based on astrology and divination. Crossley is renowned for his dark rituals, not only in Britain but also abroad. They have heard of his astral travel ability and believe they could put it to military use. Crossley has met their top brass several times to discuss training."

"Traitor," hisses Marjorie Morgan.

"But is he?" asks Captain Parker, getting to his feet. He strides towards Harold and whispers in his ear. Harold stands down, and the captain speaks again. "Crossley befriended the Nazis, gained their trust and passed on the merest sliver of understanding. But not a single member of the Nazi party can walk through walls – absolutely no one. I don't believe a single German national possesses the power. You don't need me to tell you what a rare and unique gift you have."

"Are you saying Crossley is a double agent?" asks the young man who spoke before.

"If he was, he isn't now," says Captain Parker. "Things have changed."

"What things?" Stella asks, impatiently clenching her hands, irritated by the slow passing of information. She purses her lips and ups the ante, drumming her fingers on the table. I sense a deep frustration. Stella has not been party to this intelligence and feels aggrieved.

"Crossley's allegiances are now closer to home," says Parker. After spending the last five years dabbling in and out of active service, he has left Munich for the last time."

"Why?" demands Stella.

"Crossley's common-law wife gave birth to his son last year."

"Last year?" The words explode from Stella's mouth. "How did I not know this?" she demands, a red flush creeping up her neck and flaring across her cheeks.

The brigadier coughs. "We didn't consider it necessary."

"But the man is so bloody unpredictable. Anything could happen. You should have told us."

"Perhaps," says Parker. "But fatherhood is a great leveller. We were never entirely sure whose side he was on. A quiet family life is probably a step in the right direction."

Stella draws herself to her full height. "What is the bloody point of having a psychic defence division just to recruit the biggest threat to our safety as some sort of self-appointed spy?"

"It wasn't like that," snaps the brigadier. "Crossley did volunteer, but his appointment was unofficial. He asked if he could help, and we agreed. He'd still be doing it now were it not for the child."

"Words fail me," says Stella, shaking her head. "We are working to fight Crossley and his ilk while you casually employ him."

"No money changed hands." The captain speaks slowly, emphasising every word.

"Crossley is completely untrustworthy." Stella mimics the slow, deliberate tone. "The man has no morals."

"Well, my good lady, the deed is done, and it's too late for recriminations."

Stella's eyes narrow to slits. "Don't take that tone with me."

Harold stands again. "Now, now," he says. "We really must work together."

"I thought we were," says Stella bitterly. "Things might

have gone better with a bit of information sharing. I can't believe you kept this from us. Where is this bloody child then?"

Harold takes a deep breath, then gazes at Captain Parker for reassurance. He nods surreptitiously. "In London," he says.

"For crying out loud!" Cora stands, hands on hips and stares at the captain in amazement.

"Oh, come now. It's only a child."

"I don't care if it's a duck-billed platypus. We should have known." Cora exchanges sympathetic glances with Stella, who is incandescent with rage.

"Very well," concedes the captain. "There were security issues to consider."

"Don't blame this on the Official Secrets Act," says Stella. "You had a choice."

"Be that as it may." The brigadier chews his lip and ponders. "Look, we couldn't tell you. Please accept it. Things have changed now Crossley is back in London."

Roderick Grove shrugs and looks between Stella and the brigadier with an air of conciliation. "Perhaps it doesn't matter as much as it might appear. Crossley has lost all interest in Miss Maxwell," he says.

"Crossley has necessarily faded into the background while helping British intelligence," says the brigadier. "And that is why he has left Miss Maxwell alone. But Crossley will get bored before long. He will want to do something meaningful. And with no cash gain coming his way from intelligence, he sees little point in continuing to help."

"And probably never did," says Cora. "You can be sure there was an ulterior motive for any help given to you."

"You don't know the type of man we are dealing with."

"I ruddy well do." Cora puts her hands on her waist and

fixes the brigadier with a steely eye. "Haven't you forgotten I did a bit of double-agenting myself?"

"We're going around in circles," mutters Captain Parker.

"Then I'll spell it out." Brigadier Hetherington-Shipley spits the words before taking a deep breath. "Crossley is out of our hands. He has made his feelings clear. We never altogether trusted him and now he is bored and could go rogue in a heartbeat. But we know he intends to spend time with his son. We must assume he is in London and will stay there for some time."

"Then what in God's name are we doing here?" Stella's face has turned from red to puce. She looks as if she is about to vomit.

"He won't stride into your headquarters while you're in Cornwall if that's what you're thinking."

"How do you know? You've said yourself that he's unpredictable. I would never have left the building unattended if I knew danger was afoot. Whatever happened to us working together?"

The brigadier ignores her and continues. "Crossley is off the books. And as such, he is likely to return to his former ways. God knows, he never stopped meddling in the occult. He just kept his name off the front pages for a while. But his old haunts are all over London, and unless fatherhood has tempered his ways, we can expect more of the same."

Cora stands again. "What woman in her right mind has let that animal impregnate her?"

The three military men exchange knowing looks.

"Well?"

Harold glances across the room. I catch his eye, and he shrugs uncertainly. "Matilda Donnelly," he says. Cora starts.

Her eyes widen as she struggles for words. "You mean Tilly Donnelly?"

"Yes, I believe she goes by the diminutive of Tilly."

"Dear God," Cora says, then turns and grabs me by the wrist. "Come on, Constance. We're leaving."

"But…"

"Get your stick, now. Don't argue."

"I can't. They haven't finished."

"You can, and you bloody well will."

"I don't understand. "What does it matter about a tiny baby, anyway? And who is Tilly Donnelly?"

Cora leans towards me and whispers in my ear. "You've met her mother many times. She goes by the name of Carrie Yates."

Chapter Six

OLD ENEMIES

CORA MARCHES me back to Pebble Cottage in stunned silence. She flings open the door and practically pushes me inside. I remove my coat and hang it in the hallway, stroking Teddy's ears as he rushes to greet me.

"Leave the dog alone," she says. "We need to talk."

My heart sinks as I recognise a side of Cora I have never seen before. She is usually the epitome of fun and glamour. This must be the firmer side she employed during her private investigator life. Cora strides towards the kitchen, and I follow slowly behind. The implications of her announcement are shattering. If Carrie Yates is Crossley's mother-in-law, Bosula is strictly off-limits to me. The thought of never again spending time in Cormorant House with the bohemian artists and my dear friend Mary is unbearable. This awful news cannot be true. I fling myself on a chair and put my head in my hands.

Cora ignores me and sets a pan of water on the stove. She is still silent five minutes later when the pan boils and spills onto the hob.

"Damn it," she says, pouring water into a teapot and placing it in the middle of the table. She smiles at me as she retrieves a plate of biscuits. "Ready to talk?" she asks.

I nod mutely. I am not, but it won't make any difference. I am about to get a debriefing of sorts.

"Have you ever met Tilly?" asks Cora.

"No. I didn't know she existed. I mean, Carrie discussed her family but never mentioned her daughter by name, and if she had, it wouldn't have meant anything. But thinking of Carrie fraternising with Crossley makes me sick to the stomach. She must have terrible taste."

Cora sips her tea. "I agree. They must have met. It's inconceivable to think otherwise."

"Thank God they know nothing about my ability to astral travel and my connection to the Shining Path. I have never mentioned Crossley. Not even to Mary."

"Mary isn't the problem. It's Bosula. Crossley could turn up at any time. You know you can never return, don't you?"

I shake my head. "Never is too long. I know I cannot visit soon, and that is fine. I have no plans, and Mary is otherwise occupied."

Cora raises an eyebrow but does not argue. "Have a garibaldi," she says, gesturing to the plate.

"No, thank you."

"Go on. You've barely eaten today."

I sigh and reach for a biscuit I do not want. Anything to move things on. "Stop prevaricating, Cora. What are you about to tell me?"

"I'd like to go away for a while," she says.

"Go ahead. Enjoy yourself. Elys will take care of things."

"When I say I, I really mean we."

"Me? You want me to come with you?"

"Yes, Connie. I think it's best."

"Sorry. No. I'd rather stay here."

"It's not safe, my dear."

"Nowhere is safe. The brigadier made that loud and clear."

"Yes, and he's a large part of my decision to move on."

"Don't you trust him?" I ask.

"Hardly, after today's shocking news."

"You really didn't know?"

"No. And judging by Stella's reaction, neither did she."

The front door slams, and Moggins jumps into my lap.

"Get a grip," I say to the elderly cat, stroking his head as footsteps march up the hallway. The door swings open, and Peter strides inside, his face like thunder.

"What is it?" asks Cora.

"I think the war they were predicting has just broken out. But not with Nazi Germany."

"I beg your pardon?"

"Stella apparated in front of the brigadier when he was in full flow. Marjorie and Roderick soon followed. The room is in uproar. It's one thing knowing about astral travel and another to see it."

"There's nothing to see, Peter. Their bodies don't go anywhere."

"Precisely. But three unrousable, fully grown adults slumped comatose in their seats is an insult too far for a pompous fool like the brigadier. He flounced from the room after telling anyone who would listen that he would have no more truck with the Shining Path. It's a disaster."

"How can he threaten that?" asks Cora. "There is no psychic defence division without Stella. Barely anyone else has anything but theoretical knowledge."

"I'm not so sure," says Peter. "Harold says their division has compiled a list."

"What sort of a list?" He has piqued my interest, and I am on tenterhooks wondering if I am on it.

"Names and locations as far as they know of anyone who possesses the ability to dreamwalk. Obviously, the Shining Path has the greatest numbers, closely followed by Crossley and his minions, but there are others like you, Connie, spread across the world. No more than fifty, I believe, and not all identified. The psychic division tracks everyone they find, just in case. The brigadier would like nothing more than to recruit you all to his division, especially if the Nazis push any harder. Their expectations of a worldwide war are truly frightening, and they will do whatever it takes to defend this land."

"Where did you get this nonsense from?" Cora's handsome face sets in a frown.

"Harold," says Peter quietly.

"When?"

"Just now. He stayed behind until the captain sent his batman to fetch him. He looked me out, Cora. Took me into the courtyard and told me."

"Surely this must be top secret?"

"That's what I'm worried about. Harold is fond of you, Connie. I think it's a covert warning."

"Don't be silly," I say, amused at Peter's stricken face. "I can't even walk more than a few hundred yards. What use would I be?"

"Connie, don't be obtuse. You can travel miles and go backwards and forwards in time. I can't think of a greater military asset. Especially now that Crossley has returned to his previously selfish form. They will no doubt want to keep a close eye on him as well as the warmongers. It's all very well for them to gloat about Crossley being a double agent, but who's to say he isn't working for the other side? No, this is bad news, and Stella's reaction hasn't helped."

"If I know Stella, it's a show of power," says Cora.

"There's nothing clever about abandoning your body just to make a point."

"That's not fair," I say, inexplicably feeling the need to defend Stella. "She left her body surrounded by friends and sympathisers."

"Except for the three conscription-happy military men," says Peter.

"Don't include Harold in that," I snap. "He is a good man or woman, depending upon his assignment."

"I'm not arguing with you," says Peter in as firm a voice as I've ever heard. He turns to Cora. "She's not safe here."

Cora nods. "I was saying the same thing when you arrived."

"Operation Bear Claw?"

"No. Not yet. That's too extreme. We must be out of sight but not necessarily far away."

"I'll come too," says Peter, but I ignore him, my cheeks flushing with a sudden burn of rage.

"Why are you talking about me as if I weren't here? I am thirty-three years old. I will do as I see fit. And what in the world is Operation Bear Claw?"

Cora sighs. "Nothing for you to worry about, and I am not trying to patronise you by saying that. It's just not worth explaining. Too unlikely. I know this sort of talk makes you cross, Connie. But we are living in dangerous times. You have gone from being a young girl with an extraordinary but largely unknown talent to being a hugely desirable military asset. You do understand, don't you? Porth Tregoryan simply isn't safe. And I'd rather not stay in Cornwall now we know about Tilly Donnelly."

I lower my head and reach for Teddy's ears. He looks up and rests his chin on my knee. For a split second, a vision of Jim flashes through my mind – nothing tangible, just a snip of his face, stubbled and careworn. I have never seen him like that. It can't be a memory.

"Connie?" Cora cocks her head and looks at me, waiting for a response. I shake the vision away and concentrate.

"Surely you don't think they'll come for me?" I ask.

Peter and Cora exchange looks. "I don't think they'll frog-march you off to Porton Down for experimentation if that's what you mean. But you will come under pressure to help. And I don't trust them. Saying no may not be an option."

"But I must help if war is coming."

"They may pit you against Crossley, which is too risky. Or, God forbid, trust him to work alongside you. I'm sure you can help the war effort, Connie. But quietly and safely from the sidelines. Please pay heed to this. I trusted the psychic defence division until the brigadier took over. But not now. He might be an experienced military tactician, but he doesn't understand astral travel and its limitations. Nor does he care tuppence for the danger you are in while moving unprotected on the astral plane. He is the sort of man who would be indifferent to a bit of collateral damage. There are better ways for you to assist. Truly."

I look up, trying to ignore the tears pricking at the back of my eyes as a wave of sadness lays me low. They are right. War is coming, and I am not safe here. I must leave my little cottage, my piece of Cornish paradise, and worst of all, the lonely resting place of my guardian, Vera Ponsonby. And I know this because she would insist on it if she were still alive. I will leave if only to honour her memory. "Where are we going?" I ask.

Chapter Seven

CHELTENHAM BOUND

"IS THIS IT?" I try not to frown as the car pulls up outside an unprepossessing semi-detached property on Old Bath Road in Cheltenham.

Cora removes a piece of paper from her bag and matches the address to the slate plate. "Yes. Two four six. Here we are," she says, beaming.

Peter opens the door, no doubt intent on doing the gentlemanly thing and aiding Cora from the car. But the cat box he carries on his lap impedes him, pinning him in place. I would help, but I am likewise squashed by the weight of a fidgety cocker spaniel who has grown heavier by the mile. We sit like two beached whales until the driver escorts Cora from the car. She instructs him to take our bags, and only then does she open my door and take Teddy's lead. I flex my legs, grapple with my stick, and make way for Elys, who is sitting between Peter and me and has travelled the last mile with a face like thunder. She does not like motor vehicles at the best of times, nor is she pleased about leaving her husband and baby in Cornwall for what might be a prolonged period. But Elys is dutiful and thinks her place is with me, no matter how difficult her personal circumstances are. I didn't ask her to come, nor did I expect it. But Elys insisted. I am more grateful than I can say, but we may fall out if she spends the next few weeks taking on the mantle of a burning martyr. These are strange times for us all.

Peter is the last to vacate the car. He eases himself from the vehicle and temporarily places the cat basket on the ground. Mr Moggins balefully stares back with a contemptuous look. He has never set a paw in a cat box before and has always been allowed free rein at Pebble Cottage on the rare occasions we are away. There has always been someone to pop in and feed him, and I'm sure Isla Tremayne would have been more than willing. But we don't know how long we will be away from home, which is too great an imposition, especially as her son has chosen to join us.

Things have moved quickly since the brigadier left last week, compared to our earliest inklings of war. We were shocked when the Nazis first moved into Austria. But nothing much happened after that. The government didn't intervene; any earlier panicking quickly subsided and didn't affect the price of fish in sleepy Cornwall, so we carried on as usual. But since Mrs Ponsonby's death, I have taken a greater interest in the newspapers, and they are full of speculation over whether this annexation might embolden the Nazis. Could they invade another country? I try not to think about it, but yesterday's article in the *Cornwall Advertiser* gave me a restless night with the writer openly suggesting the conscription of our young men to the war effort. And, though no longer a spring chicken, that would undoubtedly mean Peter. It is a worrying thought, and I am glad he is with me. Who knows where this might lead? I will enjoy his company while I can.

"Right," says Cora, examining her paper again. "Key under the rabbit," she reads. "What rabbit?"

Peter shrugs, and Elys ignores her while leaning against the wall with her hip defiantly jutted out. I smile and catch her eye, but she moodily adjusts her gaze elsewhere.

Cora stares from one of us to the other, narrowing her eyes. "Anyone care to help?" she drawls.

I manoeuvre towards the front door and cast my eye around the small front garden. Teddy lunges towards the flowerbed, and I spot a fallen statuette. Squatting, I turn it over. "Looks like this was it," I say, noting the resemblance to Beatrix Potter's whimsical creation, Peter Rabbit.

"Well, that's a good start," says Cora. "Where on earth is the key?"

Peter joins me, examines his namesake statue, and loses no time getting his hands dirty as he feels among the plants and soil. It doesn't take him long to find the solid, shiny key. He quickly opens the door, and we file inside.

"Better put the kettle on," says Peter, waving a folded note.

Elys raises an eyebrow in a do-it-yourself kind of way. Peter wisely does not press the point but waits for Cora to close the door before releasing Moggins into his new surroundings. I unclip Teddy's leash, and he joins Moggins in exploring the house.

"Best get unpacked," says Elys, grabbing my case.

"No need. I can do it," I say, eyeing a scuff mark that was not there before the driver so generously lugged the cases to the door.

"No. Stay here. It's my job." Elys stalks off with my case and hers, feet stomping unnecessarily loudly on the stairs.

"But we haven't chosen our rooms yet." Cora's voice

trails away as she realises Elys isn't listening. "Elys will decide, I suppose," she continues.

"Hardly," I say. "We know there are only three bedrooms. Peter will have the small one, and Elys and I will share. There's not a lot of choice for anyone."

"Sorry, dear," says Cora. "But the rent for a four-bed was astronomical, and I don't know how long we will be here. Peter dear, will you put the kettle on before we die of thirst?"

Peter glances at his watch. "Not yet. Give it another fifteen minutes, and I'll fix you a brew."

"Why? Have you some more important task to perform?" I ask.

"No. But we'll soon have visitors, and offering them a drink is good manners, even in their own home."

"Oh. I wasn't expecting the Prices?" Cora frowns.

"So, they say." Peter offers her the note he has carried since collecting it from the doormat.

"Oh dear. They want to take something from the shed. Sounds like a tall tale to me." Cora purses her lips as she speaks.

"Why is that?" I ask.

"They clearly want to check us out. It's obvious," says Cora. "As I would myself under similar circumstances. A pity. I would have liked to settle in and take a short walk, but I suppose it can't be helped."

"Just don't expose them to Elys," I say. "She's not in the mood for people."

Cora takes her car keys from the hired driver, expressing regret that he must now catch a train from Cheltenham Spa to get home. She does not sympathise enough to offer him a lift but hands over a generous tip. I leave Peter and Cora to it and navigate my way around the house, which doesn't take long. It is alright as houses go, but 246 Old Bath Road is even smaller than Pebble Cottage, with a tiny kitchen and no space for a table. Elys will not be pleased. Nor will she appreciate sharing a bedroom with me instead of Jory. But having sneaked a quick look while Elys was furiously unpacking as if her life depended on it, I feel reassured at the size of the bedroom and the fact that the two single beds are reasonably far apart.

By the time I return downstairs, Cora is relaxing on the couch while Peter lurks by the living room window, waiting for our unwanted visitors. After a while, he loses concentration, but Teddy is on high alert and starts barking as the middle-aged couple advance down the pathway. I swing into action and open the door before he can cause too much commotion.

"Do come in," I say, sweeping the Prices into the living room.

Cora stands to greet them, offers them a seat, and asks Peter to do the honours with the teapot. He obliges with a smile while I take the only unoccupied seat.

"I'm Cyril", says the man in an accent-free voice. "And this is my wife, Ida. I hope you don't mind the intrusion. I've left my tools in the shed, and they haven't equipped our new rental property properly, have they, my dear?" He turns to his wife, smiling benevolently. She pats his arm.

"No. It's not a patch on our home. I do wonder if we've done the right thing."

"It won't be for long," he says, and I wonder why they've bothered to let their house out at all. Too polite to ask, I would have died wondering, but Cora has no such inhibitions.

"Where are you renting?" she asks.

"In Charlton Kings," says Cyril, randomly gesturing in the air. Cora stares blankly.

"Do you know Cheltenham?" he asks.

"Yes. Reasonably well, although it's been the best part of three decades since I last visited," says Cora. "But I spent most of my time at the school, so my geographical knowledge is limited.

I try to withhold my surprise. Cora said nothing about a previous visit when she proposed we visit Cheltenham. She had suggested three southern towns and allowed Peter and me to choose. He wanted Chippenham, and I preferred Bath, but as we couldn't agree, Cora got the casting vote with Cheltenham. We had assumed she selected it randomly, not because she'd had previous connections. I should have known better. Cora does nothing by accident and has become increasingly like Mrs Ponsonby the more responsibilities she acquires.

"Fancy that," says Cyril. "What school were you at?"

"The Ladies' College," Cora replies. "I was looking after a young charge." Her eyes glaze over momentarily, and her face falls as if reacting to an old, painful memory.

"You should see it now," says Ida, speaking for the first time. Her voice is high and breathy, more like a young girl than a forty-year-old woman. "It's barely changed over the years."

"I'm sure I will," says Cora. "But you haven't said why you are renting a property when you have a perfectly good house here."

Cyril glances at his wife and she shifts uncomfortably in her seat. Cora's eyes sparkle as she homes in for the kill. "I sense a story. Do tell."

Cyril clears his throat. "Surely you've read the newspapers."

"Some, but only occasionally," says Cora. "They are full of horrible stories about this supposed war. I've barely come to terms with the last one, and I must admit to only skimming over articles these days. It is all too depressing."

"Then you won't have heard about the doings next door."

Cora shakes her head, and I lean forward in eager anticipation.

"Does the name Butt ring a bell?"

Cora is about to answer when Peter appears with a tray of tea. "Did you say Butt?" he asks, his glasses magnifying his widened eyes.

Cyril nods.

"Captain Butt?"

"I'm afraid so."

"What are you talking about, Peter?" asks Cora.

"The torso in the river," he replies.

Chapter Eight

A SINISTER FIND

PETER SETS THE TRAY DOWN, and I reach for a biscuit, my hands shaking with anticipation.

"What river? What body?" asks Cora.

Ida Price sighs. "We agreed not to talk about it," she says, cocking her head to one side.

"I know, my dear. But as they've asked, we can hardly refuse. Besides, if we don't tell them, somebody else will."

"That's right," says Cora. "So, you may as well fill us in. What are you running away from?"

"I wouldn't put it quite like that," huffs Cyril.

"Sorry, I misspoke. I'm far too direct for my own good sometimes. My only failing," says Cora, switching into charm mode. She leans forward, flashes a broad smile, and looks directly into Cyril's eyes. "I would appreciate a full account of anything that may affect our stay here. I promise we won't go running for the hills."

Cyril buckles and grins back with a soppy expression I have seen many times before. Cora always could make men eat from her hands. She has recently been so busy trying to be Vera that she has almost lost herself. But she has recovered admirably, and if she continues in the same vein, Cyril Price will soon hang on her every word.

"It's hard to know where to start," he says. "It's a long story, isn't it, Ida?"

"Very," says Ida, her mouth set in a thin line. I glance at Cora, silently willing her to lay off the flirtation a little, or Ida will rapidly go offside. But Cora doesn't need any interference from me.

"Of course it is," purrs Cora. "And it is so kind of you both to save us the embarrassment of hearing the story elsewhere. I do appreciate it. Ida, perhaps I could take you for a coffee sometime to thank you."

It is Ida's turn to flush, and she simpers an enthusiastic yes.

Clive Price clears his throat. "It all started back in January," he says. "Do you know Tirley at all?"

"I'm afraid I don't," says Cora.

"It's a little village to the west of Cheltenham," says Cyril. "The River Severn runs through it beneath Haw Bridge."

"I've seen pictures in the paper," says Peter, who has dragged a chair from the dining table and now perches beside me, pouring cups of tea while he speaks.

"Yes. They covered the news well at the time," says Cyril. "That picture was everywhere."

"But why would that cause you to move?" Cora's dormant private detective sensor is fully activated, and mine isn't far behind. My fingers tingle as they did when I first heard about Annie Hearn. I barely know a thing about this story, but I already feel drawn to the case.

"I'll tell you," says Cyril, taking a tea from Peter. "But I hope you have strong stomachs."

Cora nods. I do likewise.

"Well, someone had tossed a decapitated body in the water under Haw Bridge," he continues. "Now, they've never been completely sure. But Captain Butt went missing around the same time that they discovered the body, and no one has ever seen him again."

"And who was Captain Butt?" Cora drills down. She wants facts.

"Butt was our next-door neighbour."

Cyril Price looks up to see three mouths hanging open. Cora speaks first. "Well, that's a turn-up for the books."

Ida casts an anxious glance. "Are you sure it won't put you off?"

"Why should it?" asks Cora. "We're made of sterner stuff."

"And it's terribly interesting," I add, knowing that whatever they tell us, I will dig deeper. I have a fatalistic urge to find out more.

"We would love to hear the details," says Peter, as if reading my thoughts. Then his brows unexpectedly knit together as he frowns. "Did the press drive you away?" he asks bluntly.

"To a certain extent." Clive Price shakes his head resignedly. "But we probably jumped too soon. Didn't give ourselves enough time to process things, if you know what I mean."

"Are you still getting visits from nosy reporters?" Peter presses.

"Not recently. You may get the odd one or two, but they've lost interest for the most part."

"Good. Otherwise it makes the house rather conspicuous," says Peter.

"That's why we were worried it might put you off. It's such a relief to hear that you don't mind."

I flash a reassuring smile, which soon falls away at the sight of Peter's worried face. And I realise what he is thinking. We are in Cheltenham to escape the dangers of Cornwall, and the last thing we need is to bring any attention to ourselves. But Peter is worrying unnecessarily. No one will know or care who we are if they come to the door to find out about Captain Butt. He's the story, not us. I try to catch Peter's eye to send him a subliminal comforting message, but he turns away.

"Please carry on," I say, hoping Peter will not influence Cora before I hear about the crime.

"Well, as I say, William Butt lived next door. We passed the time of day with him but didn't socialise. You know how it is."

I nod enthusiastically.

"Butt would go off cruising the oceans from time to time. He always went alone. Didn't take his wife, but then she was a poor old thing, wasn't she Ida?"

"Edith was unwell," says Ida Price, tapping the side of her head. "Weak of mind. Still, you'd have thought a holiday could only help."

"He probably had a fancy woman," says Cora.

Ida blushes. "I don't know about that," she mutters. Cyril waits until his wife turns away, nods, and winks at Cora. She dons her best smile, and he momentarily loses his place in the story. I try not to sigh. Now is not the time for Cora to act up. I want facts, and I want them quickly. Peter is drumming his fingers on the table in an obvious display of impatience. Unless the Prices cannot empathise, they will soon read the mood and move on. I lean forward to take a sip of tea and firmly brush my foot into his leg. He glowers but lifts his hands from the table, cooperating for now.

"So, Captain Butt went away?" I ask with a rising intonation.

Cyril nods. "Yes, he did. Off into the big beyond, who knows where? Nobody worried, and everything continued as normal until poor Mrs Sullivan went to check on her son."

"Stop," says Cora curtly, then recovers herself, but not before a startled Cyril checks himself, wondering what he has done wrong. I can't get used to the new Cora. She is like two different people.

"I'm sorry," she says. "I only meant to ask you more about Mrs Sullivan before you got too far into the story. I don't know who she is."

Cyril continues in a relieved tone of voice. "And why would you? Silly me. I didn't say. Irene Sullivan was Mrs Butt's nurse."

"I thought she was mentally unwell, not physically ill?" I say, thinking aloud.

"Yes, dear, she was," says Ida. "And quite seriously so. The captain wouldn't leave her alone. He hired Mrs Sullivan to keep her company. She lived with them full time."

"With her boy?" asks Cora.

"Hardly." Peter interrupts as if Cora should know better. "Brian Sullivan was a fully grown man."

"How do you know?" I ask, irritated by his smugness.

"I told you. It was all over the papers. How did you miss it?"

"Just the small issue of an impending world war." I snap. Ida Price puts her hands over her face.

"There, there," says Cyril. "It's all speculation, my dear.

I'm sure we shouldn't worry." He shoots me an uncharacteristic glare. "Perhaps we should leave these good people in
peace?"

"I'm so sorry," I say. "And your husband is right. The
press is having a field day because it sells papers. There's
really nothing to concern yourself with. I'm sure the war
will never happen. Do let me pour you another cup of tea."

I snatch the teapot, trying to recover the situation with a
welcome brew. Ida uncovers her welling eyes, and Cora
reaches out and takes her hand.

"Try not to fret," she says. "Take each day as it comes.
Here." She passes the biscuits. Ida refuses them but takes
the cup of tea I thrust towards her. Even Teddy tries to
help, edging towards Ida and leaning against her leg. She
settles back into her chair. We have saved the situation
for now.

"What happened to Brian Sullivan?" I ask.

Cyril pulls a face. "He did himself in," he says.

"Next door?" Cora blurts out the question before I do.

"No. At Tower Lodge, where he lived."

"It's not far from here," offers Peter. I wish he would
stop flaunting his knowledge. It's bound to steal Cyril's thunder, and he might stop talking. But I dare not show my
displeasure. Peter is keen for this visit to end, and the harder
I push, the more likely he is to find a way to close
proceedings.

"How?" I ask.

"How did he do it?" echoes Cyril. "Gassed himself, I
think. But I'm not entirely sure. It's not the sort of thing you
like to think too hard about. Did Nurse Sullivan tell you?"

Cyril turns to his wife, who shakes her head. "I don't
remember. Irene's news shocked me so much that the details
went clean out of my head."

"My wife was the first person Irene saw after calling the police," says Cyril. "Tell them, Ida."

Mrs Price swallows, and her pale face takes on a greyish hue. She raises a trembling hand and wipes her mouth before speaking. I was dusting the lounge when Irene came knocking at my door," says Ida. "Fair frightened me, she did. I wasn't expecting any visitors that day, and she repeatedly slammed the knocker until I opened the door. She stood there, swaying, and asked if she could come in. I nearly gave her a piece of my mind until I saw that she'd been crying, bless her heart. She'd put on a face of makeup to go out, and I could see tear tracks running down her powdered cheeks."

"So, my wife let her in," says Cyril impatiently. Ida glares.

"So, I let her in," she continues. "And Irene said, 'My poor boy is dead. Brian has killed himself.' She told me how she had found her son's body and that she had telephoned her doctor for some sleeping tablets, as she would never rest easy again."

"How awful," I say. "What did you do?"

"Took her home, of course?" says Ida Price. "I put her straight to bed and told Mrs Butt she would have to manage alone. Then I left and returned here."

"That was very kind of you," I say, shivering at the thought of Mrs Sullivan's distress.

"It was nothing," says Ida.

"Except that it sent Irene halfway around the bend." Cyril Price shook his head sympathetically.

"As well it might," says Peter.

"How?" asks Cora.

"Nurse Sullivan lost all reason," says Cyril.

But that isn't a good enough explanation for Cora. "How?" she repeats.

"A hysterical outburst. Was it before or after the inquest?" he asks, turning to Ida.

She shrugs.

"After, I think," he says. "No, wait. Before." He clicks his fingers and examines the ceiling. "Oh, I can't be sure."

"Do go on," I say. "The timing doesn't matter."

"Well, whenever it was, I was getting dressed in the back bedroom. I don't like to disturb Ida when she's feeling poorly, as she was that day. And I left her to have an extra hour in bed. Anyway, I was almost ready when I heard a horrible scream coming from outside. Bloodcurdling, you know – the kind you have in a nightmare. I looked out of the window, and there she was – Nurse Sullivan pacing around the back garden in a dressing gown and slippers, screaming her head off. She was half-dressed, so I couldn't go myself. Instead, I woke Ida, and she went around to see what was happening."

Cora tilts her head and wears a puzzled frown.

"I know what you're thinking," says Cyril. "And don't worry. I kept a close eye on things. My wife's safety was uppermost in my mind."

Ida smiles, pats his arm, and takes up the story. "Poor Irene was hysterical by the time I arrived," says Ida. "Sobbing and groaning as if she was in pain. At first, I thought she had hurt herself, but then she told me that she'd been frightened in the night. I asked her how, and she said that awful man had returned. I asked her who she meant, and she said, Captain Butt. Isn't that a good thing? I asked. But she said no. He had come to her room and leaned over her, leering with a distorted face. Well, it was only a short time after Brian's death, and she was still grieving, so I assumed she had lost her reason and made it up. Although, it would be no bad thing if Butt had returned to look after his wife while Irene Sullivan was incapacitated. But she wasn't rational, and I was unsure if she was telling the truth. So, I asked my husband to come inside and check."

"Which I did immediately," says Cyril. I inspected her room and looked around Mrs Butt's. I even examined the captain's bedroom. Nothing. Not a man in sight. She had completely imagined it."

"I called out her doctor," said Ida. "Doctor Condor, it was, and he came right away and gave her a sedative. He said she had been hallucinating. But then Irene said something extraordinary."

"What was that?" I lean forward, hanging on to Ida's every word, conscious that my obvious interest is unedifying, but I don't care. Visions flit through my mind of cases past, and I know with certainty that I am meant to get to the bottom of this thing.

"Irene Sullivan said that she might have made a mistake, and the body at Tower Lodge might not have been her son at all."

Chapter Nine

THE TIRLEY TORSO

"HOW UTTERLY RIDICULOUS." I blurt out my opinion without considering the impact of my words. Mrs Price purses her lips and crosses her hands over her ample chest.

"She did say that I tell you. Didn't she, Cyril?"

"So, you said, my dear."

Ida cast a glance his way. "It really happened."

"I don't doubt it."

"Neither do I," I clarify. "But how can a mother not know her own son?"

"You'll have to ask her about that," says Ida.

"I might if I can find her."

"I heard Irene is still at Tower Lodge getting it ready for sale. Whether she will speak to you or not is a different matter," says Mrs Price.

Cora uncrosses her legs and draws a deep breath. "We appear to have come full circle," she says. "What has the Tirley torso to do with Brian Sullivan?"

Cyril Price nods. "Isn't that the question?" he replies.

"Quite." Cora leans forward, awaiting a more satisfactory response.

Price shrugs. "Nobody knows," he says. "They're not completely sure that it's Captain Butt's body. It was not in a good state. By which I mean all the normal identifying features were missing."

I discreetly grab my handbag and feel around inside, grasping a notebook and pen. Then I wait for Cyril Price to look away before listing the salient points of the conversation before I forget them. I am still scribbling away when Cora asks Cyril Price if they found more body parts. He curls his lip before shaking his head. "I don't know, and I don't want to know. The whole thing leaves a bad taste in my mouth. And it's not a fit topic for mixed company."

I inwardly groan, frustrated at his apparent reluctance to discuss details in front of the ladies. If we weren't here anonymously, I would have proudly told him that Cora was a private detective, and I am also one of sorts. But I know he would disapprove. Cyril Price is certainly not the kind of man to understand my unique abilities if they still work. The jury is currently out on that.

"Other than the captain going missing, is there any reason to assume it's his body?" Cora asks.

"Yes," says Cyril. "They found shoes near the corpse, which they believe belonged to Captain Butt. The police were satisfied that Butt was their man."

"But was it proved beyond a reasonable doubt?"

"No. They couldn't prove it at all. I said the police were satisfied, and they were. But I believe they based their decision on the balance of probability. There were no defining marks or scars. Nothing that nailed identification."

"Excuse me," says Peter, getting to his feet and placing empty cups on the tray.

Clive Price takes his action as the pointed reminder it is and turns to his wife. "Time to go now, my dear," he says. "We've intruded on these good people for long enough."

"Who could tell us more about the body?" I ask, desperate for further information.

Price ponders for a moment. "I have a friend at the Chronicle," he says. "A chap called Huggins. Daffy Huggins. He's currently working for the graphic section of the paper, but he's big on crime and has written several articles for the main rag." Price claps a hand to his mouth and faces his wife. "Best not repeat that. Daffy hates anyone referring to the Chronicle as a rag. But it's not a top-drawer news source, although I'm sure it's perfectly trustworthy. Here, have this," he says, removing a card from a silver holder he takes from his pocket.

I reach for the item, and Price suddenly snatches it back.

"Not that, this," he says, thrusting the original into his pocket and turning beetroot red. Ida Price follows the trajectory of his hand, narrows her eyes and peers into his flushed face. Clearly, she has banked the moment and will no doubt ask questions later. I check the card. Donald Huggins, Correspondent, *Cheltenham Chronicle*. I am unfamiliar with the address, but Cora will know where to go. I stow the card in my purse and watch Peter escort the Prices from our temporary home.

Cora follows him to the door, and they soon return. Peter is sitting on the arm of my chair, and Cora has resumed her original position.

"Well, that's a turn-up for the books," I say brightly.

"No," says Peter. "Absolutely not. Don't even think about suggesting it."

"Are you sure?" asks Cora. "It will give Connie something to do."

Peter snorts. "We're supposed to be anonymous, as you very well know. It's bad enough that we've managed to rent the next-door semi to a seemingly infamous house without going out of the way to signal our arrival. Leave it alone, Connie. It's too much to risk."

"But nobody will care who we are. They're only interested in Captain Butt," I reply, frustration welling inside me.

"Connie has a point." Cora looks earnestly at Peter.

"Whose side are you on?" he demands. "Stella McGregor would have a hairy fit if she knew about this. Not to mention our friends in the intelligence service."

"They're no friends of ours," I say, wondering how Peter could have forgotten the events of last week so quickly.

"Even so. Tracking down killers would be foolish, and you know it. Please don't go chasing unsolved crimes for the sake of entertainment, Connie. We may as well take out an advertisement in Crossley's latest magazine."

"Does he have one?" asks Cora.

"I don't know. He did once. The man writes for a living in between his more heinous deeds. I was making an example. Can you please stick to the point, which is keeping Connie safe?"

"Can't be done," I say. "Sorry, but this investigation is inevitable."

"What do you mean?" Peter rearranges himself onto the arm of the chair and stares me full in the face.

"I have the same feeling I had with Annie Hearn and all the other crimes I've encountered. It's impossible to explain, but the moment I hear about them, I know I must play a part in their resolution."

Cora reaches into her handbag and perfectly applies lipstick without using a mirror. She purses her lips together and makes a duck face. Satisfied, she speaks. "What about the black mark?" she asks.

I pause and consider her words. "Crossley has marked every murderer I have encountered. They cannot see him, but he is there, poised and waiting to apply a black mark to their forehead for every life they take. And I'm usually there to see it." I open my mouth again, determined to offer reassuring words about my future safety, but I can't find any. They are right. It's a risky business.

"You see," says Peter. "You can't put yourself in danger. It's impossible."

"I can't not," I say, and this time, I'm sure. "We're here for a reason. The crimes find me; I don't seek them. I know I gave the Prices the third degree, but the murder had already happened. And I didn't choose to come to Cheltenham; Cora did. It's fate, and you can't fight something destined to happen before we ever arrived. You must accept this as I have, Peter. I must resolve this murder one way or the other."

Cora smiles. She has now moved on to her nails and is expertly filing them with confident strokes. "Connie is right, of course. The best we can do is mitigate the danger. Nothing will stop fate."

"You are so irresponsible," snaps Peter. "Just admit you're as interested as Connie. Once a private detective, always a nosy busybody."

Cora raises an eyebrow. "Temper, temper," she says.

"Sorry. I didn't mean to be rude. But someone must look after Connie's interests."

"Yes. You and I, Peter. We will. But we must accept facts. You know what happened last time," says Cora calmly.

"I'm not a child," I protest again, knowing they are

referring to my tendency to run away when things get complicated.

Peter sighs. "Very well," he says, resignedly. "But with conditions."

"Name them," says Cora.

"One of us must accompany you at all times, Connie."

I nod happily. There is nothing too onerous about that. "And the other?"

"Absolutely no astral travelling whatsoever. You cannot risk it. And I expect you to back me up on this, Cora."

Cora nods. "Agreed."

"Connie?" She glances my way.

"Absolutely," I say, knowing neither one of them can see my fingers firmly crossed behind my back.

Chapter Ten

TOWER LODGE

"WELL, I DIDN'T EXPECT THAT," Peter says as we loiter against the dry-stone walling abutting Tower Lodge. I examine the mullioned windows regimentally set into a sturdy square building with the disconcerting appearance of a military fort.

"It looks exactly as it sounds," I say, in the building's defence.

"Even so." Peter does not elaborate as he shifts from foot to foot. The temperature has dropped, and it is unusually cold for May. Though dressed in a warm coat with a scarf tightly wound around my neck, I am far from comfortable and internally debating gloves. "We'd best press on," I say.

"Must we?" Peter could not look more ill at ease if he tried. He does not appreciate the concept of calling without an appointment and deems it bad-mannered. On the other hand, asking provides the opportunity for refusal, so I have dragged Peter up Leckhampton Hill to call on Irene Sullivan if she is still in residence, as Ida Price suggested. It took a monumental amount of persuasion. I couldn't walk for obvious reasons, and Peter tried every trick in the book to dissuade me from using the bus. After yesterday's fiercely debated exchange of views, he hoped I would change my mind about digging into this crime, but he ought to know better. I cannot help myself. Something drives me from beyond my consciousness, and I cannot rest until I have completed the task. So, with Cora's understanding, if not her blessing, we caught a bus from a convenient stop near the house and disembarked a walkable distance from Tower House, where we are now standing in the biting wind while Peter debates whether he can go through with it. I advance towards the building and decide for him.

My rap on the partly boarded window makes a loud noise reverberating from beyond as if the building were empty. It is not a good sign.

"What did you do that for?" hisses Peter.

I shrug. It's a fair question. But Tower House, amongst all its other oddities, lacks a front door. I press my nose to the window and peer inside, but something obscures my view, and I am none the wiser.

"I suppose we'll need to go through the gate," I say.

Peter raises his eyes heavenward and follows me through the gap flanked by sturdy stone quoined pillars. I advance to the side door and knock upon it with my stick. We wait in silence as a dark cloud crosses the sky. Peter holds out his hand and sighs as a fat raindrop plops into his palm. "That's all I need," he grumbles.

I smile sweetly. Peter, my long-time friend and protector, is not his usual, cheerful self. I first noticed his changed demeanour towards the end of last year. He seems anxious and lonely, even relinquishing his membership of the dramatic society. Peter has forgotten how to live, and it makes me sad. He seems so bored of life.

Peter does not return my smile, so I reach for his hand and squeeze it. He forces a grin and quickly drops my hand as we hear a shuffling noise coming down the corridor. The door opens, and a stout, matronly woman appears, glaring at us from beneath a black hat. I wonder why she is wearing it indoors, but Peter coughs nervously and re-sets my focus.

"Mrs Sullivan?" I ask.

"Yes. I am she."

"I'm Connie, and this is Peter. We've taken two four six Old Bath Road for a few months."

"Oh." Her eyes narrow, but she says nothing further, and I know I will have my work cut out.

"Mr and Mrs Price dropped by yesterday," I continue. "They send their regards."

"Do they really? That's far-sighted of them, considering I am rarely here and will soon leave Cheltenham altogether."

"They said as much," I continue. "But suggested you might drop by to finish clearing up."

"What else did they say?" asks Irene Sullivan, her terse voice bristling with suspicion.

"Not much. Just small talk."

"You're lying. Now leave me alone."

"Alright," I say. "Please don't shut the door on us. Of course, they told us about Brian. And the captain, for that matter. I wondered if you would talk about it."

"Absolutely not. Good day."

I glance at Peter, willing him to help. He steps forward and speaks softly. "We're not journalists," he says.

"So you say."

"I mean it. I work in a library. Take this." Peter offers her a card I did not know he possessed.

"A librarian? What can you want with me?"

"Not only a librarian, an actor too."

Irene stares at the card, and the ghost of a smile flickers momentarily on her face. "Brian would have enjoyed speaking to you."

"I hear he was a dancer," says Peter.

"Oh, he was. A very good one. Brian danced at the Winter Gardens. He was very popular with the ladies."

"I wish I'd known him," says Peter. "I can perform on stage, but I've two left feet on the dance floor. I'm sure your son could have taught me a thing or two."

I watch Peter admiringly. He is acting for all he's worth. I am the one with little rhythm. Peter is jolly nifty on the dance floor.

"I've been clearing Brian's room," says Irene. "I should have done it months ago, but so many people were coming and going. And by the time they left, I couldn't face it. But the land agent is pressing me, and needs must. I wish I hadn't left the job for so long. There's a thick layer of dust to contend with now. Anyway, I found Brian's old photograph album. Would you like to see it?"

"I'd love to if it's not too much trouble."

Peter follows Irene down a passage and through a door into the small, dark living room. I lean past Peter, and my eyes adjust to the barely lit space.

"Wait a moment," says Irene, fumbling in her pockets. She removes a matchbox, strikes a light, and ignites a gas lamp. "Sorry. I wasn't expecting visitors," she says. "There's no electricity, which isn't a problem upstairs, but it's no good in this room."

"Why have you boarded the windows?" I ask.

Irene sniffs and turns her head away.

"What a lovely room," says Peter.

This time, she smiles. "I think so, too," she says. "I had many happy times here until Brian died."

"I'm so sorry," Peter murmurs.

"It's the road. It's dangerous," says Irene randomly.

Peter frowns.

"You asked about the windows," says Irene, turning to me.

"Yes. I wondered why you would board up such a lovely room." This time, I am on a full charm offensive, gesturing enthusiastically towards the outside.

"Sit down," says Irene abruptly. Peter and I take seats on a worn settee. "Someone had boarded the windows up when I got here," she continues. "But they looked so ugly, I had them removed. The room looked lovely for a while. I could look out and wave at passersby. We see a lot of walkers around here, as it's so scenic. And I didn't mind them nosing at my beautiful living room. I was very proud of it. But Brian was worried about the traffic because Tower Lodge lies directly on the roadside. He said if anything came down the hill too fast, it might hit the house and shatter the glass. A few months passed, and I hoped he would forget all about it, but just before Christmas, he boarded them up from the inside. I really didn't like it, but Brian was unmoveable on the subject."

"That's a shame, but understandable that he would want to protect you," says Peter. Once again, he utters the right words, and Irene's tentative smile takes full form. She beams at Peter.

"I have been a little naughty, as you can see," she says, gesturing towards the right-hand window where a loose board has been snapped away.

"Good for you," says Peter. "Are those Brian's

photographs?" He points to a faded green album by the undamaged side of the fireplace.

"Yes. And I said you could see them. Here, take a look at my boy."

Irene passes the album to Peter and takes a seat a little way from us, staring at him with an odd expression I can't initially fathom.

"Thank you," says Peter, turning the first page. And all becomes clear at the sight of a bespectacled young man standing tall and proud with an elegant partner on the dance floor. With his swept-back sandy hair and earnest face, it's like looking at Peter's twin brother – no wonder he can do no wrong in front of Irene. Even Peter appreciates the resemblance.

"Goodness me," he says. "Don't we look alike?"

Irene doesn't speak, and for a moment, I think Peter has talked out of turn and upset her. But her eyes fill with tears, and she gulps down a sob. "I thought so the moment I saw you. That's why I wondered if you would like to see his photograph."

"It's an honour," says Peter, quietly turning the pages. "Nice car," he continues, pointing to a dark automobile.

Irene peers across the room. "You mean the Daimler? It belongs to Keith Newman, Brian's friend from London. My son had an Austin Tourer. Not so grand, but still his pride and joy."

"Brian seems like a nice young man," says Peter, closing the album. "I would like to have known him."

Irene shakes her head, seemingly on the verge of tears. But a scratching at the door relieves her introspection.

"That must be Bimbo," she says, heaving herself from the chair. "Excuse me for one moment."

"Who's Bimbo?" mouths Peter.

"Never mind that," I say. "What on earth has been going on in this room?" I nod towards the gaping hole on the right-hand side of the fireplace where bricks and rubble are piled on the floorboards.

"Some kind of excavation," says Peter.

I stand and make my way towards it, kneeling and eyeing the space in the wall. "There's a hole all the way through," I say.

"Sit down," commands Peter, hearing a patter of foot-steps up the hall. I return to my seat just in time for an excitable spaniel to throw himself towards me with Irene Sullivan hot on his tail.

"Get down, Bimbo," she says, and the dog obediently sits at my feet.

"There's something on your dress," says Irene coldly. I glance down to see a large patch of soot where I knelt by the fire.

"Can I use your bathroom?" I ask, forgoing any attempt at explanation which, however carefully worded, could not make me look less guilty.

"Down the passage and to your left," she says curtly before turning towards Peter. I leave the room, confident she will be far happier without my presence.

The passageway occupies far more of Tower Lodge than is practical and contains an alarming pit in the centre where further excavations have occurred. I pass a sink and stairs before turning right towards the bathroom. It is cold, dark, and dusty, and the only light comes from the open door. I forgo any personal ablutions and make a poor attempt to clean my dress using cold water and an old floor rag. By the time I finish, I smell like a tramp and have only succeeded in redistributing the soot to a different location. But Nurse Sullivan is observant and would have noticed if I had not tried. I can now spend a few minutes nosing around before returning to the front room.

I locate the other side of the gap on the back wall by the end of the bath. Someone has attempted to replaster the hole from this side, which has been partly removed, exposing an old flue. It's nothing sinister, just poor workmanship and an unsettling mess that's not worth any more of my time. There being nothing else to see, I return to Peter, who is chatting in full flow with an entranced Irene Sullivan.

"I was just telling Irene about your book," he says.

I raise an eyebrow, wondering if this is some kind of elaborate code.

"It's fascinating," she says. "You don't look like a writer, if you don't mind me saying."

"We are many and varied," I reply vaguely, wondering what kind of book I would have authored.

Peter enlightens me. "Exposing injustice is a worthy cause, isn't it, Connie? It's a shame you must conduct so much of your work in secret."

"Well, yes. That's why I didn't say anything." I flash him a glare as if concerned about his indiscretion, and Peter plays up as only an actor could.

"You know I would never do anything to draw undue attention to you. But Irene is a nurse. Confidentiality comes with her profession. You can rely on her to be circumspect, I promise."

I raise an eyebrow and wait.

Irene Sullivan eagerly leans forward. "I won't breathe a word, not a single syllable, if you will only listen to my side of things. I want to clear Brian's good name. Please help me."

Chapter Eleven

SUICIDE OR MURDER?

"OF COURSE," I say, retrieving my notebook from my handbag. I quickly turn a page, so Irene doesn't see yesterday's jottings taken from the Prices' recollections.

"What do you want to know?" Irene speaks eagerly, her speech growing faster as if yearning to rid herself of an inner burden.

"Anything. Everything. Why don't you start at the beginning?"

Irene sighs, as if she has often heard this request.

"Don't rush if it's too hard," says Peter sympathetically.

"It's not that. I've had time to become accustomed to my loss. But for all the times I've told this story, nothing ever comes of it. I'm weary of repeating the same old words in the hope someone will pay the price for murdering my son."

"You seem very sure of foul play," I say.

"Well, I am. Brian did not take his own life, I can assure you."

"Wasn't there a note?" Peter leans forward, his eyes never leaving hers.

71

Irene nods. "Yes. But it was all wrong."

"How?"

"The wrong tone, the wrong words."

"Did you recognise the handwriting?" I ask.

Irene snorts. "It was Brian's all right. But he must have written it under duress."

I lower my notebook and try to select the right words. "No mother ever wants to believe their child might take his own life."

"I'm not stupid," says Irene. "But I know the difference between wishful thinking and a mother's instinct. Brian would never have written the note in that tone."

"But if Brian were unhappy enough to end his life, he wouldn't behave normally. His demeanour, his writing – everything would be different." I persevere with my point. Irene can't be objective, so I must.

"It felt staged," she mutters.

"What did?"

"The room, the note, and there were things all over the lodge that shouldn't have been there."

"Go on," I urge.

"Oh, I don't know." Irene puts her hands to her face and covers her eyes. She pauses for a moment, deep in thought. "It's so foggy now. The captain left, then they found his remains at Haw Bridge, and from that moment, I felt a black cloud bear down on me. It's still there and always will be now with both my children gone. How is this a fair burden for an elderly lady? I don't deserve it; truly, I don't."

"Both your children?"

"I lost my dear daughter before she came of age. And now Brian. It's more than a body can bear."

My heart aches for the woman before me. Smart but dowdy, plain with a stern face, Irene's demeanour does not naturally garner sympathy. Until a few moments ago, I found little to like about the dumpy nurse. But her frown lines tell a story. Her sad decline to old age is now unfettered by motherly duties. She looks empty, careworn, and sorry to the bone. Her only purpose now is to find out what happened to her son. And I know I can help her. I abandon my assumption that he died by his own hand and start practising the objectivity I had wrongly assigned myself.

"Did you see Brian?" I ask.

"When?"

"The day he died."

Irene nods. "Yes. I found him. I thought you knew that."

"I've phrased my question badly," I say. "I meant, how did he appear?"

"Oh dear." Irene Sullivan covers her mouth with a shaking hand. "Oh dear," she repeats. I wait, and she pulls herself together. "Brian had lain there for a few days," she says. "I don't know if you have ever seen a dead body, but decomposition strikes quickly. The body swells, and rigor mortis sets in. I've often seen it," Irene continues. "It's part of nursing, but nothing prepares you for the sight of a loved one lying there, motionless and so obviously out of this world."

"Would you like a hot drink?" Peter offers, reverting to his standard remedy for all things unpleasant. Irene shakes her head, and Peter turns away, disappointed. I suspect he struggles with this line of questioning and would rather be elsewhere.

"Where was I?" asks Irene. "Oh yes. My dear boy. I didn't linger by his side. Perhaps I would have held him if I weren't a nurse. But I knew how it would be, and I wanted to remember him full of life."

"You didn't touch him then?" I ask.

"Briefly. I lifted Brian's hand to check his pulse, but his skin was cold as I expected. And his head had lolled away from me, so I didn't have to look at his poor, dead face. I ran to fetch help, and Constable Merry did the rest."

"You've said you don't believe Brian killed himself. Why is that?"

Irene looks up and points towards the fireplace. "You've seen that mess," she states, gesturing towards the large hole.

"Yes."

"That's where they dug for evidence. Excavations according to that chief inspector. Ruddy vandalism, I told him when I saw what they had done to my lovely house. But he doesn't care, that one. No emotions, as cold as ice. I'll never forget his lack of empathy."

"What was the inspector's name?" I raise my pencil expectantly in anticipation of a possible contact.

"Chief Inspector Percy Worth, damn him." A spark of anger ignites as Irene practically spits the words.

"Right," I say, scribbling down the name.

"He comes to my house, all high and mighty," says Irene, "demanding the key to Tower Lodge. Well, I was in bed in the semi at Old Bath Road, recovering from my ordeal. The doctor had given me some pills, and I was trying to get through the day when Worth turned up with one of his bobbies and insisted that I hand him the key. I would have refused if I had known what he wanted it for. But he was clever and said nothing until it was too late."

"What were they looking for?" I ask.

"Bits of the captain's body," says Irene. "They thought Brian had cut him up at Tower Lodge and then killed himself in remorse, as if my boy could ever do such a thing. So, they pulled the house to bits and found nothing except an old overcoat belonging to Captain Butt."

"Isn't that rather suspicious?" I ask, mentally allocating it a solid nine out of ten for concerning activity.

"Not in the least. Captain Butt often stayed here."

Peter glances quizzically at me, and I feel his sympathy evaporate. I don't know how to phrase the question without offending, so I offer one word.

"Why?"

Irene sighs. "Captain Butt was a dreadful payer," she says. Receiving my wages was like getting blood from a stone. Now Tower Lodge is mine. I lived there until I started looking after Mrs Butt. Well, I couldn't be in two places at once, now could I? And one day, when I was pressing Captain Butt for unpaid wages, he suggested he might take over the housing payments and use the place himself every now and again if I wasn't at home and Brian didn't need it. So that's what we did. If you look, you will see his shaving foam bottle is still in the bathroom."

"How extraordinary," I say.

"Not really." Irene is on the defensive, so I ask another question.

"Might I assume the police came away empty-handed?"

"Correct," says Irene. "Nothing apart from the coat. No blood, no tools, nothing. They wasted their time but made a right old mess."

"I'm sure they'll put it right," I say brightly.

"Are you?" Irene raises an eyebrow. I'm losing her coop-eration.

"Can you tell me anything else?" I ask.

"I was trying to. You need to know about the gas pipes."

"Do go on."

"They said Brian gassed himself. He died from asphyxi-ation. And they expect me to believe he did this by lugging a huge marble-topped washstand across the floor all on his own just to get at the floorboards beneath."

Irene cocks her head and looks at me as if waiting for my agreement.

"Really. How unreasonable."

"Isn't it? What an unnecessarily convoluted way to go about it."

She pauses, and I wait, realising I have lost the conversation thread somewhere. Peter picks up my confusion immediately.

"Are you saying that the police think Brian did something to the gas pipes?" he asks.

"Well, that's what they wanted me to believe," Irene replies. "But I don't. They said Brian had peeled back the linoleum and raised the floorboards so he could sever the gas pipe to kill himself. But why would he do that? It's silly."

"Somebody did," I say.

"I don't dispute that." Irene Sullivan thrusts her chin forward. "It's clearly damaged. You can see for yourself if you like. I'm simply stating the obvious fact that Brian wouldn't have gone to such ridiculous lengths."

"But why?"

"Because there was a gas fire upstairs when I first moved in. Brian took it away when they fitted the electric light. He thought the two things had no business together. So, he employed someone to remove the fire and make the gas pipe safe. All Brian needed to do was knock the stopper out, and the gas would flow freely. So, why would he go to the lengths of moving a heavy object and prying up floorboards?"

"He wouldn't," I say. The penny drops, and I now appreciate Irene's point of view. Brian had no logical reason to take the more complicated route. A shiver of fear traverses my skin.

"Is that what you mean by staged?" I ask.

Irene nods. And there's something else," she says. "This place was not empty in the days leading up to Brian's death."

"Well, no. Your son was here."

"I mean someone other than Brian. When that hound Chief Inspector Worth marched me back here to ask for my impressions, I noticed dozens of cutlery pieces in the drainer. Well, Brian alone couldn't have used that many items. And the draper's boy said he heard a dog barking and saw a man in the house, but Bimbo was in the car?"

"In the car? What do you mean?"

"I hadn't seen Brian for a while, so I visited Tower Lodge a few days before finding his body. I saw milk bottles outside, but Brian had the key, and I didn't have a spare, so I left and returned a few days later. The milk had gone, and someone had shut Bimbo in the car. The poor boy was lying in his own mess and had been there for several days."

I angrily scowl, thinking of everything I would like to have said to her precious son if he thought leaving a frightened dog alone in the car was acceptable, but Irene pre-empts me.

"Bimbo was Brian's baby. My son loved him like a child. Brian would never have shut his dog away. It isn't possible. Whoever killed Brian put Bimbo there."

"I believe you," I say.

Irene Sullivan bows her head in relief, then glances at her watch. "Oh dear. I really must go. I'm running very late."

"That's a shame. I would have liked to look at Brian's bedroom."

"Please do. You can see what I mean about the gas pipe. Here. Take the key and let yourself out. Oh, hang on. No. The agent needs them."

"We can deliver the key," says Peter.

"Are you sure?" Irene doesn't wait for confirmation but roots in her pocket and pulls out a card. "There you go. You'll find him in Cambray. Thank you. That saves me a job."

Irene hands me the key, and I open my mouth to thank her. But the words don't come. A feeling rushes over me, bringing waves of certainty that Brian did not kill himself. No suicide took place in these four walls. I am in the grip of the same sensation I had with Annie Hearne, and I know I must resolve this case, no matter what.

Chapter Twelve

SEARCHING FOR CLUES

"LET'S MAKE THIS QUICK," says Peter impatiently. He has just returned from accompanying Irene Sullivan to the door and is sporting unusually red cheeks.

"Still cold outside?" I ask.

"I didn't notice."

"Fair enough. You look odd, though."

"Don't, Connie." Peter shakes his head sadly.

I say nothing. Something has plainly disturbed him. He glares at me. "What now?"

"We look upstairs," I say confidently. "Come on then."

I limp towards the staircase. Peter follows behind.

"She kissed me," he mutters.

"Who, when?"

"Irene Sullivan, just now."

"Oh dear," I say, imagining Peter's natural antipathy to spontaneous human gestures. "What did you do?"

"Hugged her back. It's all I could do, the poor woman."

I pause and lean on my stick while clutching the banister. "Don't get too fond of her. You'll lose your objectivity."

"This is your investigation, not mine. If it were up to me, we'd be somewhere else taking a proper break and not exposing ourselves to unnecessary danger."

"Come on," I say, ignoring his concerns. "The sooner we do this, the sooner we leave." I reach the top of the stairs to find two doors leading to two bedrooms, one notably smaller. We enter the larger bedroom directly over the living room to find it fully furnished with a made-up bed still in the centre. I step back and almost fall into Peter.

"What's wrong?" he asks.

"Nothing. It must have been my imagination. I thought for a moment that I could see the body."

"Where?"

"Lying on the bed, right in front of me."

"You silly old thing," says Peter, ruffling my hair in an uncharacteristic display of affection. "There's nothing here but us."

I take heart at his words and walk inside, but my skin is still crawling. And every time I look away from the bed, something lurks in the corner of my vision.

"I think we should leave," says Peter.

"Can you see it too?" I try to disguise the tremor in my voice, to no avail.

"No. But you're as white as a sheet, Connie. Don't carry on if it's making you fearful."

"I must," I say, but every instinct in my body screams at me to leave, though I don't know why. "Look. There are the lifted floorboards."

I advance to the corner of the room and use my stick to support me as I squat to my haunches. "I can't see properly," I say.

Peter reaches into his pocket and removes a cigarette lighter.

"You don't smoke," I say, bemused.

"You never know when you might need one." Peter hands me the lighter, and I make a few attempts to create a flame.

"Be careful," he says anxiously, glancing between the flame and the pipe.

"Don't worry. They'll have stopped the supply by now. Look," I say, pointing to the gas pipe below. "It's cut clean through."

Peter crouches down to join me and examines the evidence. "Deliberately severed. No doubt at all. I wonder if…" he continues.

"What's on your mind?"

"Nothing. It's just a fleeting thought. Brian would protect his mother if he intended to kill himself, but not to this extent. Somebody else tampered with the gas supply. Someone who didn't know there was a handy gas tap over there." Peter stands and points to a protruding pipe, jutting ever so slightly from the wall at floor level.

"When you know, you know," I say. "But I wouldn't have seen it if you hadn't pointed it out."

"And I wouldn't have looked for it but for Irene's remark."

"I wonder how Brian paid for the gas?" I ask.

"By coin. I saw the meter downstairs. Takes a shilling, I would guess, judging by the slot."

"Right," I say, traversing the room. I approach the wardrobe, gazing away from the bed, and the door swings open to reveal three suits hanging neatly beside a woollen coat and a pullover. "We should have asked Irene if any clothes were missing," I say.

"I doubt they are," Peter replies. "But what difference would it make? He hardly needs clothes in the afterlife."

"Keep an open mind," I remind him, but Peter grunts noncommittedly. He is going through the motions, and a growl from his stomach tells me his mind is on other things.

I gladly turn my back on the main bedroom, still feeling the pull of dread at the thought of the malign influence within, and head towards the spare room. The bed is neatly made with an incongruous pink candlewick counterpane, on top of which is a carefully folded suit.

"Must be the clothes Brian wore the day he died," says Peter.

I grimace, but without the accompanying fear, I noticed in the front bedroom. Peter and I examine the tiny room, opening and closing a chest of drawers with nothing inside. Then we gaze through the window across the garden towards the hill.

"Time to go," says Peter and I must agree. There's nothing else to see in the bedrooms.

We return downstairs and turn towards the rubble-strewn hole when the strangest feeling draws my attention to a large piece of linoleum still on the floor near the bathroom.

I stop and stare.

"What is it, Connie?"

"Why is that still there?"

"To protect the floor. That's usually how lino works."

"No," I say, shaking my head. "Look, someone's cut it."

Peter follows the line of my shaking finger and squats down. "Yes. The fitter, no doubt. Honestly, Connie. You're letting your imagination run wild." Peter sighs, then in a gesture of appeasement, he prises back a section of lino, and hurls it to one side. We stare in horror at the image below – a chalked unicursal hexagram that someone had gone to great lengths to hide.

Chapter Thirteen

TESTING THE LIMITS

PETER and I left Tower Lodge and caught the next bus back to Old Bath Road, mulling over the incident in silence. Then, after helping me off the bus, Peter sought out Cora, and they disappeared for an hour-long walk.

I briefly fell asleep, waking to find myself alone and thoroughly bored. I am distractedly staring from the window when Elys appears.

"What have you done with them?" asks Elys as I drum my fingers on the windowsill, still looking for signs of Peter's existence.

"Nothing," I reply.

"Well, Mrs Pennington said she would take me into town," Elys grumbles, still addressing Cora formally, even after all this time. "And it's pushing two o'clock. The shops will shut if we don't go soon."

"For goodness' sake, you've known us long enough, Elys. Call Cora by her name. We're all friends together."

"So, you'll be cooking tea then?" asks Elys, raising an eyebrow.

I ignore her. I would, but Elys knows the limitations of my cookery skills and wouldn't chance it. "I'll come along and keep you company if you like," I offer.

"No," says Elys firmly. "Cora wouldn't like it. Anyway, tell me what happened this morning, Connie. Peter left the house with a face like thunder.

"That's Peter all over at the moment," I reply. "He worries too much."

"With good reason. And you don't appreciate it."

I sigh. Elys's comment has hit the mark, but she's only half right. I do understand it, but I don't much like it. No fully grown woman appreciates a babysitter, no matter how dark her nemesis.

"Shall we play cards?" I ask, now bored and frustrated.

"Some of us must get on with dinner if we're not going out," snaps Elys. "You'll have to entertain yourself."

Elys stalks off to the kitchen, and having nothing better to occupy my time, I head upstairs.

The room I share with Elys is heavily draped with thick curtains and mustard-coloured flock wallpaper, creating an uneasy combination of claustrophobic and cosy. I am still tired from this morning's exertions and decide to lie down again for another short nap to pass the time until Cora returns. But no sooner does my head touch the pillow than a reckless thought worms into my mind. I try to dismiss it as foolish, but the idea has stuck, and I cannot evict it. *Go on, Connie. Have a go. See if you can still do it.* Intrusive thoughts undermine any prospect of sleep as they taunt me with the notion I have long feared. Can I still dreamwalk?

I last tried at Pebble Cottage and might have succeeded but for the sudden appearance of Mr Moggins. But that was at home, where things felt safer. And even if safety was a false premise, the cosy, familiar surroundings made me feel protected, nonetheless.

I close my eyes and listen for the swell of waves breaking on the shore and imagine the odour of the salty sea air. I miss Porth Tregoryan more than I could ever have imagined. But if I fired up the astral travel engines again, I could go there now. I promised Peter I wouldn't risk setting foot on the astral plane, but he isn't here and will never know. I rise and check the room. Mr Moggins is downstairs with Elys while Teddy clings to me like the proverbial shadow. He won't disturb my efforts as long as it's just the two of us. So, I shut the door, and switch on the main light, hoping it works like a candle.

I try to remember what dreamwalking feels like. But it's been so long that I can't properly recall. It used to be so spontaneous, sometimes happening when least expected and often at great inconvenience. I would find myself on the Porth Mawgan cliffs, arms outstretched and running as if my life depended on it. Happy days. What has happened to inhibit my abilities so suddenly? It must be apathy or my mindset. I've been miserable since Vera died, but now marks the turning point for change.

I stare at the ceiling light, but it is too bright. I look away to find orange cylinders momentarily burned on my retinas. I need a candle, and I can hardly ask Elys to provide one, especially in broad daylight. Then I remember the portable wall light on the upstairs landing hanging on a hook, no doubt for when the electricity supply is unreliable. I tiptoe and get it, ignoring Moggins, who stares balefully from the foot of the stairs. I strike a flame using the lighter I have conveniently forgotten to return to Peter and place the lamp on the dressing table at the foot of my bed. Narrowing my eyes, I gaze towards it and feel a pull towards the flickering flame. It stirs a memory, a feeling of calm tranquillity, and I let it take me. But five minutes later, though sleepy, I am still very much present in the room, my hands on the bed, my feet grazing the bottom bedstead. It isn't working. Why? I try again, this time focussing on the candle while remembering my room in Pebble Cottage. I project my sea-facing window onto the mirrored dressing table, imagining the dark sky beyond. A smile involuntarily plays on my face at the welcome memories, so poignant I can almost feel the pathos of Vera's empty room. I see the sea sparkling beneath a waning crescent moon and feel the gentle breeze against my skin. And all at once, I am falling backwards into the pillow. As if by magic, I stop and rise upwards, floating above the bed until my head bobs along the ceiling. I will myself down and turn towards the single bed nearest the window where my sleeping body lies. This may not be Cornwall, but I have finally done it, and I test myself by slipping a finger into the wallpaper. It disappears.

Chapter Fourteen

NOCTURNAL WANDERINGS

I GASP and pull back my hand, momentarily baffled by the lack of reaction to what should have been a cold exterior. It has been so long since I left my body that I have forgotten I can't touch or feel anything in my astral state. I am like a novice again, a newborn foal faltering on unstable legs without understanding how the world works. I stop for a moment and consider my next steps. I want to run along my little beach and stand outside the empty cave I once used as a second home. I close my eyes and think of myself standing there. Nothing happens save a slight pull on the back of my head, evoking a long-forgotten memory – my body's reminder to rejoin it. Not yet, I mouth, watching my sleeping form. But it is hard to pull away, and I find myself standing close enough to see my fluttering eyelids surrounded by the first faint signs of crows' feet. I am wearing well, still youthful and reasonably slim, despite my lack of physical prowess. But my temples are already showing the early signs of greying hair, and frown lines are present even in repose. I move away, feeling weirdly egotistical at my fascination with myself. But it is hard to move, and I don't know if I can overcome the pull between my body and soul. I screw my eyes shut once again and aim for the hotel in my mind's eye. But I can't see it as it was in the good old days, only as it is now, run like a military unit by Roxy Templeton. No warmth, no fun, and no appeal. Perhaps that's why my attempted dreamwalk has become an abject failure.

I snap open my eyes and decide on another tactic. Even if I can't access the astral plane, I am still separate from my body and should be able to move around at will. I push my hand through the wall again. I might as well visit Captain Butt's house while I am here. It will be a lot easier than acquiring a key. I close my eyes and push through the wall, meeting no resistance, and find myself in a large front bedroom similar to mine.

The space belongs to a man. I first suspect it from the sparsity of personal effects and am confident when I peer into a half-open wardrobe containing male garb. I spy a coat with a bulging pocket and automatically reach my hand to explore the inside. It passes straight through the fabric, and I sigh. For a second, I had forgotten how useless my body is in the astral form. Simple tasks are beyond me and become highly frustrating. I curse the irony of my position. Either a hopeless cripple who can touch but barely walk or a lithe spirit who can pass through walls while being unable to pick up so much as a bunch of keys. Life is unfair.

Still, I am in his room, and I spare a thought for the captain or the pieces of his broken body still remaining in this world, wondering how he came to such an unhappy end. Who would go to the lengths of cutting up a man and throwing him into a river? Someone who didn't want him identified, I reply aloud. I think of counterarguments and bank them for later. I must visit Haw Bridge if Peter will take me. Important questions nibble on the edge of my consciousness and may break through if I'm in the right surroundings.

My hand naturally flies to my heart at this overt mention of geography. In the old days, the thought would have been enough to spin me towards the destination, occasionally passing backwards through time. Now, I don't budge an inch. My powers have faded, succumbing to the apathy of a false sense of security. No wonder Stella McGregor became frustrated. The psychic defence division is all talk and research. They have no agents in the field. God knows they wouldn't have needed Crossley if they had any talent, Harold aside. I shiver at the thought of the jowly, dome-headed Felix Crossley. What was the brigadier thinking in placing his trust in the man? The whole notion is the antithesis of common sense. But it's not just the military at fault. I can't remember the last time The Order made any serious attempt at training their external forces. Perhaps they routinely carry out dreamwalking drills at HQ but haven't asked me yet. Not for a while, anyway. They lost interest when I started making excuses about going to London. But Vera had died, and things were difficult. I couldn't raise the enthusiasm.

But I'm here now, gazing around the dark green room with its solid, wooden framed portraits of India. Captain Butt must be an ex-officer of the Raj. The paintings are heavily anglicised with hero soldiers and colonial surroundings, more befitting a large manor than this small semi-detached house. Have his fortunes fallen, I wonder? I drift towards his chest of drawers, frustratedly swishing my hand inside, annoyed that I can't open them and have a good ferret around. But wishes won't get me anywhere, so I try another room.

The door to the bedroom mirroring Cora's is firmly shut. I march towards it and stride through, feeling more confident in my astral form. This room is different, cluttered, dusty, and has a hypnotic, pattered wallpaper of entwined cornflowers and daisies. A wall clock ticks sonorously, and for a moment, tiredness overwhelms me. I shake my head, trying to rid myself of the soporific feeling and glance towards the window. The lady of the house uses this room, and if the contents of the dressing table are anything to go by, she wears little makeup or perfume. Dark hairs interspersed with grey cover the hairbrush, which needs a good clean. It sits carelessly above a lace handkerchief bearing an ink mark. Nearby, a lidless fountain pen has spilt its contents onto a pamphlet for the cinema, which lays upon a water-stained piece of blotting paper. Clearly, Mrs Butt is untidy and bordering on chaotic, and I wonder what she is like in the flesh. A glance at the windowsill reveals nothing of her personality but gives a good insight into her physical form as I spot a double silver frame, handily inscribed Polperro 1937. Mrs Butt occupies the right-hand side, her eyes tiny slits in a puffy face above a formidable bust. The black-and-white photograph may not convey the colours of her flesh, but it is good enough to see that her skin is the palest white. She looks unhappy and unhealthy, her dumpy frame no doubt the result of eating to combat unhappiness. I shudder at the thought of going the same way. Back home, I often tell Elys I am one of her Hevva cakes away from being officially plump. She says it's nonsense, but then Elys likes feeding people and is never happier than when dishing out baked goods.

Captain Butt faces his wife in the photo frame. He is tall and rangy with little more than the merest nod to middle-aged spread. He stands erect, at ease with his hands in his pockets, gazing from a little white cottage. He is not hand-some; his features are too big, and his ears stand out from his head. But on the attraction scales, he is notably higher than his poor, downtrodden wife. My eyes refocus on the blotting paper. On closer inspection, the stains I noticed earlier are not water marks. They are tears, likely shed by Mrs Butt. My heart aches for her.

Prickles form on the back of my head, and I grow irri-tated at the nagging tug from my body as it urges me to return. I am enjoying this saunter around 248 Old Bath Road, using my detective skills to probe into the lives of the Butts. But this three-bedroomed house has a further room, doubtlessly unoccupied and likely devoid of possessions. Still, I would like to see where Irene Sullivan lived for so long as a gooseberry between a warring couple.

I locate her room with ease. The door stands open, and I enter, surprised to see her effects still in place. Nurse Sullivan must have started packing and been disturbed midstream, for a carpet bag sits open on the bed containing an old pair of shoes and some stockings. A narrow mahogany dresser sits opposite the single bed, and a dense dust patch indicates where someone has moved a book, no doubt for packing. I see a receipt for a prescription dated last week marking the book. Nurse Sullivan must have secured a key and is moving out, which is hardly surprising as she indicated her days in Cheltenham would soon end.

I attempt to sit on the bed, not usually comfortable in my dream state. But standing has become burdensome in a way I cannot fathom. The bedside drawer is wide open and contains a letter folded over with the top half sprung back. I read the few lines I can see.

Oh, and Betty. Captain Butt is the meanest man I ever met. No matter how often I ask, he will not pay my wages. He has made dear Edith sign money over to him again, no doubt to fund that jezebel, Ida. He has intimated he will take Edith to the Barnwood Asylum, but she will not entertain the idea. Brian is coming to dinner…

I crane my neck and try to read on, but it is too dark in the drawer to see any more, and I give it up as a bad job. Still, a mere two lines of Irene Sullivan's writings has told me everything I need to know about her feelings towards Captain Butt. He sounds thoroughly disagreeable, and it's hardly surprising that he came to a bad end. I check myself at my shameful thoughts. Nobody deserves his fate, nobody.

There is nothing else of any interest in this tiny third bedroom, and I look out of the window and think about the contrast between this suburban property and the hilly outlook of Tower Lodge. How strange it must have felt for Irene to go between one and the other. The captain, too, for that matter. And as I think of Tower Lodge, my thoughts turn unexpectedly to the discovery I had been trying to avoid thinking about since first seeing it yesterday – the familiar symbol lurking beneath the lino. Nothing about the Bath Road house suggests anything dark other than the captain's apparent bad temper and disdain for his wife. Aside from that, I have seen no archaic symbols or suggestion of an affiliation with the dark arts. I'm sure Irene did not create the unicursal hexagon hidden at Tower Lodge, and there's no reason to think the captain did, either. For a moment, I wonder if it might have been Brian. If so, what would that imply? Was he a member of The Order? Did he know Felix Crossley? I shudder at the thought of Crossley's name, and his image evolves suddenly in my mind, overlaid with the unicursal hexagon. A jolt of fear shudders through me. I am rooted in terror as icy tendrils snake down my spine. And all at once, I plunge through the floor and down into the darkest whirling black.

Chapter Fifteen

SUMMONED

AND JUST LIKE THAT, I am in the middle of the astral plane, wondering in awe as star clusters glow and fade in the indigo realm. I am entranced and afraid, my heart racing, my breath shallow, trembling with an adrenaline rush as I contemplate my foolhardy actions. The last time I travelled this path was with my eyes tightly shut to block any chance of seeing Crossley, who had dogged me through time and space. Now, I am alone, in splendid isolation, not another traveller in sight. Why? However lonely my route through the celestial sphere, I have always passed others. They rarely acknowledge me, but I am aware of their spectral presence. This time, I am alone with the stars. It could be worse. Crossley could be on the horizon. But I feel a deep, indescribable loneliness from which I may never recover.

I marshal my thoughts and try to stay positive by remembering a time when I feared I would be stuck here, alone in this transcendental dimension forever. From experience, it never lasts. Fate brings me here to deposit me elsewhere. I've never understood how or why, but I take comfort in knowing it does. I passively wait, suspended in this twinkling, starlit world, for the next part of my journey to begin.

It happens quickly. I feel myself floating up, then rapidly sinking, spinning in a vortex until I arrive disorientated in a darkened room. I wait until my eyes adjust to the light and contemplate my surroundings. I have materialised in a narrow nursery with a low range of drawers and a wooden crib at one end. Puzzled, I creep towards it and lean over to see a sleeping child snuggled under a blue blanket, his chest rising and falling to the sound of gentle breathing. The room, papered with chunky giraffes, is illuminated by an outside lamp flooding light into the uncurtained nursery. How this poor little child gets to sleep, let alone stays that way, defeats me. Mrs Ponsonby always drew my thick bedroom drapes closed at bedtime to keep the room safe and snug. I didn't appreciate it then and rebelled by sleeping with both curtains and windows open in my teenage years, but I understand now, feeling the vulnerability of the little child exposed to all manner of monsters lurking in the shadowy corners of the half-lit room.

I smile as I look down on him, his little mouth twitching, eyelids silently flickering as he dreams his innocent dreams. Then suddenly, his eyes snap open and he sees me. He overtly reacts to my unknown face, eyes opening wide as he anxiously stares at the stranger before him. His lips quiver in silent rage. Then suddenly, he screams, and I stare aghast as his tongue vibrates in a wide, angry mouth. Tears stream down his creased cheeks, and he wails in abject terror. A door slams, and I hear footsteps thundering down the hallway. I am rooted in fright as the door opens and a woman appears, arms outstretched as she reaches for her child.

The woman walks right through me, sending a shiver of

revulsion through my body. Her presence does not hurt me, nor can she know I am there, but there is something unnatural about the earthbound crossing paths with the astral. It's as disconcerting as fingernails down a chalkboard. A feeling of nausea takes me, and I instinctively flatten myself against the far wall, watching as she tends to her infant.

She picks him up and rocks him, but he is inconsolable. She cradles his head and draws him into her, then moves him to her shoulder and strokes his little head. He is inches from my face, staring towards me as if I'd walked straight out of his latest night terror. He draws a breath, gasps as he meets my gaze, and releases another ear-piercing shriek. His mother sings a lullaby, her voice rising ever louder as she competes with his shrill wail. But it is not to be. A deep, male voice booms down the hallway. "Will you shut that child up, Matilda? I need my bloody sleep."

The woman glares at the door, scowling at her inconsiderate partner. "Hush now, Chatan," she soothes. "Daddy will be cross. Come now." But no kind words can stop the screaming. Her son is distraught, and it's all because of me.

"Damn you all," says the male disembodied voice from afar. I hear a door slam and footsteps on the landing.

"Now you've done it," whispers the woman, nuzzling the child's head. "Daddy is angry." She holds the child protectively to her chest, and as she does, an icy fear grips my insides, rising ever higher as the steps get closer. And all at once, I understand. I know where I am and who I am with. My heart almost stops in mortal dread; for a moment, I am transfixed, unable to move. Then, just as the door slams open, I slide behind it. The wooden door slips through me, and I peer down the room as the man stomps towards the crying child.

"What on earth is wrong with him?" asks Felix Crossley,

reaching for his boy. Tilly Donnelly sidesteps and turns towards the window, protecting him with her body.

"What do you think you're doing?" asks Crossley. "I won't hurt my own son. Give him to me."

"He needs his mother."

Crossley snorts. "A fat lot of good that did. He's bellowing like a cow in an abattoir."

Tilly Donnelly blinks angrily, still holding her boy close to her chest.

"I said give him to me." Crossley stares hypnotically towards her, and she silently hands the child over.

Crossley yanks a chain from his neck and speaks soothingly to his son while twirling a gold symbol over his head. The little boy stares at the spinning, glinting metal, and his cries stutter to a halt, replaced by a breathless rasp as he calms. Crossley continues until the child's eyelids close. Minutes later, he lies in his father's arms, now in peaceful repose.

"Thank you," whispers Tilly.

"Take him," says Crossley, handing over the child. Tilly places him in the crib, and Crossley turns towards her, sniffing the air.

Tilly reaches into her pocket and passes him a handkerchief.

"What's that for?"

"You might be coming down with a cold."

"I think not," says Crossley, thrusting the item in his pocket. "Something smells wrong."

"Chatan is teething, I am sure of it. You upset him a few nights ago when you stayed out all night at the club. But not as badly as this. I will rub some brandy on his gums."

"Is that some veiled objection to my nighttime activities,

Matilda? Are you unhappy at home while I am out tending to my followers? You could have come with me."

"And so I will, when the time is right. Chatan needs his mother."

"Not as much as he needs my protection," says Crossley, curling his lip in disgust. "The time is drawing close. We have played happy families for long enough."

"Between your time in Germany and the nights spent on Calicum Aureum business, you've barely been with us. I can look after my son whether or not you're here."

"Have you learned nothing from my teachings?" Crossley moves backwards, his head swaying like a cobra about to strike. I cower in the corner of the room, barely daring to look.

"Yes, but your expectations are too dark. I can't bear to think of them."

"The alternative is worse. Our son dies, and you spend the rest of your life grieving."

"Why can't we move away and live a normal life?"

"Don't be ridiculous, Tilly. You knew what I expected when you joined The Order – a life for a life. I made a pact a long time ago. Many years before we ever met. I covenanted to perform a rite that demanded the sacrifice of the child of a man of God. That was nearly thirty years ago, and I am still to deliver; I tried and failed to keep my end of the bargain, and it has taken me until now to have the stomach to try again. I might have given up were it not for our son. But you must understand, I cannot keep him for much longer without attending to my obligations."

Tilly visibly shudders, but not as much as I do. My heart flips, and I tremble as I consider my position. Why am I here? Why is Crossley having this strange conversation in his son's room in the middle of the night? Tilly must have heard this before. Why does he need to tell her again?

"Naturally, it's for your benefit," says Crossley, turning towards me with a malevolent smirk. I hold my breath, willing him not to see me.

"Oh, for goodness' sake, come out of there," Crossley continues. "I haven't summoned you for the sake of my health."

The game is up. My quickening heart settles a little. The worst has happened, and it makes me brave. I take a deep breath and move a pace forward. Crossley examines me from top to toe.

"What a disappointment," he says. "I expected so much more than this. Look, Tilly. She's a bloody cripple."

Tilly Donnelly stares at Crossley. "I don't know what you're talking about."

"Of course you don't. Your powers don't extend that far." He points directly at me with a fat, nail-bitten finger. "If you were as gifted as I am, you would see my arch nemesis, as she once was, about a foot from the door. I haven't been able to find her by the usual means. But I have spent many nights studying ancient texts, and I successfully forced her hand tonight. She's in my house and now belongs to me."

Crossley closes his eyes and his body stills. His lips move, and I realise he is trying to detach himself from his body. Crossley is an expert who can easily morph into the astral plane with little effort. I have seconds to make my move, and I do it suddenly and without warning. I can't access the celestial realm alone. Not yet. So, I turn and run, scrambling pell-mell downstairs, through the wall, and out into the road. I run into the path of a passing carriage and slither inside, trying to contain my ethereal form within its wooden sides. I am only a few seconds ahead of Crossley and have barely any options. He will catch me in seconds if I don't act now. I screw my eyes closed and try to think of a plan, and suddenly, it comes to me – a nearby place of safety.

I hurl myself from the carriage and tumble to the floor, pick myself up and look behind. Crossley thunders towards me, riding the evening skies like a rocket. I wish the world could see him as I do; then, they might step in and stop him. But people saunter by unseeing, uncaring. Crossley gains ground, sneering at me through his whirlwind form. But I know where to go. I run and run, stopping, starting, twisting my path unexpectedly through buildings, parks, and trees making an unpredictable zigzag towards Queensborough Terrace and the only safe place I know. Crossley is almost upon me when I reach my destination and hurl myself through the wooden door of the Shining Path headquarters.

Chapter Sixteen

THE SHINING PATH

I FEEL a force as Crossley's astral self meets resistance at the door, impeding his progress. I peer through a tiny window and see him standing outside, his face a mask of fury. He raises an arm, bunches his fist, and waves it threateningly. Though tempted to gloat, I walk away without changing my facial expression. The door has withheld Crossley's attack for now, but he is the strongest member of Calicum Aureum, and I won't push my luck. As I walk backwards, eyeing the door uncertainly, I notice the worn symbol of protection Stella chalked on the back of the door years ago. It has held up against this latest onslaught, and I thankfully conclude that the Shining Path headquarters are truly safe. But they are also worryingly quiet. No one is on duty in the living room, watching for trouble. They have become complacent. In the old days, Stella would take control, her eyes out on stalks, every nerve aflame and ready for action. Now, I have sailed through the front door without meeting a challenge. It is a good thing I am friend, not foe.

I glance through the wide living room window. Crossley

is still outside, lurking by the streetlamp and shooting scowls towards the building. The pavement seems to ebb and swirl beneath him, but a closer look tells me that his spider hordes are on the march again. They ripple towards me like a tidal bore, surging forward at Crossley's command. I turn away when the first hairy legs reach the window, and a mandible slavers over the glass. I know the power of their lure, and I will not let them draw me outside.

But the night creatures are only one of my problems. My scalp is tingling as a sudden headache screeches through my temples. A pain so intense that it feels as if someone has taken my hair and viciously pulled it, reminds me I must reunite with my body, and soon. But I cannot control myself. Getting into the astral realm is more by luck than judgement, and I can't risk leaving the headquarters while Crossley's creatures are so close. They would follow, and God only knows what they would do to me. I shudder at the thought, back out of the living room and run down the hallway, searching for signs of life.

The kitchen is empty, but I hear voices in the back parlour and recognise Marjorie, who is talking to a young woman I have never met. I wait for them to stop so I can politely announce myself, then think better of such a rash action. If I speak to Marjorie, she will tell Stella I have been dreamwalking. And Stella will take it upon herself to rebuke Cora and Peter for not taking better care of me, which will be grossly unfair considering I am a fully grown woman, and they don't know I am here.

I decide to walk away from Marjorie and her friend. Aside from their casual attitude towards potential attacks, I am perfectly safe in the headquarters. And if I go about my business quietly and don't draw attention to myself, I can benefit from a respite before setting off again as if I had never been here. Content with my plan, I retreat before Marjorie notices my astral self, and I detour upstairs, finding the room I once stayed in, which is happily empty.

I attempt to lie on the bed, which is always challenging in the astral form. Sometimes, I settle on the mattress surface but often lie uneasily in rather than on the furniture. But my current state of casual acceptance has positively affected my astral form, leaving it to follow a conventional gravitational pull. I find myself the right way up and occupying a comfortable position on the bed. Tired, I stretch out, hands behind my head, trying to think peaceful thoughts. My quiet serenity does not last long. Thuds and bangs interrupt my contemplation as objects strike the window. My soul shrinks in terror at the memory of the last time I heard this unholy noise in Oliver Fox's house on Worple Road. Once again, Crossley's night creatures, spiders, bats and flying insects have defied their usual aversion to daytime and now surround the building, united in their malevolent attempts to gain access. I clutch my hands together and try to brave it out as the noise increases in intensity and the windows rattle. The sounds grow louder with each passing minute. I close my eyes and try to still my beating heart. I sing to myself – a gentle sea shanty that Vera would whistle as she went about her chores. Eventually, the noise quietens, the thuds drop away, and silence reigns. I lick my lips, daring to hope that this is the end of the onslaught. Tipping my head to one side, I listen, still aware of the quietness beyond. Then my ears pick up the merest hint of noise, a reptilian whisper like a gentle hypnotic hiss, which increases as a rhythm beats on the glass pane. I could peel back the curtains and check to see what's outside, but there's no need. Hilda, or rather Harold Grady, told me more about this creature than I could ever wish to know the last time I stayed in Wimbledon. It is Crossley's snake, his faithful serpent, loyal to his bidding and with craven determination to lure his victims away from safety.

Panic fills my chest. Oliver Fox himself could not resist the snake. Peter and I barely got away with our lives the last time we encountered it. I have been away from my body for too long to be strong enough to resist it. I must find Marjorie and ask for her help. Crossley cannot breach the walls of the headquarters, but if I'm not careful, I might give in to serpentine temptation and open the window myself.

But fear has rendered me immobile again. Though I know I must go to Marjorie, I dare not move from the bed. A beguiling, almost musical hissing fills my ears, and I feel myself smiling for a moment before sanity settles. *Fight it, Connie. Bring the shutters down.*

My mind fills with memories of Stella's training. I imagine heavy metal doors and slam them down, segmenting the serpent's body. But it is not enough. The pieces skitter away, reassembling into a misshapen, blood-ied, mightier opponent. I recreate the doors, but the snake swishes its tail, smashing a dent into the metal. A chill shivers down my spine. The serpent is stronger than I am. I cannot fight it on the astral plane, and it is slowly infiltrating my thoughts and breaking my defences. What can I do?

I half hear a voice, neither real nor imagined, telling me to think beautiful thoughts, and I try to follow its bidding. First, I think of Vera, but memories of my childish tantrums consign her image to oblivion. Then I think of Teddy, but a stomach-churning knot of fear grips me as I wonder how he is and whether he is in danger, standing guard over my soul-less body. I summon Peter, Cora, and Elys to mind in quick succession, but they are thin and insubstantial. It is not enough. So, I allow myself to remember my happiest memory, long held at bay deep in my subconscious mind, to stop it from breaking my heart. I take a jewel-encrusted key, unlock the box, and shake it out. A cherished image of Jim reaching slowly towards me, his arms around my waist and placing a soft, gentle kiss on my lips. My heart flutters at the memory, and a million rose petals drift from the sky. The snake screams as if it's on fire, instantly sloughing its skin as it retreats post haste. I hear a thud, not against the window but on the path below, as if a large creature had plopped to the ground. I feel buoyant, safe, loved and in love. The creatures have gone, but an awful pain on the back of my scalp burns into my brain like acid-coated shards of glass. Jim is the last thing on my mind as I hurtle backwards to my body.

Chapter Seventeen

DUALITY

EXCEPT I DON'T. My body tried to call me home, but my heart was elsewhere. I am sick, weak, and badly in need of becoming whole when my astral form drifts straight through the celestial realm and drops onto a patch of grass yards from a cliff edge. I am on my hands and knees, and it takes a few moments to make sense of my surroundings. At first, I think I am back in Cornwall, and a surge of relief passes through me. Glorious, beautiful Porth Tregoryan, my child-hood home. But the grass is different, and the sea air smells wrong. The cliffs are a different colour. Puzzled, I get to my feet and spin around in a circle. *Where am I?*

Something is coming in the distance; a man leaning heavily on a woman. She is marching him forward while he staggers uncertainly beside her. And what is that behind them? It looks like a ghostly, ethereal form.

A shiver of fear passes through me as I comprehend the scene ahead. With thoughts of my beloved Jim in mind, I have found my way back through time to Seaford, where I stand on top of the cliffs as Grace Duff drags a drugged and helpless Jim towards the edge. I watch with horror, and a certain knowledge of a looming fate I cannot escape. The insubstantial form behind them is me. I remember now. I saw them pass, but I couldn't stop them. Something happened. Something so awful that I nearly died, causing such profound memory loss that I have never fully regained it. To lose Jim was bad enough, but the thing that almost killed me was seeing my form at another moment in time. My memory has protected me from this realisation until now.

But I can't avoid what has already happened. I am standing in the middle of a cliff stretching far around me with nobody else in sight. Even if I weren't rooted to the spot, even if I could run, it would be too late.

The party of three are coming straight for me. I can only watch in terrible silence as Grace Duff and Jim, walk past, and I find myself face-to-face with an earlier version of myself. My 1932 astral body takes one horrified look before crashing to the floor. She lies there, barely breathing. Grace marches onwards, Jim trailing at her side. I touch my face and check my breath. Somehow, I am still here. I have survived the encounter, but the old Connie cannot endure the dichotomy while I am still conscious. I should go to her and help her on her way, but I have a chance to do something I could not before. Find out what happened to Jim.

I run towards Grace Duff, arms raised, screaming at her to stop. She does not hear me and carries on, shoving Jim to the side as she supports his weighty body. He is getting weaker and walking forward like a mythical zombie, unknowing, unseeing. I run ahead, plead with Grace, and beg her to stop. She does not hear me and continues walking, intent on her inhumane task. And then it is over. She gives Jim one almighty shove, and he tumbles over the clifftop, crying out as he falls below with a sickening thump. I scream his name as I fall to my knees, sobbing tearlessly. Grace Duff wipes her hands together and strides off with a satisfied expression from a job well done. I rock back and forth on the grass, hardly able to believe that fate could be so cruel as to show me Jim's final moments in this despicable manner. But though deep in grief, I rationalise that I am here for a reason, for closure. I can finally say goodbye to Jim's broken body. Still kneeling, I push myself to the cliff's edge and peer over. Then, from the depths of despair, I feel a tiny frisson of hope. Jim has landed only twenty or thirty yards down and is lying on a ledge, his arm at an unnatural angle. But even from here, I can see the rise and fall of his chest. He is alone, injured and in dire need, but Jim is alive. If only someone could find him and take him to hospital, they might yet rid him of the poison. I must help. How can I help?

But a savage pain in my scalp tells me it is too late. My head is spinning, my vision blurred. My heart slows as my fingers tingle. Jim may not be dying, but I am. I have no form or function. I cannot speak to the living, and I cannot help Jim. But I could spare one life tonight – my own. I crawl towards my 1932 version, painfully inching forward until I am almost within touching distance. I lean forward, and my fingers brush hers, and as they do, we meld together and break apart, hurtling backwards into the astral plane. And I know when I wake up at 246 Old Bath Road that my alter ego made it back to Cornwall, too.

Chapter Eighteen

CAVENDISH HOUSE

I WAKE up twisting and thrashing on the bed to find a warm spaniel nose in my face. Teddy whines, then licks my cheek, trying to comfort me as every synapse in my brain flares in recognition of my newly acquired knowledge. I remember everything. Every tiny detail of my time on the astral plane. And more besides. My memory has returned in vivid detail. I am whole again.

I sit up in bed and check my watch. It is six o'clock and early morning, judging by the light outside. I have been out of my body for the best part of a day. I contemplate all that has passed as I watch Elys's chest rise and fall as she sleeps in the bed beside mine. Elys exhales with a low noise like a horse's whinny. She is enjoying a well-deserved sleep, but I am buzzing with uncontained excitement and cannot settle. So, I quietly rise and collect my dressing gown from the back of the door before heading downstairs.

Morning has broken, and the first pale shards of sunlight grace the south-facing lawn of our little rented house. I set a kettle to boil and make myself a cup of tea before stepping outside to perch on a conveniently placed bench, where I stare out across the neighbour's back garden. The morning is balmy and unusually hot for May. I sit in quiet contemplation as I sip my tea, trying to collect my thoughts.

I don't know if Jim is alive or dead. Logic tells me he must have eventually expired from his injuries, or he would have tried to find me. And if he didn't care enough to track me down, he would have asked Mrs Douglass about Teddy. Jim's poor mother now lives in a nursing home. She took a tumble last year and broke her hip. I took Teddy to see her soon after, and she mentioned how much she missed Jim and hoped she wouldn't die without knowing what had happened to him. I wanted to reassure her but couldn't. I wonder what I would say now, if she asked me again?

Seeing Jim, albeit in the past, fills me with joy. I feel giddy like a schoolgirl and buoyed with unjustified hope. Where could Jim be if he were still alive? How could he have left us to carry on, never knowing where he was? More importantly, how will I ever find out?

All these questions should lay me low, but they don't. My feelings for Jim, which have increased with my newfound memories, have filled my heart to the exclusion of anything else. I must return to Seaford, find him, and stay a little longer than my recent dreamwalking allowed. But even as I consider this, I am overwhelmed by the obvious flaw in the plan. I arrived in Seaford by accident, unintentionally accessing the astral plane. But I have no control over my movements, much less the ability to manage time travel well enough to arrive at an exact place within a tight schedule. I've more chance of walking to Gloucester. There must be another way.

"Do what?" says a voice behind me. It is Peter, and I realise I have been muttering aloud.

"You're up early," I say.

"It's too light to stay in bed. Besides, I had an early night last night. Not as early as you, though. What happened? You missed a jolly good supper."

My stomach rumbles in time with Peter's words. "I was tired. Too tired to eat, and you were out all afternoon. Where did you go?"

"Out and about," says Peter noncommittedly. I sense we are both keeping secrets.

"And today?"

"I am entirely at your disposal," Peter replies. "Shall we take a trip somewhere?"

"I'd love to."

"Do you fancy a visit to Broadway? It's a quintessential Cotswold town and very attractive. Or we can see Gloucester cathedral?"

"Another day," I say. "I must deliver some keys."

Peter's face falls. "So you must," he replies, remembering our promise to Irene Sullivan. "Cheltenham it is, then. We'll go via Cavendish House."

"What's that?" I ask.

"A department store like no other," Peter replies. "It's huge. If you like shopping, you'll love this."

"I don't particularly."

"Well, I do, and if we're confined to Cheltenham, I'm dropping in for a bargain. Look at this old threadbare thing. I badly need another." Peter pulls at the tartan-checked tie around his neck, flipping it open to reveal a large tear.

I sigh. "Point taken," I say. "Shopping it is."

I toast a slice of bread before dressing and returning

downstairs to find Peter waiting impatiently in the living room.

"Come on. The bus is already outside," he urges, opening the front door.

"Run ahead," I say. "You know I can't do anything quickly."

Peter pulls a face, but does as I ask, stepping back once he's spoken to the driver to wait for me on the pavement. We board and embark on a pleasant journey across town, arriving at The Promenade ten minutes later.

"Where's the agent?" asks Peter, reaching for the keys. I pass them over, and Peter locates the address of a smart townhouse not far from the bus stop.

"I'll take them," says Peter as we reach the building and look up to see a steep set of stairs to the front door.

"I can manage," I say.

Peter shakes his head. "The office is on the third floor."

"Right," I mutter disappointedly. I would have liked to speak with the agent, too, but managing three flights of stairs is too much, especially after last night's little escapade. I have gone from animated to barely functioning since breakfast. My body might have enjoyed a night's repose, but my mind was too engaged to reap the benefits. I lean against cold metal railings while waiting for Peter and gaze towards the town centre, noticing a small wooden stand with people milling around it in the distance. I wonder what it is, but Peter interrupts my musings as he runs down the outside steps, taking them two at a time.

"Well, that was enlightening," he says.

"Go on."

"Nice chap, but my goodness, he could talk. Or should I say gossip. Salacious, too, I might add. I'm not sure I should repeat it."

"Well, you've started, so you must continue. I am a woman of the world."

Peter laughs. "I think not," he says. "But I will tell you as long as you promise not to be too shocked."

"Carry on."

"The agent says Brian Sullivan and Captain Butt were up to no good."

"You mean dodgy business practices?"

"No. I mean personally."

"Sorry. You've lost me."

Peter sighs and marshals his thoughts. "You know. The things that men and women do."

My face flushes, and I turn away, annoyed at my body's betrayal. "You mean they are? What's the word?"

"Homosexuals," says Peter.

"I don't believe it."

"Nor did the agent's assistant, if it helps. He said Butt was a great strapping man without an effeminate bone in his body."

"Not that it matters," I add, turning away and hoping Peter has not noticed the colour of my face. We don't talk about Peter's private life. But he's had several male friends, some of whom he has been extremely close to. I have always assumed he is of that persuasion, which makes discussing things in this context rather uncomfortable.

Peter touches my face and makes a fizzing noise.

"Don't," I hiss.

"Come on, Connie," he says, opening his arms wide. "You know how it is."

I sense an unburdening, an offer to talk and get it out in the open. I am flattered, but I can't. Not now, not like this. I divert the conversation. "I'm starving," I say.

Peter's smile slips away for a second, but then he speaks.

"We'll eat something at Cavendish House. But I haven't told you everything yet. And you will need to be especially worldly to digest this rumour."

"Do tell?" I say, relieved at the slight change of subject.

"Word has it that Nurse Sullivan used Tower Lodge for medical matters. Specifically, the removal of unwanted foetuses."

"Surely not?" I say as a wave of nausea rushes over me.

"I'm afraid so."

"Fact or fiction?" I ask.

"A bit of both. It depends on who you speak to. The agent says he's heard it all over town. His assistant says it's tittle-tattle."

"I don't like the sound of this land agent. Irene Sullivan is his customer. This careless talk is unprofessional."

"For what it's worth, I don't believe a word either. I liked Mrs Sullivan."

"Not as much as she liked you."

"Only because I remind her of Brian."

"That's a good enough reason."

We banter together as we walk towards Cavendish House, and I stop about twenty yards from the front entrance to admire flags and bunting across the building. Several large boxes of spring flowers grace the outside, and a proliferation of fashionable mannequins fill every window.

"My goodness," I say.

"Impressive, isn't it?

"How did you know it was here?"

"Cora told me yesterday."

"She'd know, of course."

"Oh yes. Cora knows every inch of this place."

"Let's take a look then."

We enter the large door at the front and see a wooden staircase to our right. "Race you," says Peter, jovially.

"Very funny."

"Come on. There's a lift at the rear." I follow Peter, and we ascend to the second floor, where Peter selects three ties and a waistcoat.

"Last of the big spenders," I say, surprised at his profligacy.

"Mum slipped me a few pounds."

"I'm sure she'll approve."

Peter finishes and then ushers me back to the lift for a short journey to the top floor. The dining room is half empty, and we select a table near the window overlooking the front. Peter orders two cream teas, which the waiter brings over on pretty china cake stands. We polish off two scones with cream and strawberry jam, washed down with Darjeeling Tea and a chocolate macaroon. I feel stuffed and sleepy as I gaze from the window while Peter visits the little boy's room. He returns presently, and we chat a while before I am distracted by a low buzz of noise coming from outside.

"What's that?" I ask, pointing to the wooden stall consisting of a trestle table with a banner erected above.

"Not sure," says Peter.

"Someone just threw an egg at that poor chap."

I stand incensed, watching a blond-haired man scraping yolk from his jacket.

"Rough crowd," says Peter.

"They're all dressed the same," I continue, pointing to the stall. "I wonder who they are?"

"I don't know." Peter gets to his feet and offers me his arm. I stand, and he helps me up. "No idea who they are at all, Connie. But we've nothing better to do. Let's find out."

Chapter Nineteen

THE COTSWOLD BRUDERHOF

"*WILLKOMMEN,*" says the tall blond man as we approach the stall arm in arm. He smiles engagingly, and I lock eyes with Peter, exchanging unspoken surprise at the man's friendliness after his recent hostile encounter with the egg thrower.

"Are you hurt?" I ask as he wipes glutinous albumen from the front of his breeches. They are short and tied at the knee, exposing hairy white flesh from his calves to the top of his coarse, heavy boots. The man strokes a well-trimmed beard and nods his head.

"Yes, *danke. Du bist sehr art.*"

"I'm sorry?" I say, failing to recognise the language. I should have guessed the man was foreign by his dress. I gaze at the other people surrounding him. The men dress similarly in breeches and linen shirts, some with stockings, others bare-legged, while the women's attire is uniform, comprising blue dresses and bonnets. They remind me of historical photographs of Cornish farmers I have seen in Peter's library, out of place and out of time.

"Kind," says the man in heavily accented, broken English. "It is kind of you to ask."

Peter offers his hand. "We saw what happened," he says. "Nobody should suffer that sort of loutish behaviour."

The man accepts Peter's handshake with a firm one of his own. "*Ich heisse* Kurt," he says. "And don't worry. We are used to it."

"I am Peter. This is Connie," says Peter, introducing me with a nod. Kurt bows his head before reaching for my hand. He shakes it vigorously, but I barely notice. A shiver flashes through me as it did the first time I encountered Annie Hearn, and I know with certainty that fate has drawn me to this odd little man. Somehow, he will be part of my future. Kurt feels it, too. He withdraws his hand, cocks his head, and examines my face. "*Das schicksal*," he says, gazing beyond with faraway eyes.

"Who are you?" I ask, feeling an urgency to know that takes me by surprise.

An older woman marches stridently towards Kurt. She wears the standard long blue dress, but the addition of a gingham shawl sets her apart from the other females. She pulls it tightly around her shoulders and addresses Kurt in a Germanic-sounding language, the hard-edged consonants streaming harshly from her lips. Kurt smiles and pats her shoulder, uttering the only word I understand throughout the conversation. "*Nein*," he says.

I step back nervously, wondering if she is angry with us. But Kurt places a guiding arm behind her back and urges her our way. "This is my sister Ursel," he says. "Her English is good, better than mine. Ursel will answer your question.

"You want to know who we are," Ursel says coldly, failing to offer a hand or soften her words. She is direct and to the point, and I suspect Ursel would not give us the time of day but for her more amiable brother.

I nod, almost regretting my earlier question.

"We are Bruderhof," she replies, placing her hands on her hips. She waits for a reaction, and I flounder.

"Ah," says Peter, a wave of enlightenment passing his face. "Well, I never. I have heard of the Bruderhof. But I didn't know you travelled."

"We would not, but for the evil in our homeland," says Ursel. Her features slip into a frown, worry lines etched over her face, and her eyes flicker as if disguising a heavy pain. "No. We would not, but we must accept the inevitable."

"You mean the Nazis?" asks Peter. He chews his lip, and I reach for his hand, recognising the gesture as a familiar indication that he thinks he has gone too far. Too direct a question for people who have fled their country for reasons beyond their control.

Kurt does not take offence. "We do what we must," he murmurs. "We are godly people, and the Nazis do not like us. They, the soldiers... I cannot find the words." He turns to Ursel and spreads his hands.

"They threaten us," she says. "Tell us to abandon our Christian ways or move on. Some of us do, some do not. And those who stay suffer for their beliefs. At first, our tormentors used only words, then they took our belongings and used force upon us. So, we left to start a new life."

"Here, in Cheltenham?" I ask.

Ursel shakes her head. "No. We are here today to sell our wares. Our new home is farther south. We live in a small holding in Ashton Keynes."

"I know it," says Peter, and I wonder how he can, but I don't articulate my doubts. Sometimes, Peter can be too clever for his own good. Others, he likes to appear that way, and I would not put it past him to pretend.

"Come. Break bread with us," says Kurt. "To thank you for your kindness."

"But we haven't done anything," I say.

Kurt jerks his head towards a group of young men farther down The Promenade, flashing angry glares at the Bruderhof. Their pent-up anger bubbles like a simmering volcano. "People don't understand our ways. They are afraid. And so *freundschaft* is *gut*."

"Friendship," Ursel gently corrects her brother. We value friendship." She meets my gaze and sees a reluctance. "Unless you are afraid of reprisals," she continues. We would understand."

Peter grimaces, and I recognise his need to protect me. But I have encountered far more serious threats in the astral zone. A group of intolerant men are the least of my worries. I feel an unaccountable bond with the Bruderhof. "We would love to join you," I say. "And perhaps you can tell us more about your community."

Kurt leads us towards a trestle table tucked away behind an old milk float. He reaches into a wooden container and removes two rough loaves from a sack. Ursel appears behind him with a jar of honey, and within moments, they have created a rudimentary meal. Kurt pours fresh milk from a small urn into hand-crafted wooden beakers before saying grace. Peter and I have only just eaten and have little appetite. But we both understand the heartfelt gesture of breaking bread with guests and share their fare willingly. The simple food is delicious, and although we are full to bursting, we enjoy it. As we finish, more brethren join us, helping themselves to the remaining bread.

"I hope they will not go hungry on our account," says Peter anxiously.

"There is more bread in the sack," says Kurt. "We grow all our food and have plenty to go around."

"Self-sufficient," says a grey-haired man who has just joined the table. He speaks with a heavy West Country accent, English, not German.

"I'm from Somerset," he continues, registering my puzzled expression.

"I don't understand."

"May I?" asks the man, deferring to Kurt.

"Please," says Kurt. "But speak slowly. I wish to follow the conversation."

"Jacob Morris," says the man, turning to shake our hands. Peter responds, but I am sitting too far away to reach.

"We'll take your greeting as read," says Jacob, smiling at me. "I heard you ask Kurt about the movement."

"We did," says Peter. "But only out of curiosity. Don't feel obliged to answer if it's difficult."

"It isn't for me," says Jacob. "Quite the best thing that ever happened in my godless life. My wife had just died. I was a lonely old man with nothing to look forward to when I met Kurt."

"Not old," says Kurt. "Never old."

"Thank you, my friend. But old enough and dispirited. I had a little money but what's the use of that with no family? Anyway, the Bruderhof were welcoming and evangelical. They aim to expand their community and open their world to those who wish to live a more godly life."

"Have you been with them for long?" I ask.

"Nine months," says Jacob. "Which is as long as any other English man. Kurt, Ursel and some of the other far-sighted Bruderhof arrived last year. They could see what was coming and fled persecution while they could. Sure enough, things got worse until the Nazis forced the remaining Bruderhof from their country. They used the little funds available to purchase a farm at Ashton Keynes, land that would help them support themselves and provide food and accommodation, health care and a committed Christian life."

"Impressive," says Peter. "Very admirable. It can't have been easy."

"It isn't," says Jacob, slowing down as Kurt glances his way.

"Excuse me." Ursel leaves the table and walks towards the banner to relieve those who haven't eaten yet. Several well-dressed ladies approach the stall but quickly leave when they hear her accent.

"Do you see what I mean?" asks Jacob.

"Perhaps they don't understand?"

"Or they're hostile to strangers. There never seems to be a middle ground. People either fear us, dislike us, or want to join us. Few are prepared to simply accept our ways."

Jacob scratches his head. His hair is thinning, and a bald patch on his head looks sore with sunburn. He wears heavy sideburns, badger-like, with more white hair than black. I estimate his age to be around sixty. Yet he seems athletic, slim, and wiry. "Do you work on the farm?" I ask.

Jacob nods. "I do now, even though I am a master printer. But the farm has no use for such things. Not yet. It may do so in the future, and we have plans for a periodical in time. But I currently work the land as there is much to do. We have livestock, an orchard, crops, and hives. We make baskets, weave linen and cook food to eat and sell."

"It sounds idyllic," says Peter.

"Then join us."

"I can't. I have a library to run."

"Too bad," says Jacob.

"Is everyone welcome?" I ask, impressed at the ethos behind this community striving for the means to live comfortably within their faith. It is appealing; so appealing that, for a moment, I consider joining. But what would they want with a cripple?

"Everyone who wants to work and follow our ways is welcome," says Kurt, who has followed the conversation very well. "As long as they toil hard and commit to our rules."

"Indeed," says Jacob. "The last of the German and Dutch contingent arrived in March this year. A young English man joined us from the Romanies just after I did, and there have been twenty or more since then, both men and women. Admittedly, our life does not work for everyone. One recently arrived man only lasted a few weeks before moving on, saying it wasn't what he expected. But that is rare. Most people who join stay with us. It is a good life and one I could never leave."

"We would not allow it," says Kurt, embracing Jacob. Kurt is a naturally tactile individual, forever shaking hands and hugging. Peter looks slightly uncomfortable whenever he sees it, but I appreciate the warmth of his gestures.

"We have kept you long enough," I say, my eyes growing weary from last night's exertions.

"Yes. We must go." Peter stands and takes Kurt's hands.

"Come and see us," says Kurt.

"We will."

"I mean it. Please come."

Jacob stands and approaches me, shaking my hand for the first time. And suddenly, I am momentarily outside my body, standing in front of a large barn. Inside, a man pitches hay from a bale, standing with his back to me, hunched over in concentration. Then, task accomplished, he strides farther into the barn. But there is something familiar about his walk. Something I can't quite put my finger on.

Chapter Twenty

THE WINTER GARDENS

I AM NO SOONER OUT of my body than back in it, absent for only a fraction of a second. My hand is still in Jacob's when my awareness returns and I cast a guilty glance at Peter, expecting a covert admonishment. But he is busy talking to Kurt and has not noticed my momentary slippage. And why would he when I remained upright and seemingly conscious?

The time differential while dreamwalking never ceases to amaze me. Time runs slowly on the astral plane and speeds by in the real one. And I marvel at my ability to keep going without giving myself away. Had I fainted, I would have fallen to the floor, but unless something dramatic occurs, I usually remain upright and functional. And I am thankful for it. I have never come to terms with the embarrassment of dreamwalking. I would die of humiliation if anyone who doesn't already know found out. Perhaps astral travel will become more commonplace in the fullness of time. After all, the ministry is working hard to weaponise it.

But they are doing it covertly. And not just to protect military secrets. Most people don't believe your consciousness can leave your body. I have only realised, in recent years, the rarity of my gift.

"Ready?" asks Peter as he shakes Kurt's hand for the final time. I nod.

Peter places a guiding arm around my waist, and we slowly stroll down The Promenade.

"How are you feeling?" asks Peter.

I stiffen, hoping he is not about to enter into a discussion about my recent bodily absence, no doubt, with an accompanying vacant expression.

"Well," I say suspiciously.

"Legs functioning? Movement up to scratch?"

"As much as they ever will be," I reply tartly. I'm crippled with limited walking ability, as Peter knows full well. I don't appreciate the stupidity of the question.

"Simmer down," says Peter, sensing my displeasure. "I was going to ask if you thought you could make it over there?" My eyes follow the direction of his finger, pointing towards a huge domed building in the distance.

"What is that?" I ask.

"The Winter Gardens," says Peter. "A former hangout of Brian Sullivan and this morning's intended destination of our dear Cora."

"Oh," I say distractedly while trying to estimate the distance between us and the building. It's not a million miles away, though it's too close to my walking limit for comfort.

"I'm not sure, Peter. "It's risky."

"Then we'll take a cab."

"That seems like a terrible waste of our time and money."

"I'd rather that than have to pick you off the pavement if you fall."

Peter raises his hand towards the passing traffic, but I reach out and lower it again.

"I can try," I say.

"Are you sure?"

"I'd like to. It's high time I pushed myself."

"Don't think like that. Better safe than sorry."

"Better active than lose the little ability I have."

"Very well," says Peter. "But you must take my arm."

I do so willingly and lean into him as we slowly pass a nearby fountain where Neptune sits, regally thrusting his trident before him. I pause, marvelling at the stone-carved seahorses frolicking before their master.

"Beautiful," I say.

"Very skillful."

I sigh and sweep my hand through the sprinkling water. "Just look at those mermen. Whoever carved their shells was a true craftsman."

"Conches," says Peter.

"Whatever you say." I set off again, lips pursed. Peter might think it is helpful imparting his greater knowledge, but it's spoiled the moment. I increase my pace, greatly regretting it a few moments later when my leg cramps and the old familiar feeling of weakness strikes.

I stop and rub my leg.

"Just a little while longer, Connie," says Peter. "We're in Imperial Place. The Winter Gardens are only a few yards away."

But a few yards for Peter can range from a little longer to an eternity of hard slog for me, depending on the day. And bearing in mind we have been in town for a while, both shopping and visiting a distinctly unsavoury property agent,

I have already expended most of my energy. I cling on harder to Peter's arm, grit my teeth and force myself one baby step at a time until we reach the steps of the Winter Garden. And as I stop and finally appreciate the towering structure before me, I am glad we came.

I stand in awe, following a trail of ivy as it creeps along the buttresses upon which iron spans hold an enormous glass roof. The sun is out in earnest, casting its rays onto the central atrium and reminding me of a distant view I once had of the Crystal Palace.

"I didn't expect it to be this big," I say. "It seemed smaller from afar."

"Isn't everything?"

I shake my head. Peter is in a proper know-it-all mood today, but I can't be bothered to disagree while there is a stunning building to explore. Assuming I can navigate my way around it without falling over.

"Can we go in?" I ask.

"Absolutely. I'm hoping Cora is still here. She had a luncheon appointment."

"Lucky her."

Peter opens the door and ushers me inside. I limp into an enormous courtyard full of palm plants of all sizes in heavy clay pots. I run a finger around my neck and loosen the knot on the new beau blouse I bought last month in Newquay. The temperature is several degrees warmer here than outside, doubtless from the greenhouse effect of the sun on glass. In fact, the room feels like a giant orangery until we reach the gaudier end, where heavily draped curtains and bright linen weave cushions create the effect of a Middle Eastern boudoir. I stare open-mouthed at the luxury, marvelling as we move onwards. My legs have stopped bothering me, and now I am preoccupied with the grandeur of the ever-changing decor. We pass Egyptian hieroglyphics and carved statues, soon slipping into an Anglo-Indian theme of Hindu gods and goddesses standing incongruously alongside black-and-white photographs of British soldiers in the Raj.

"It's remarkable," I say. "How I wish I could travel to some of these places."

Peter frowns. "Don't say that. Be careful what you wish for."

I don't reply. I know what Peter fears, but he is not aware of my recent uncontrolled dreamwalking and I have no intention of telling him. Peter mothers me like an old hen at the best of times. I swear part of Mrs Ponsonby has entered his soul to keep me in line. And I smile as I think of her and realise, for the first time in a while, that Vera's memory brings smiles and not the usual tears.

"It's not quite so impressive if you take a closer look," says Peter, pointing beyond the magnificent entrance hall to an even larger room. I follow as he strides towards it, and my heart drops as I see an almost empty auditorium with a few feeble displays of costumes and dancing paraphernalia.

"This must be where Brian strutted his stuff," says Peter. "And it is clearly not used very often. Rather a lot of wasted space, I fear."

"How sad," I say. "Such a magnificent building, but all lace and no knickers."

"What a horrible expression," says Peter, looking down his nose.

I place my hands on my hips. "The last person who said that in my hearing was your mother."

"She should jolly well know better."

"I thought it was funny."

"And look at the ironwork. It's all rusty. A pane of glass

is missing, and I can't count the number of cracks." Peter has moved on from my coarse remark and is giving the building his full critical attention. Sadly, he is right. The Winter Garden, so magnificent from the outside, is a crumbling behemoth. I feel disappointed and ever so slightly cheated.

"Why would Cora come here then?" I ask.

"To eat," said Peter. "There's a cafe somewhere, I imagine. Unless she's brought a picnic."

I scrutinise his face, trying to decide whether he's serious, but Peter's expression remains impervious, and I won't give him the satisfaction of asking.

"Come on then. We'll look for Cora, but can we please go home if we don't find her quickly? I am beyond tired."

"Of course," says Peter, eyeing me with concern. For all his faults, Peter cares and would feel horribly responsible if I became incapacitated.

He takes my arm, and we slowly pass through the cavernous space into a further small room and then another, which opens into a pleasant seating area filled with small round tables and pot plants. A wooden counter runs the length of the room behind which several women industriously prepare food.

"Cooee," says a voice, and we immediately spy Cora dressed in her latest bright red turban head wrap, teamed with a tight-fitting tailored suit finishing at the calves and with a long line of oversized buttons down the centre. She sports a slick of scarlet lipstick and has pencilled her already impressively arched brows a darker shade of fair. Cora does not dress like your average middle-aged woman, and no man would guess her age or even dare to try. She carries herself upright, with a straight back and head held high. Her slender figure and military deportment give her a ten-year advantage over her peers, and she is more than capable of competing with much younger women. Heads turn as she waves towards us, beckoning us over to the table she shares with a portly man in his fifties or sixties.

Her gentleman friend has the air of an overfed wolf caught in the act. His thin lips set into a frown as we approach.

"Charles. Meet Connie and Peter," says Cora, bounding to her feet and enveloping me in a warm hug. I disentangle myself, and she does the same to Peter.

"Do join us," says Cora. "You don't mind, do you?" she asks Charles, daring him to deny her with the twitch of an eyebrow.

"I'd be delighted," he says, looking anything but.

Peter pulls out a chair and does the gentlemanly thing, settling me down and taking my stick before finding an inferior chair with a missing cushion at the next table. He removes his handkerchief and cleans the wrought iron base before perching on the edge.

"How lovely to meet you," says Peter.

Charles forces a smile. "Likewise," he growls.

We sit for a moment while Cora beckons a passing waiter and insists that we choose something from the menu. I feel nauseous, and Peter pales as we contemplate yet more food.

"Thank you, but we've eaten," says Peter, waving the waiter away.

"Two coffees and a plate of cakes," says Cora, brooking no refusal. "Our puddings will be along shortly, won't they, Charles? And we can't possibly eat in front of you."

"I really can't..." says Peter, his words trailing away at the futility of his protestation as the waiter marches off with the order.

"Now, you've just missed the most thrilling violinist," says Cora. "He played a few solo pieces by Vivaldi. It set just the mood for lunch."

"How pleasant," I say, glad to have avoided the moment. I like music as much as the next person, but I have no great love for stringed instruments unless at the lower end of the scale. They are only marginally less painful than the mouth organ, accordion, and bagpipes, all of which set my teeth on edge.

Peter winks, knowing my aversion to instruments that sound like yowling cats and opens his mouth to speak. I think he might mention it for one horrible moment, but instead, he turns to Cora and says, "How do you two know each other?"

"From the distant past," says Cora. "We met when Charles gave a talk at the Ladies College many years ago. I was boarding while looking after a young charge. The head-mistress asked if I would like to attend the event. Charles and I got talking, and he invited me to an open evening. We've been friends ever since."

"Really?" I say, wondering at how little I still know about Cora despite our years of acquaintanceship.

"Were you a teacher?" asks Peter.

Charles splutters a reply. "Not at all. I was an architect. Ms Cream came to my first demonstration at the town hall. I was showing off plans for a new building. Sadly, it did not come to fruition."

Cora smiles sympathetically. "Most unfortunate. It would have been a notable piece of work."

"Their loss," says Charles. "Anyway, I gave it all up soon after that."

"The property?"

"No. The career. Too much dependence on other people."

"And your occupation now?" asks Peter.

"I'm a politician."

"Oh," says Peter, as an uncomfortable silence descends. "Good for you," he adds when too much time has passed for comfort.

"We're not a popular breed," says Charles. "Look." He produces a folded flyer from his inside pocket and slams it on the table. A spoon in Cora's coffee cup rattles and jumps from the saucer. Charles opens the paper to reveal his image on the front underneath the words *Vote Charles Ince*. Four tiny holes at each corner suggest that drawing pins once held up the document. And some bright spark has drawn a pair of blacked-out glasses, a hearing aid, and a gag across his face. "Sheer bloody vandalism," says Charles, then catches himself. "Sorry for blaspheming, Cora. It just slipped out. But this is the sort of nonsense we must put up with. No respect anymore."

Charles shakes his head while Cora pats his shoulder, and I wonder why she has so much tolerance for this man-child. Charles Ince is brusque, moody, and without self-awareness. He has no redeeming qualities, lacking both good looks and charm. Yet Cora hangs on his every word, patting his shoulder and reassuring him that politicians are valuable and necessary. It makes me wonder if she's holding a candle for her now ex-husband, Andrew Pennington, who still occupies a position in parliament. The divorce scandal did not touch his career prospects, and, to the best of my knowledge, he is happily settled with his new family. But Cora knows the demands of a public service life from her time as a politician's wife and perhaps feels for Charles Ince despite the fallout from her cheating reptile husband.

"It's very childish," says Peter, pointing to the defaced print. Charles nods his gratitude, and I look away, fearing that gallows humour might strike. It wouldn't be the first time, and it's almost impossible to recover from. No excuse is ever good enough. Fortunately, the waiter returns with two cups of coffee, the promised plate of cakes, and Cora's desserts.

"Delicious," says Cora, spooning cream into her mouth. "Would you like to try some?"

I shake my head and utter a firm no.

"What is it?" asks Peter.

"A rum baba."

"Then no."

"Good. More for me," says Cora, taking an even larger spoonful. I don't know where she puts it. Annoyingly, Cora can eat unlimited food with negligible effect on her waistline. If I take so much as a lingering glance at a pudding, my weight will immediately increase by several pounds. I distractedly take a piece of vanilla sponge, cut it open, and start spreading extra jam before remembering that I don't really want it and that my dress is already too tight. But I eat it anyway. Tiredness has rendered my spirits low, and I'll fall asleep if I don't watch it.

"Charles has offered to help with your little problem," says Cora.

My heavy eyelids flutter open. "What problem?" I ask.

"Your investigation."

"Really?" I ask. "How might he do that?"

"Charles has many connections," says Cora.

"Fabulous. Police connections?"

A flicker of annoyance crosses Charles Ince's face. "Possibly. What do you need to know?" He sounds unenthusiastic, and I suspect he has no interest in helping me but is motivated to please Cora.

"Anything about the torso case. Information about Captain Butt or Brian Sullivan. Ideally, I would like to speak to one of the officers concerned with the investigation."

"Charles can arrange that," says Cora.

Charles Ince pats the back of her hand. "I can try," he says. "No promises, though."

"I'm sure you'll do your best," smiles Cora, flexing her hands catlike as she looks deeply into his eyes.

"Anything for you, Coralie," he says, briefly lost in the moment.

I try to disguise the revulsion crossing my face. Peter looks away, thoroughly embarrassed by the public display of affection, and I push my plate away. The cake had little appeal to start with, and now it has none.

"Thank you," says Cora, taking her spoon and polishing off the rest of her pudding. Charles Ince's face falls as her interest diverts from him.

"I'll tell you something for free," he says, returning to me.

"Yes?"

"Young Sullivan regularly danced here." Charles vaguely waves towards the auditorium.

"So I hear."

"He was a proper ladies' man."

"We heard the opposite," says Peter, a flicker of interest replacing the glazed-eyed look of a man with an overfilled stomach.

"What? One of them? Good Lord, no. I saw the man in action. He was a regular heartthrob. The ladies queued out of the door to get a spin around the dance floor with Brian. Or should I say, Byron?"

"Should you?" I ask, nonplussed.

"His nom de plume."

"A stage name?" I ask.

"More or less, not that he was consistent. It depended on the day. Sometimes, he called himself Brian Sullivan, and other days, Byron Smith. Look over there," says Charles, pointing to a corkboard by the double doors.

"At what?"

"Go and see."

I glance at my stick and shake my head, but Charles is oblivious to my disability. I am pleased on the one hand but frustrated by the fact that I am so tired that the board might as well be a mile away.

"I'll go," says Peter, jumping to his feet. He returns moments later with a poster advertising an exhibition dance at the Palais de Danse, Winter Gardens. The poster is faded, and upon closer inspection, I see that the exhibition happened before Christmas.

"And now he's dead," I say, remembering the tragic look on Eileen Sullivan's face and her pathetic attachment to Peter, bearing more than a passing resemblance to her deceased son.

"The world moves in mysterious ways," adds Cora, taking a none-too-subtle glance at her watch.

"I always thought he'd come to a bad end," says Charles.

"Did you know him?" I lean forward, half interested, half combative. Charles Ince is displaying the same know-it-all traits that Peter did earlier. I feel the need to challenge him and find out whether he is repeating gossip or has something of genuine interest to impart.

"Not really," says Charles.

As I suspected.

"But I heard Chief Superintendent Wayman thought differently."

"Why?"

"As a high-ranking police officer, he was naturally party to the investigation, including one or two unsavoury facts about Sullivan's friends in the capital."

"What about them?"

"I can't tell you details," says Ince curtly. "Suffice it to say that they were operating on the fringes of the underworld."

"Is that why Brian died?"

"Of course not. He killed himself."

"His mother thinks not," I say.

"Then she is wrong. He killed Butt and did himself in. No other way out, do you see?"

"It's not as hard and fast as that," says Peter, coming to my aid.

"Only if you avoid the obvious facts." Charles Ince scowls and purses his lips like a recalcitrant child.

"Not much point in us pursuing this case," I blurt out, unable to stop the words I know I shouldn't utter.

"That's exactly what I said when Cora first mentioned it," says Charles.

"But you said you would help anyway." Cora smiles sweetly, takes her spoon and dips it into the pot of cream accompanying the cakes. She offers it to Charles, who obediently opens his mouth and swallows it.

"When will you know?" she asks as Charles licks his lips.

"Know what?"

"Whether your policeman friend will be able to help."

"In a day or two," says Charles, noncommittedly.

"That would be such a help, wouldn't it," says Cora.

Peter and I nod in unison. "Absolutely." I am heading to

the point of not caring, but for reasons unknown, Cora is putting every ounce of effort into keeping Charles onside. I wonder why? Is she worried about me and wants to keep me occupied? Or is it that the ex-private detective in her has never really gone away? Either way, she is grimly determined to get as much help from Charles Ince as is humanly possible. And with little else to go on, Peter and I must gratefully accept any assistance we can get.

Chapter Twenty-One

MORAL SUPPORT

I SLEEP like a baby and wake the following day to a cock crowing from a nearby garden. I rub my eyes and squint at my bedside clock. It is only a little after six. I roll over and try to get back to sleep, but thoughts of Jim lie heavy on my mind, spiralling from an optimistic certainty that he survived the fall to a grim fear that he died alone on the cliff in the night. Neither thought is conducive to sleep, so I turn my thoughts to the torso murder, trying to recall everything I have learned.

I mentally sieve the facts and discard some of the sillier notions, leaving me with an overwhelming desire to see the bridge where they found Captain Butt's remains. It seems relevant somehow, and I can't work out whether it would be an easy place to discard a body, both physically and in terms of the likelihood of being seen. Did his killers get lucky and find the bridge empty? Or was it seldom used anyway? Processing this information does not help me sleep. I give up, dress, and go downstairs to the living room, where I find Peter grimacing and holding his stomach.

"What's the matter?" I ask as Peter emits a little moan.

"Too much food yesterday, I think," he replies, sitting heavily down as his dressing gown splays open. I avert my eyes, grateful for the invention of male undergarments, as Peter struggles to re-fasten the cord.

"Ask Elys for something to make you feel better."

"She isn't up yet?"

"Must be," I say. "She's not in our room."

"Odd," says Peter. "She's not in the kitchen either."

"I know where Elys keeps her remedies," I say. "I'll look them out. You shouldn't move too far in your condition."

"No, I'll do it," says Peter, but I ignore him and make my way to the kitchen, leaning heavily on my stick. My incapacity from lameness varies daily, but it is tiresome this morning, probably because I overdid it in Cheltenham yesterday. Persuading Peter to go for a drive would be an excellent use of our time, as neither of us would need to walk. So, dragging myself to the medicine cupboard is in my best interests to help him feel more in the mood for a drive. I reach the kitchen and rummage around in a closet. Peter is right, and Elys is nowhere to be seen, but I quickly lay my hands on a small green bottle marked 'ginger and peppermint stomach remedy'. I unscrew the stopper and sniff, recoiling at the unpleasant stench. Then, I place a teaspoon and a jar of honey on a small tray to take away the taste. I inch into the living room, balancing the tray in my left hand while using the stick in my right.

"Connie, you shouldn't have," says Peter, viewing my painful progress with concern.

"It's fine. I should look after you for once."

Peter takes the bottle and glugs it back without reading the label. He wipes his hand over his mouth and pulls a face. "Grim," he says. "Let's hope it works."

I hand him the honey, and he sucks the teaspoon dry. "I might go back to bed," he says as his stomach growls.

"Poor you," I sympathise, sensing my trip to Haw Bridge slipping away before my eyes. But I test the water anyway. "Are you doing anything later?"

"Possibly. It depends how I feel."

"What might that be?"

Peter eyes me suspiciously. "I'd like to finish my book. Failing that, a trot up the street. But nothing too tiring after yesterday. I feel like a rest."

"That's a pity," I say.

"Why?"

"I would have liked to visit Haw Bridge."

"I doubt there's much to see."

"Even so, it's bound to help. I can't picture how someone managed to toss a torso into the water."

"The body was in pieces," says Peter. "Bound to make it easier."

"But they couldn't have carried it there by hand."

"I agree. The police are sure the killer transported it by vehicle. I still don't understand how viewing the location would help."

"It's just a feeling."

"Fine. We'll go. But not today."

"Tomorrow?"

"I'm playing golf."

"Doing what? You hate it."

"I'm largely ambivalent to the game, and before you say it, I know I'm not very good, and my handicap is dreadful, but Cora's isn't, and she's asked me to keep her company."

"What about me?"

"Come along."

"Don't be silly. I can't walk that far."

"But you can join us on the eighteenth and sit in the clubhouse while we play."

"Oh, really, Peter. I may as well be alone here. You never think of me."

Peter scowls. "Oh, I do. And probably more than is healthy. Elys isn't coming either, but she hasn't made a fuss."

I restrain myself from further argument and try one more time. "Perhaps you'll feel like a drive later if your stomach ache improves."

"I wouldn't count on it," says Peter, heaving himself to his feet. He puts the tray back in the kitchen and slowly climbs the stairs.

"I'll be in my room," he says.

I wander into the kitchen and start making myself a cup of tea before noticing a shape down at the bottom of the garden. I ignore it until it moves, then realise someone is huddled on the garden bench, leaning forward, with their head in their hands. I strain for a better look and recognise the figure as Elys. Judging by the way she is hanging her head, Elys is not in good shape. I set out another cup, boil the kettle and make a pot, all the time watching her. Elys barely moves, staring fixedly at a point on the ground. Once brewed, I fill two mugs and slowly walk down the garden. By the time I arrive, my knuckles are raw from the heat of the cups, both carried in one hand with my stick in the other.

Elys looks up as I approach her. "Oh, it's you," she says.

"Sorry. Were you hoping for someone else?"

"Not really."

"I've brought you a hot drink," I say, almost dropping the cup as it burns my skin.

"Thanks." Elys takes it, and absent-mindedly sips.

"You'll burn your lips."

"Least of my worries," she replies.

"What's wrong, Elys?"

"How long do you think we'll be here?"

"It's hard to tell."

"It already seems like forever."

"Missing Jory?"

Elys nods.

"And Lowenna, too?"

Elys turns away as tears prick her eyes. I park my stick and sit beside her, placing an arm around her shoulders.

"I'm sorry, Elys, and so grateful you came here. I know how hard it is to leave your family and how worried they must be with you away while you are in the family way. I don't know how long it will take, but we will be back long before your baby comes. Cora will decide on the finer details of our trip, more's the pity. I'd leave for home tomorrow if it were up to me. Not that I'd have left Cornwall in the first place if I had any say in the matter."

"I know," says Elys in a small voice. "And everyone must make sacrifices in these times. But I miss them. I hope Lowenna won't forget me."

"Oh, Elys," I say, taking her hand. "Your daughter adores you. She is safe and well with your mother and Jory. Why not send a postcard? Jory can read it to her."

Elys laughs. "Not his strongest skill," she says. "But I take your point. Lowenna would love that. And I saw some cards in the little corner shop yesterday. I'll take a walk there later. Would you like to come with me?"

I bite my lip, remembering the proximity of said shop. "Maybe later," I say. "I did too much yesterday, and I'm paying for it now. I was hoping Peter would take me for a drive instead. That way, we could both recover."

"Recover from what? Is Peter ill?"

"Yes, but it's probably indigestion," I say. "Although you can never tell with Peter. He either underplays or overplays his illnesses. No consistency."

"How will you get to wherever you're going? Will Cora lend Peter the car?"

"I expect so. But as Peter has refused to take me, it's a moot point. Which is fair enough if he's poorly, but I doubt he would even if well."

"Where were you going?"

"Haw Bridge."

"Where?" Elys looks blankly.

"Near Tirley. It's where they found the torso. You know, Captain Butt's dismembered body."

Elys shudders. "You are a strange one, Connie. I don't know why you want to get involved in such horrible matters."

"I can't help it. Unsolved crimes follow me. It's just one of those things."

"And you can't fight fate." Elys glances towards a single magpie and covertly salutes.

"Peter would call that superstitious nonsense."

"And I would call him a fool," says Elys. "Anyway, you can talk. You're as superstitious as I am."

"No point in tempting fate," I say.

"Exactly."

"I suppose there's another way."

"For what?"

"Visiting Haw Bridge."

"Is there?"

"Yes. But I'd need someone with me."

"I can't, Connie. It's not like I wouldn't appreciate a bit of time away from the house, but I've duties to perform. Besides, you may not be able to get there by bus?"

I sigh. "Maybe, maybe not. Then plan C it is."

Elys narrows her eyes. "Plan C?"

"I'll dreamwalk."

"No, you won't," says Elys emphatically. "You know what they've told you. It's too risky."

"It's the only possible way."

"Of course it isn't. Just be patient. Wait until someone can drive you. You're not a child, Connie. You can't stamp your foot and expect people to come running."

"I can't stamp my foot because I'm lame." I take my stick and slam it into the ground. It's all very well taking lectures from people with two functioning limbs, but neither Elys nor anyone else can understand the frustration of not being independent.

"Oh, stop feeling sorry for yourself," Elys shouts.

I sit calmly for a moment, anger simmering beneath. But I keep a lid on it and speak gently. "You are the one who feels sorry for yourself because you're missing your family. But in a few weeks, you'll all be reunited. I will never be independent no matter how hard I try, however strong my character is, or how stiff a lip I show to the world. You can't fairly compare our situations when yours is temporary and mine permanent. You expect too much of me sometimes, Elys."

I get to my feet and turn to walk away, but Elys calls me back. "Connie, I'm sorry," she says. You're right. There's no comparison between my problems and yours. I shouldn't have said those things. I will help, but I honestly can't go today. I must shop and clean, among other things."

"I understand," I say. "But Elys, would you consider a supervised dreamwalk?"

"What do you mean?"

"I am safer astral travelling with someone watching over me. I've done it before with Peter. He sits beside me and helps me focus my mind on the where and when of how I will travel. It's quite straightforward and safe. I just need someone to keep me focused. I could try alone, but I haven't successfully navigated the astral plane recently. I've lost my accuracy over the years, not to mention my confidence. It's been a long time, and I'd almost forgotten how to do it until the other day."

"If it's that safe, then why not ask Peter?" asks Elys, eyes narrowed.

"Because he'd say a flat no without considering a safe way to help."

"But you've been told not to dreamwalk, and you promised you wouldn't. Tell me you haven't tried."

"I'd like to, but I can't. It wasn't my fault."

"Did it happen accidentally?"

"Whatever you'd like to think."

"I can't help you, Connie. I'd be in all kinds of trouble if anything happened to you."

"Please, Elys. As long as you watch me, I'll be perfectly safe. If I become agitated, you wake me. It's really that easy."

"Then why won't Peter…"

"Because he's taken control, and the power has gone to his head. It's my life, not his."

"I don't know. It's a risk."

"And being unable to control my dreamwalking is equally hazardous, but nobody thinks about that. Sooner or later, the ministry will monitor all astral travellers and persuade them to join forces, placing them in harm's way. Those who refuse must defend themselves alone. I have lost so many skills from lack of practice that I am practically powerless in either scenario. I must start building my defences again, whether or not Peter agrees."

Elys sighs and stares into the distance before turning back to me. "I hate to say it, Connie. But you're right."

Chapter Twenty-Two

HAW BRIDGE

TIME PASSES at a snail's pace while Elys prepares everything she needs to produce two meals swiftly, clean the house and collect fresh bread from the nearby bakery. I wait upstairs in my room, eager to avoid Cora, who has an uncanny knack for knowing when mischief is on the horizon. Once, I could count on Cora to turn a blind eye to discipline. At times, she actively encouraged rebellion, acting as more of a friend or confidante than a woman old enough to be my mother. But since Vera left us, she vacillates between behaving like an indulgent aunt and a Doberman pinscher. And I wouldn't like to take a chance on whether she'd permit my intended course of action, no matter how logical it seems.

Since speaking to Elys, my argument for practising dreamwalking skills has solidified in my mind. Quite why it has taken me so long to come to this obvious conclusion defeats me. As soon as the words left my mouth, I realised I should have been honing my gift all along. Grief for Vera had laid me low and stopped my passion for dreamwalking.

But instead of encouraging me to strengthen my gift, Stella and the other members of the Shining Path accepted my decision without protest. This may have been an easy choice for them. I would not need constant surveillance if I lived an ordinary life. Crossley wouldn't have the means to track me if I avoided the astral plane altogether, and they could tick me off as a problem solved. But in a world with limited dreamwalkers and an insurgent Nazi party determined to use any means at their disposal to forward their cause, in hindsight, this was a poor strategy. Lame, I might be, but I am stronger and more determined than many able-bodied travellers on the astral plane. I lean against the window ledge, watching an overloaded automobile make its way up Old Bath Road and ponder what would happen if we did go to war.

Though I miss the golden sands and towering cliffs of Porth Tregoryan, the view across regency Cheltenham towards the distant rolling hills lifts my spirits. My vantage point only allows a glimpse of the countryside from a street lined either side by unremarkable houses. But I can't complain. I saw the best of Cheltenham yesterday, a town chock full of historical buildings with a sympathetic blend of complementary styles. I was lucky enough to take a quick limp around the Winter Gardens abutting the classically designed town hall with stunning gardens beyond, which I enjoyed despite the deterioration inside. Similar handsome towns surrounded by green and pleasant countryside flourish across the length and breadth of England. My heart swells with pride as I consider my progress from a young girl who had never set foot beyond Newquay to a woman who has successfully navigated parts of Britain alone. And today, from nowhere, I realise I am in the unique position of being able to help my country and place myself at the disposal of those who need me. First, I will find a way to crush Crossley. And then I will volunteer for whatever comes next.

I hug myself as a shiver of hair stands up on the back of my arms. I feel alive and in control, and images of Vera Ponsonby flood into my mind, moments from the past where she has shown pride in me and her last loving words. I don't feel sad any longer, only empowered.

Crouching, I remove my case from under the bed and open a little box I took from Vera's trunk. Inside is Vera's precious last letter to me, a ruby brooch in the form of a crescent moon and a postcard depicting a Greek monastery at Mount Athos, which has always intrigued me. I open the letter and read Vera's words. They leave me joyful and feeling strong, and I fold the paper with a smile, returning it to the box with the postcard. I am not one for jewellery, but I pin the ruby brooch to my dress directly over my heart to acknowledge Vera's memory.

The door opens as I push the trunk back under the bed, and Elys returns, her apron stained with gravy. She removes it wordlessly and hangs it on the back of the door before smoothing her dress over her bump. Elys flashes a half smile and rubs her fingers over fine crows' feet at the corner of her eyes. She yawns before sitting heavily on the bed, hands cradling her stomach.

"You look exhausted," I say. "Do you need a rest?"

"Now is not the time," says Elys. "Peter is still in bed, and Cora has been out for a few hours. It's now or never."

"Are you sure?"

Elys nods. "I've thought of nothing else all morning, and your logic makes sense every way I look at it. The Nazi threat is real, and sacrifices must be made. I hope with all my heart that danger won't find you, Connie. But we will all pay if they conscript our men as rumours suggest."

"Jory is a fisherman. He should be safe."

"I'd rather not take the chance." Elys heaves herself to her feet. "Where do you want me?" she asks.

I remove the chair from our dressing table and drag it to the end of my bed. "Sit down," I say. "Have you eaten?"

Elys nods.

"Here," I say, thrusting the latest copy of *Home Chat* magazine her way. You'll need something to do while I'm gone."

Ely takes the magazine and perches on the chair. I recline on the bed, fingers brushing the tufted counterpane as I try to relax.

"Can you light a candle?" I ask, having already secreted both candles and matches on the trunk at the foot of Elys' bed.

She reaches over and strikes a match. "What next?" she asks.

"I'll use it to concentrate. You can extinguish the flame once I've gone."

"How will I know?"

I consider her question and try to remember the many occasions I have glanced at my prone body. "I'll appear to be asleep," I reply.

"And how will I know if you are in trouble?"

"Wake me if I seem fitful, cry out or move around. If all is well, I should lie quietly. You will know if anything is wrong. Peter always does." I point to a glass of water on the dresser. "Throw this at me if you are worried."

Elys frowns. "Whatever you say."

"One last thing, Elys. I need to focus on arriving at Haw Bridge. I've memorised it on the map, but it would be helpful if you chant the name while I try to connect with the astral plane. Keep repeating it for as long as you can."

"Right." Elys holds the now-lit candle and chews her lip. She is nervous but determined, and I make a mental note to buy her a thank-you gift to show my appreciation for her trust in me. Her decision couldn't have been easy.

I recline and adjust my pillows to a comfortable height before watching the candle flicker beneath Elys' faltering breath. I clear my mind of all extraneous thoughts, concentrating on a mental image of a photograph I found of Haw Bridge earlier that day. And in my mind's eye, I superimpose it on the candlelight. Seconds pass before déjà vu overtakes me, and my pillows feel lighter and less substantial. I barely need a point of concentration, so focused am I on the mission at hand. My fingers slip easily into the mattress, and I feel myself floating upwards. I look down to see Elys smoothing her hair, and then I drift through the ceiling, onwards, upwards, and ever higher until darkness surrounds me as I arrive on the astral plane.

Stars swirl in a violet haze as I linger on the periphery, waiting for the celestial heavens to do their thing. I have never understood why there are moments of hesitation, periods of non-activity, sometimes seconds, others lasting so long that I wonder if I will ever leave. But instead of a futile drift while I make sense of it all, I tightly focus on my objective. Haw Bridge, Tirley. Captain Butt. I think of myself hovering above the river, and then I drop down and put myself in the same position as Clive Price when he found the first telltale bloodstains. I envisage the photograph of the iron railings stretching along the bridge with a red brick cottage beyond. And before I know it, I am moving again, spiralling downwards, and landing precisely as if someone had painted me into the photographic image in my mind.

I stand there in my short-sleeved dress, watching the nearby treetops shimmer. The iron rails shine with recent rainfall, but I don't shiver. I cannot touch or feel in the dream state. But I can look and learn. And I am here for a reason.

The blood stains were purportedly in the middle of the bridge. I glide along, examining each iron bar to no avail. I did not expect the evidence to be obvious, but a blood mark would have been a valuable aid in locating the body. I peer over the edge to the swirling river beyond. The water level is high – far higher than I would have expected in May. Now that I am closer, I see that the rails are not wet but sparkling as if frosted. I turn to face the cottage. Smoke billows from the nearest chimney. The location is quiet; not a car in sight or a pedestrian, and barely any birdsong. Any noise comes from the fast-flowing river. This means that I have successfully answered at least one question. The bridge is quiet enough to dispose of a torso without being seen.

A distant thrum interrupts my thoughts. I don't react at first, but then I realise that the noise is getting closer. It sounds like an engine, probably a car, as a tractor would be too noisy. My first instinct is to hide. I don't know why, but the sound troubles me, making me feel threatened. So, I run towards the cottage and secrete myself behind the hedge.

The car slows as it approaches my destination, and for one awful moment, I fear discovery. But the gears grind, and the motor stutters across the bridge before the car pulls over. I wait for a few seconds, immobilised by the shock of the unexpected arrival. Then a distant splashing noise breaks the spell, and I suddenly realise that not only have I found my way to the exact location, but my concentration was so accurate that I arrived at the right moment in time. The river is high because it's January, not May. And I have just witnessed someone dumping the torso. If I can see the car's occupants, I can solve the mystery.

I peer from behind the bush as the car door slams shut and realise I have left it too late. The perpetrators are getting away. And I have been needlessly crouching behind foliage as if anyone could see me when I know full well that they can't. I dart from my hiding place like an Olympic runner and watch as the black car speeds off into the distance. I clutch my forehead, furious with myself. I could chase after it, but the car is already a hazy shape in the distance. I didn't even manage to note the number plate. So, I glide to the centre of the bridge and find a ruby red blood-stain across several rails with a purplish fibre embedded between. I lean over, peer below and see a marble-white chunk of something unidentifiable drifting downstream. I contemplate following its course but baulk at getting closer than necessary. I know what it is, how it would smell and that it would have started putrefying. Instead, I search my immediate surroundings, finding a canvas shoe, twine, and a glove. I decide to look closer, but a figure moves in the distance. Someone is coming towards me. But my reason has returned. I am only visible to fellow dreamwalkers and needn't worry. The man won't see me. I keep on track, kneeling for a closer look at the glove, when suddenly, the earth moves, and my shoulders shake as if I were in the middle of an earthquake. I feel myself falling backwards, whipping through time and space at a mind-bending rate. I abruptly stop and my eyes snap open to see Peter standing before me, an expression of fury across his face.

Chapter Twenty-Three

POOR ELYS

PETER HAD BEEN SO angry that he'd stormed off, clomped downstairs and slammed the door before striding up the street in his dressing gown. I'd spent the next half an hour comforting a stricken Elys, who had been shocked at the strength of Peter's rage. With Cora still out and Elys feeling the weight of Peter's disappointment, I had decided that bed was the best place to be and had exhaustedly fallen into a dreamless sleep. I'd woken around midnight to find the house still and quiet. A glance to my left had told me Elys was in bed, and I'd debated getting up to see if Cora's car was in the drive. But it was all too much effort. I lay in bed until sleep finally took me, drifting in and out of consciousness until dawn, when I awoke to find Elys had gone downstairs.

It is now nearly eight o'clock, and I have taken an age to get dressed, procrastinating like mad as I screw up my courage to face the inevitable storm. I go downstairs and open the living room door to find it empty. The same is true of the dining room and kitchen: no Cora, Peter, Elys, and no car. I feel a rising tide of panic swell within my chest, and my heart beats a little louder as the first spikes of dread chill my blood. Yesterday, I felt invincible, certain I was pursuing a sensible and logical course of action. But I had gone against everything I'd agreed. Had I overreached? Were Peter and Cora so angry that they had abandoned me? Surely not?

I pace the living room, limping from one side to the next, and soon, my leg begins to drag. My calf isn't painful today; it's just lifeless as if controlled from elsewhere. But the butterflies in my stomach leave me restless, and I can't bear sitting alone with my thoughts. So, I keep relentlessly plodding the length of the room, wondering why everyone would leave me alone if I truly were in great danger. Unless they are so angry, they don't care anymore.

Ten minutes pass, and the clock chimes nine. I have been moving for the best part of an hour, changing location long enough to brew a pot of tea. But I have reached the point when I must sit before I fall, and I almost tumble onto the couch, drawing up my legs and clutching my knees like a small child, feeling utterly bereft.

By the time the door goes, I have given up all pretence of bravery and am sobbing like a baby when Cora finds me.

"What on earth is wrong?" she asks, placing an arm around my shoulders. "Are you ill?"

"No. But where were you? Why did you leave me alone?"

Peter appears from behind her, lips pursed, face impassive. "Don't be ridiculous," he says. "We left Elys in charge."

"She isn't here," I say, wiping my eyes.

Peter raises his eyes heavenwards and strides into the kitchen. "Elys?" he calls.

I hear the door slam as Peter enters the garden. He returns moments later. "Cora, come quickly."

Coralie removes her arm, shoots me a worried glance, and runs wordlessly from the room. I collect my stick and follow them to the garden to see them crouched at the end of the stony path.

"Get the doctor," says Cora and Peter runs past me, and through the garden gate.

I reach Cora, who is kneeling beside Elys, holding her hand as she lies on her side. "I'm fine," Elys growls. But I can see that she isn't. A large, angry lump bulges from her temple, a line of dried blood is crusted on her cheek.

"Oh no. What happened?" I cry, stroking Elys's hair.

"I woke up feeling dizzy and came outside for some fresh air," says Elys. "I must have fallen over." She clutches her head as she speaks. "Please help me up. I need water."

"No," says Cora firmly. "You may have a concussion. We're close to the hospital. Peter will fetch help in no time."

We wait anxiously, and sure enough, ten minutes later, Peter arrives, accompanied by a bearded man carrying a doctor's bag. He shoos us away and crouches by Elys, feeling for her pulse and checking her eyes.

He beckons Peter over. "Help us to the car," he says. "I'd like to properly examine this young lady at the hospital to be on the safe side."

Peter and the doctor support Elys as she approaches the car. "Don't tell Jory," she pleads. "He will only fuss."

But Cora turns to me the moment the car pulls away. "Surely we must let her family know?"

I nod. "Jory would never forgive us if we kept it from him."

"I'll get Peter to send a telegram to the hotel as soon as he returns. Roxanne will get it to Jory."

I scowl at the name of my arch nemesis, still resentful that I am indebted to her. "You should do it immediately. Jory might want to come to Cheltenham."

"Patience, Connie," says Cora. "We don't know how Elys is yet or if there will be any consequences."

I gaze in horror as the impact of Cora's understated words hit home. "You mean the baby might be hurt?"

"Let's hope not," says Cora, turning away.

Tears prick my eyes. I try to hold them back and fight the urge to feel sorry for myself while Elys is in dire straits. But try as I might, tears flow down my cheeks, and I cover my face with my hands. "Jory will hate me," I wail.

Cora places a gentle hand on my back. "Don't be silly. Why would he?"

"Because it's all my fault." My shoulders shudder as sobs rack my body, even more heartfelt than earlier when I had felt abandoned. Now, I know my behaviour would have justified their desertion.

"Look at me," says Cora, but shame has immobilised me and I hide my face from sight.

"I said, look at me," Cora barks, her words clipped. She has never shouted at me in all the years I have known her. I look up.

Cora pulls an expensively embroidered handkerchief from her sleeve and wipes my face. "Whatever happened to Elys is not your fault," she says.

"But I made her watch me dreamwalk, and Peter was furious. Elys was so upset. I convinced her she was doing the right thing when deep down she probably knew she wasn't."

"Elys knew exactly what she was doing," says Cora. "She is highly intelligent, and I value her opinion. You would have heard my views if you'd come downstairs to face the music last night. Elys explained your point of view, and I agreed with her. And I said the same to Stella McGregor when I telephoned her from town this morning."

"But Peter?"

Cora tilts her head. "It's fair to say that Peter does not concur. But then he never has been terribly objective where you're concerned."

"I don't know what you mean."

"Peter is an only child. You are his best friend, and your relationship is as close to that of siblings as Peter will ever know. He is overprotective, in my opinion. And he has overexerted his influence on The Order. You are their greatest asset, and we all appear to have lost sight of this simple fact."

"So, Elys wasn't in trouble?"

"Not with me, and that's what matters. Peter will soon calm down and will doubtless apologise. I expect he's feeling awful now. But Elys told you she's been feeling dizzy for a few days. I should have made her see the doctor sooner."

"Thank goodness," I say, but my relief does not last long. "What if she loses the baby?"

Cora sighs. "We can only hope that the fall caused no harm. For what it's worth, I found Elys on her back. She must have clipped her head against the bench on the way down."

I thank Cora and sink back onto the settee, letting the cushions take my weight. We sit in silence, neither of us knowing what to say or do next. Cora finally jumps to her feet. "I'd make a hot drink, but we need something stronger."

She tinkers around in the dining room, emerging moments later carrying heavy glass tumblers filled with an amber liquid.

"Bottoms up," she says, handing a glass to me.

"What is it?" I sniff the liquid and wrinkle my nose. It does not smell appealing.

"I don't recall saying bottoms up if you please, my lady. Just drink it. It will do you good."

I follow Cora's lead and slug back the contents, gagging as it goes down. But moments later, a surprisingly pleasant warm glow settles over my throat, and my hands stop shaking.

"Another?" asks Cora.

"Most definitely not."

"Ah, here he is." Cora turns her head as a car pulls up outside. Peter emerges, opens his wallet, and drops a few coins into the driver's hand.

I lean forward, heart racing as Peter enters the house, slamming the door as he strides into the living room.

"Well?" asks Cora.

"I don't know," says Peter. "I left Elys tucked up in bed. They can't tell if she has a concussion or not, so they'll keep her overnight."

"What about the baby?"

"It's moving," says Peter. "Elys said the doctor had a good feel of her tummy and seemed satisfied. She isn't worried, so neither am I."

I'm so relieved I start crying again. Peter shakes his head. "Why the waterworks? You haven't stopped all morning."

Under any other circumstances, I would put him right, but nothing can spoil my joy, knowing the baby is safe and well.

"Isn't it marvellous?" I say, reaching for Cora's hand. She is a little more cautious.

"Encouraging news," she says. "But let's keep everything crossed. Peter, would you mind popping into the post office?"

"I already have," he says. "I know Elys said not to, but Jory has a right to know."

"We thought so too," beams Cora. "Now, sit down, Peter. I've spoken to Connie about our friends at the Shining Path. Let's get this out in the open so you and Connie can be friends again. We'll have no more tears today."

Peter scowls. "You've outvoted me," he says. "A ridiculous decision, but one I must abide by. Don't blame me if it all goes wrong and you find yourself stuck on the astral plane with Crossley."

I shiver at Crossley's name but find yesterday's inner resolve. "It's inevitable, though, isn't it? I can't avoid my fate forever."

"You sound like a bad actress," says Peter. "You are not Joan of Arc. Crossley is not Satan."

"And you have never set foot on the astral plane in your life. But you have seen enough of Crossley's creatures to appreciate the danger. And if you don't see me as much of a warrior, think about the last time we were in London. You must remember the assault on the Shining Path headquarters?"

"Not like you do," snaps Peter. "It's invisible to me. I can't see what you see, and I can't step in to help. All I can do is protect your earthly body. But that's not good enough, is it?"

Peter turns his head, but it's too late. I have already seen the tears in his eyes. And I finally understand. Peter is bigger and stronger than me but impotent to protect me on the astral plane. He wishes he could offer more and takes my independence as a rejection of his help. I reach for his hand, but he snatches it away. And as the doorbell rings, the moment is lost.

Chapter Twenty-Four

ALL IS NOT AS IT SEEMS

"AH. A VISITOR. JOLLY GOOD," says Cora, opening the door.

A familiar figure, casually leaning against the doorpost, doffs his hat before turning to greet her.

"Do come in," says Cora, waving Charles Ince ahead. He gazes unappreciatively around the small living room and steps inside, awaiting further instructions.

"Would you like some tea?" asks Cora. Charles Ince nods in the affirmative, and Cora moves towards the bell before exclaiming. "Oh dear. Poor Elys is in hospital. I rather think we'll have to do without."

"I'll make it," I say, in no mood for small talk with Cora's friend.

She looks doubtfully towards me. "Can you manage?"

"Of course, she can't," snaps Peter waspishly. "I'll go."

Peter disappears, and Charles Ince takes a seat. He answers a few general questions about the weather before Cora swoops in for the kill.

"Did you get anywhere with the inspector?" she asks.

"Sadly not."

"Oh." Cora does not try to hide her disappointment.

"Don't worry. I didn't give up," says Charles eagerly.

"Really?"

"Of course not. Where there's a will, there's a way."

"You clever thing," trills Cora, placing her hand on his arm. If Charles Ince had a tail, it would be wagging. He smiles and edges closer to Cora on the settee. I look away, hoping he doesn't lean in and try to kiss her. An air of grim anticipation settles across the room.

Cora smiles but moves out of range. "Tell me all about it," she says.

"Well, I visited the police station as promised," says Ince. "To no avail. Too much red tape. The inspector wouldn't cooperate. But I am well connected, and he introduced me to the next best thing."

"Which was?"

"A particularly well-informed journalist."

"Oh." Cora looks doubtful again, but Charles continues. "No, really. A chap called O'Donnell. He's a regular newshound, I tell you. And he's been sniffing around this case since it went to trial, preparing for some dubious exposé with Mrs Sullivan."

I listen in and engage with the conversation now that things have moved on from the earlier flirtation. "How do you know that?"

"I spoke with him, young lady," says Ince, fixing me with a stern eye.

"And who does O'Donnell work for?" I ask cynically.

"*The Empire News*," he says.

"Ah."

"Ah, indeed. The man has decent credentials. You should be grateful."

I rearrange my features into something resembling gratitude and thank him profusely. His face softens. "Anything for Mrs Pennington," he says.

"What did you discover?" asks Cora, just as a scowling Peter carries in the tea tray. He is clearly in low spirits, having made little attempt to clean up tea slops where the overfilled pot has sloshed over the tray. And there is not a biscuit in sight. Peter asks Charles Ince if he would like a cup of tea and takes Cora's and my acceptance for granted, pouring two cups without asking. I pick up the insipid brew, which has barely seen a tea leaf, and hope my face does not reflect my feelings. My stomach growls, and I think about the gingerbread Elys baked earlier in the week and wish Peter had had the foresight to bring it through.

Charles Ince slurps his tea and launches into details of his meeting with Bernard O'Donnell at a small tea shop in The Strand. He brags that although O'Donnell had no initial interest in revealing details of his story, Ince wooed him with his charm and undeniably valuable connections. I let out an unbidden sigh and immediately cover my mouth with a well-positioned handkerchief to the nose. I am already weary of his boasting and wish he would get on with the story. Cora prompts him with a few well-chosen words.

"How thrilling," she says. "Do go on."

"O'Donnell kept some of his theories close to his chest," says Ince. "But was more than happy to share those of Chief Inspector Worth, of whom he does not have a high opinion – a tricky matter, as I consider Worth to be more than a mere acquaintance. But I thought of you, Cora, and hoped a neutral stance would help. So, I listened without comment."

"Thank you," says Cora with a smile that does not reach

her eyes. Even Cora is getting bored now and is eager for details.

"Well, Worth was initially of the opinion that the body in Tower House might not belong to Brian Sullivan."

"I've heard similar," says Peter.

"Apparently, there was a height discrepancy," continues Ince. "The coffin was several inches bigger than the body."

"Are you sure?" I ask.

"I didn't measure it myself," snaps Ince. "But Worth had a bee in his bonnet about the alleged anomaly. Brian Sullivan was five foot seven and a half, but the coffin measured five foot eleven, according to O'Donnell. Worth investigated and tried to tie up the loose ends, as it were. Anyway, Bernard Spilsbury measured the body during the autopsy and said it was the right height."

"So why the excessively long coffin?" asks Peter.

"A mistake by the undertaker, I suppose."

"Costly, though," I offer.

"Possibly. It's a pity there were no satisfactorily recorded notes around the measurements, or it might have settled that particular issue."

"What about the identity of the torso?" asks Cora.

"Hard to tell without the head," says Ince. "They never found it. Probably never will."

"Did they establish a cause of death?" I ask.

"Spilsbury noted evidence of injury. Possible vehicle impact."

"The body was struck by a car?" I ask, remembering the dark vehicle speeding away from Haw Bridge.

"Could be," says Ince. "Spilsbury thought so, and quite a fast-moving one, in his opinion. But again, that was conjecture rather than fact."

"So, Brian Sullivan might have run over Captain Butt and killed himself rather than face the music."

"That's one theory," says Ince.

I feel deflated. If true, then one death would be accidental, and the other a suicide. The case feels more sinister than that.

"But O'Donnell had another theory, borne out by Irene Sullivan's evidence," says Ince. "He is certain that Brian was not alone at Tower House. At least one other person stayed there, perhaps more."

"Two," I say. "There were two." I cast my mind back to the misty winter morning of yesterday's dreamwalk. My vision had been hazy, but with hindsight, I was sure there were two shadows in the car. And the hulking shape pushing the torso from the bridge could have been two people close together.

"Indeed. O'Donnell tells me there is no shortage of theories," says Charles Ince.

"Do be a dear and summarise them all." Cora, who briefly disappeared, has returned with a plate of biscuits. I could hug her. She offers them around, and I take two.

Ince coughs. "We touched on one theory a few days ago," he says, shifting uncomfortably in his chair. Cora and I exchange glances. Ince's face has turned puce, and it's clear he would rather not elaborate.

"Was there any evidence?" asks Cora, taking his impossibly vague reference as an allusion to rumoured homosexual activities between the two men.

"Butt's name came up in a sodomy case at the Gloucester Assizes a few years before – a chap by the name of Nelson Gardner, who worked in a greengrocer. O'Donnell thinks it's a red herring. Follow it up if you want, but I did not ask, nor do I require any further details."

Ince's face is now scarlet. He reaches into his pocket, removes a handkerchief, and mops his brow. I let him off the hook.

"Anything else?" I ask, changing the subject.

As Charles Ince stuffs his handkerchief back again, he pulls a notebook out, withdrawing a small piece of lined paper and placing the notebook on the coffee table. He narrows his eyes and tries to focus on his lightly pencilled notes.

"Unaccounted for people at the lodge," he says. "I think we've covered that."

"Not in any detail," says Peter. Ince sighs.

"Sullivan spent a lot of time in London," says Ince. "He had friends there. One in particular, called Newman, drove a Jaguar SS. Look, here's the registration." Ince points to a careful sequence of letters and digits. DXT 375.

"Nice car. I take it his friend had a bob or two more than poor old Brian," says Peter.

Charles Ince nods. "You're right in part. Brian Sullivan was hard up for cash. How did you know?"

"I read a few articles in the press. Irene might have said something, too. We met her, you know?"

"So Cora said. Sullivan died with little cash to his name, but he had his car and holiday cottage, of course."

"Why didn't he sell them if he was short of money?"

Ince shrugs. "Who knows? The cottage was an asset that Brian and his mother used. She's been there recently, I hear."

"Where is it?" I ask.

"Somewhere in Polperro," says Ince. "Here. Take this. It belonged to Brian Sullivan and should go back to his mother. You won't find much in the way of useful information, but the address of the cottage is somewhere inside."

I reach forward and take the notebook into my custody before Ince can change his mind. He continues talking.

"Yes. Sullivan was not entirely broke by any means. As for his friends, I have already told you they were treading a fine line between lawful and criminal. And there is reasonable evidence to suppose they were in Gloucestershire in January."

"Definitely?"

"I believe so. And Keith Newman may well have had a hand in the torso disposal.

I lean forward. Now we are getting somewhere.

Ince continues. "They couldn't find much evidence, but police searching the river below Haw Bridge found a man's chamois glove."

"It could belong to anyone," I say.

"Yes, were it not for the laundry mark. But that was revealing, and it wasn't from a local laundry. It took a bit of tracing, so they told me. But the police tracked the laundress down eventually."

"Who was she?"

"A woman called Celia Greilly, Newman's estranged wife. She ran a laundry business from her premises in Langton Street or perhaps Glasshouse Street in Piccadilly. She used several properties. Ince clicks his fingers as he tries to remember.

"Is it in the notebook?" I ask, flicking through. I find it a few pages in. "Here we go. Twenty-seven Langton Street and twenty-six Glasshouse Street, Piccadilly."

"I say. That's rather close to our friend Crossley," says Peter, tracing his finger down the page.

"Felix Crossley?" asks Ince.

"Yes."

"Hardly surprising," he continues. "Crossley is one of Newman's acquaintances. Look. It's all here in the notes."

Chapter Twenty-Five

UNEXPECTED ENCOUNTER

TWO DAYS HAVE PASSED, and we are now on the move. Everything changed yesterday when Elys arrived home looking tired and pale. After rallying from the fall, she left her bed to visit the bathroom and almost fell in a heap on the floor. Fortunately, a diligent nurse spotted her swaying and darted to her side to hold her up before it was too late. They put Elys back to bed, but she had reached her fill of the hospital and insisted on being discharged the following day. Peter picked her up at almost the exact time Jory arrived from the station, having left Lowenna with his mother-in-law. We held a pow-wow, the upshot of which was that Cora would drive Elys and Jory back to Porth Tregoryan while Peter and I would hire a car and visit Ashton Keynes before heading north to an as-yet-unknown destination.

Seeing Elys more frail than usual was bad enough, though we could have coped had everything else been normal. But hearing Felix Crossley's name in conjunction with the torso case has set us all on high alert. Crossley has cropped up in every case I've ever worked on. And he has daubed his black mark on every perpetrator I've unmasked. This leads me to think that destiny is pushing us in the same direction again. Though the thought of seeing him brings me out in goosebumps, I accept it as inevitable. But whereas I am prepared to meet my nemesis now, Peter is still against me returning home to Cornwall or going anywhere I might encounter Crossley. As I have an inexplicable desire to visit the village where Kurt and the other Bruderhof reside, I have used this to my advantage, and Peter has agreed to drive me there while we decide what to do next.

It's late morning when we pass a pretty lake on the outskirts of Cirencester. Peter breaks his silence.

"Mother sends her love," he says.

"How kind. I miss Isla. When did you speak to her?"

"I didn't. Jory passed on her regards, amongst other things."

"Such as?"

"News from home," says Peter. "And the library in particular. Mother is such a stalwart. Mr Whitstable can't run the library on his own. Rather than summon me back, Mother has stepped in, but I worry she is taking on too much. Jory says she's rather good at it."

"You'd better not stay away too long, or she'll take your job."

Peter flashes a wry smile. "I'm missing it. I want to get back sooner rather than later."

"Then let's just go home. I'm not afraid."

"No, Connie. It's not worth the risk."

"What's the latest intelligence?" I ask.

"Crossley is still in London. Rumour has it he'll soon be on the move, but we don't know where."

"Short of leaving England, no one place is safer than another."

"But Cornwall is the riskiest. Please, let's stay away a little longer."

"Fine," I say, saving the battle for another day. I have already stupidly revealed that I would like to visit Brian Sullivan's cottage in Polperro. The fact that we are leaving Cheltenham is not an excuse for abandoning the case. I have done what I can here, but my instinct tells me to hasten south. It might be nothing, but I feel drawn to Sullivan's cottage. Unfinished business, perhaps. Peter, of course, thinks otherwise. He doesn't care whether we find the torso killer or not. And if he can keep me away from my beloved Cornwall, he will. I fear we will end up in some godforsaken grim industrial town up north where he can hide me away among the masses. It won't happen. I won't let it.

"Not far now," says Peter as we drive past an old wooden sign pointing to Ashton Keynes. We travel for another half a mile while I admire the lush green fields shimmering from a gentle breeze below a golden sun. It is a truly magnificent day, and we could hardly have picked a better one for visiting our new acquaintances.

We drive on optimistically through Ashton Keynes and out the other side. Peter stops and scratches his head. "Odd," he says. "We must have missed it."

"What are we looking for?"

"A two-hundred-acre farm," says Peter.

"That shouldn't be difficult."

"It depends if they thought to make a signpost."

We turn the car and trek back through the village again, before finding a tiny sign almost concealed beneath a rambling bush.

"Ah. Bet this is it." Peter spins the steering wheel and inches the car up the narrow, pitted drive.

I watch as we pass a couple of cottages with a third under construction. A man waves down the car and stops us.

"Jacob," says Peter.

The man drinks us in and cracks a smile. "Hello, my friends," he says. You came to see us after all."

"We said we would. Is it convenient?"

"Of course. Park the car over there. It will be perfectly safe."

"Can I bring my dog?" I ask as Teddy sticks his face through the open window.

Jacob ruffles his head. "Sure. No need for a leash, as long as he doesn't chase the livestock."

"He's got better manners," I assure him.

Peter helps me from the car, and we join Jacob, Teddy trotting at my side.

Jacob checks his watch. "We break for our midday meal in a moment," he says. "You must join us again."

"We'd love to," I say. "Peter, fetch the basket, would you?"

"Sorry. I forgot," says Peter, heaving a wicker basket from the boot.

"We've just vacated our rental property earlier than expected and thought we'd empty the larder. Please take this towards lunch."

Jacob smiles and opens the lid. His eyes widen at the sight of a large ham and the remains of Elys's gingerbread, among other useful items. "Follow me," he says. "You will be especially welcome when my brethren see this."

Jacob takes us to a lengthy, narrow cottage with a slate roof. Inside, a long, narrow dining table occupies an equally long, narrow room, where Urcel and another lady are setting baskets of bread on the table. A delicious-smelling stew bubbles in a large pot on a rudimentary range.

"You," says Urcel, abruptly. "Sit," she gestures.

"Thank you," says Peter, guiding me to the table, where he settles me down before taking a seat. Urcel eyes Teddy suspiciously but says nothing when he slinks under the table and wraps himself around my ankles. I smile, and she nods. Urcel does not waste words. She is curt, but it is her way, and I realise she means nothing by it.

"Look," says Jacob, depositing the hamper on the kitchen table. Urcel examines it and raises an eyebrow. "*Sehr gut,*" she says, nodding her head.

"Ready?" asks Jacob.

"*Ja.*"

He advances outside the building, and I watch through the window as he takes a rope and loudly jangles a bell. A few moments later, the drive fills with women and men dressed almost identically. They surge through the door, taking their seats at the table. When those are all full, they occupy a row of chairs around the fire. Nobody speaks to us, although they acknowledge our presence and seem perfectly content to tolerate us.

"Here he is," says Jacob as Kurt strides into the dining hall. He sees us at once, advances, and vigorously shakes Peter's hand.

"Welcome, welcome," he says in broken English. "We are honoured."

Urcel interjects in a stream of words I don't understand. Kurt nods at the hamper as she tips it towards him so he can see the contents.

"Very kind, *danke,*" he says before addressing the room.

"Please welcome our friends who will join us for our meal," he says. "Who will lead grace?"

"I will," says a tall, black-bearded man. We bow our heads, clasping our hands in prayer as he thanks God for our meal. My stomach is rumbling by the time he finishes, as the smells from the range titillate my tastebuds.

Urcel scoops the stew into bowls, which she passes to the other woman. They circulate them around the room with military precision, and within a matter of moments, everyone has food and eating irons.

"You may begin," says Kurt, and the room falls silent while the hungry workers demolish lunch.

Kurt, who has been standing, draws a chair to the corner of the table and sits between Peter and me.

"I will show you around the farm once we have eaten," he says. "Would you like that?"

I nod, my mouth too full of delicious meat and potatoes to risk talking.

"Is everyone here?" asks Peter. "They can barely squeeze into this space."

"I know. We need a bigger house. Always people coming. Some leave too, but we gain more than we lose."

Jacob shuffles his chair over from the fireplace and joins the conversation. "And to answer your question, we are only one man down. Dougie is attending to a cow in calf. He won't leave her until she is safely delivered. Dougie loves animals… more than people I suspect. And he's at rather a loose end since leaving his Romany clan."

I'm disappointed. For a moment, I had felt such a strong pull towards the Cotswold Bruderhof sanctuary that I half expected to find evidence about the case, possibly in the shape of a mysterious stranger who might have been Brian Sullivan in disguise. After yesterday's talk about misleading coffin sizes and Irene Sullivan's admission that she hadn't seen Brian's face, I was starting to wonder if the dead body was actually his, and what better place to hide than with a self-sufficient community welcoming the persecuted and destitute. But Brian could hardly be described as a traveller, even with a few weeks of beard growth. And the idea that he wasn't really dead was fanciful; no doubt conjured up in my imagination for fear I wouldn't solve the case. I sigh.

"What's wrong, my dear?" asks Kurt.

"Nothing. This is delightful," I say, scooping the remains of my stew with a chunk of homemade bread.

"Where are you going?" asks Kurt as Urcel disappears with another bowl.

"Cow shed," she grunts.

"Ah, *gut*. I can take it." Kurt makes to stand, but Urcel places her hand on his shoulder.

"No need. Finish your meal."

We chat for a few moments while the bowls are cleared, and before long, Urcel returns. She washes her hands before producing two large platters of apples.

"Bertha has calved," she says unemotionally.

"Is it healthy?" Kurt looks up and stops eating momentarily, listening with concern, and I realise how precious their livestock must be.

"A fine young heifer," says Urcel.

"Then we must celebrate." Kurt's face is wreathed in smiles. "Would you like to see the new life?" he continues.

"Yes, please."

Kurt crunches his apple, and we follow suit before leaving the dining room and heading towards the byre. The barn door is open, and Teddy darts inside. I hear him whining long before I reach the cow shed.

We enter, and I look ahead to see a tousle-haired man

wiping down a young calf while the mother licks its face. Teddy curls into him, almost merging together as if they were one.

"Good job, Dougie," says Jacob, following behind. Dougie turns and grins, and my heart almost stops as I gaze at a dear and familiar face, blankly returning my stare.

"What's wrong?" asks Peter.

I try to speak, but such is the shock that I nearly pass out.

"What is it, Connie?" he demands.

"I gesture towards Dougie with trembling fingers. "This man is Jim Douglas," I say.

Chapter Twenty-Six

MISSING RECALL

"YOU MUST BE MISTAKEN," says Jacob. "This man is called Dougie."

"It's Jim." My lip wobbles as I protest my truth, leaning into Peter for fear I will fall.

"Well?" asks Kurt, palms up, brow furrowed,

Jim steps forward and offers his hand. "Dougie Callaway," he says. "Pleased to meet you."

"Calloway? That's Bertha's name. Oliver and Bertha Calloway. Your next-door neighbours."

Jim shakes his head. "Sorry. I must have a doppelgänger."

"But what about Teddy?" I ask, swallowing a sob. "Look at him. He knows you."

Jim squats and ruffles Teddy's ears. The little dog tries to climb into his lap, licking his hand vigorously. Jim or Dougie pauses momentarily, his eyes narrowing as he gazes into the distance. His mouth tenses as he squeezes his eyelids shut. I can almost hear him thinking.

"Did you say, Teddy?"

"Yes. Don't you recognise him?"

"Should I?"

"Or me? Can't you remember me?"

"No. Not at all. Sorry, but you're mistaken. I'm not the person you think I am."

I gulp, trying to swallow my tears, but it doesn't work, and I flee the barn at a snail's pace. Peter follows.

"Come now," he says, taking my arm. "What's all that about?"

"He doesn't know me," I sob.

"Let's sit down," says Peter. "Look. There's a lovely patch of shade beneath that old oak. We can rest and talk." Peter releases his top button and wipes a bead of sweat from his temple.

"There's nothing to say." Tears stream steadily down my face as I realise that there are worse things in life than a missing sweetheart. Who knew finding him could be so painful? I am so shaken up I can barely stand and slump on the ground, head bowed.

"Come here," says Peter, placing a brotherly arm around my shoulders. I cry it out until the tears stop. Only then does Peter speak again.

"Are you sure that man is Jim?" he asks.

"You should know. You met him when you collected me from Worple Road."

"True," said Peter. "But that was a while ago. I was in a rush and barely registered his features. I'm afraid I couldn't pick Jim Douglass out of a lineup."

"You may not recognise him, but I do. Did you see how Teddy reacted?"

Peter nods, and I realise my little dog isn't with me. He has stayed with Jim.

"Did you part on good terms?" asks Peter.

"Yes, although distance and my stupid dreamwalking complicated matters."

"Did you tell Jim about it?"

I nod.

"Did he understand?"

"That's the golden question," I say. "I don't know. He was cynical at first. You know how hard it is to believe in something you can't see."

"Perhaps it was too difficult for Jim to deal with," says Peter, gently.

"That might explain his reaction. Perhaps he's embarrassed to know me and hopes I will go away."

"There is a more obvious solution."

"Sorry, what?"

"That Jim has simply forgotten who he is. After all, he was in dire straits the last time you saw him."

"I know. But how could Jim lose his memory for this long? It's been years."

"Why shouldn't he? You did?"

I pause and consider Peter's response. "A good point, but I more or less recovered my memory within a year," I say.

"It took some doing, though. And even now, you struggle to remember certain things."

"And Jim was full of poison. I thought he must have died."

"Even more reason to consider amnesia," says Peter. "It's a pity you can't remember exactly what happened in Seaford."

"I can," I say.

Peter cocks his head. "Since when."

"I wasn't going to tell you. I knew you would worry."

"Oh, Connie. So, Haw Bridge wasn't the first time you entered the astral plane?"

"No."

"For goodness' sake." Peter sounds exasperated but checks his temper. "I don't want to know how or when. Just tell me about Jim."

"I apparated back in time to Seaford and clung on for about five minutes longer than I'd originally managed to stay the first time. She was there."

"Who?"

"Grace Duff. I watched her push Jim towards the cliff edge. She'd given him poison."

"You've always known that."

"Yes. But I didn't see what happened next. Jim fell, and Grace returned to her cottage thinking she'd got away with it and killed the one man who knew what she'd done. But she was wrong. Jim fell onto a ledge. I could see him lying there, barely conscious and writhing in agony, with poison seeping through his veins. I wanted to help him, but I couldn't. I should have gone to him, but he wouldn't have seen me. And then I realised I wasn't alone. Someone was lying on the ground. A young girl. Me."

Peter pales as he returns my gaze. "You saw yourself?"

I nod.

"There are bound to be consequences," he says.

"There were – to my memory."

"It's different for Jim, but probably just as traumatic. I can only imagine how he felt, poisoned and alone on a cliff edge. A catastrophic memory loss is hardly surprising."

"I know." I sniff, tears tumbling down my face again.

"But what should we do?" asks Peter, steepling his hands.

"I don't know."

"Do you have any doubts about Jim's identity?"

"None at all."

"Then you should talk to him."

"He already thinks I've come from the funny farm. You saw his face."

"Connie. Even if Jim can't remember anything, we can try to work out whether your theory is feasible."

"It must be," I say. "I know Jim. I recognise him. I loved him." My voice falters as I consider the awfulness of my situation. I'd always hoped to bring good news to Maud Douglass one day. To bring her son to visit her as she lay ailing in the nursing home with memory problems of her own. I know she would recognise her only son, regardless of her state of mind. But what's the good of it if Jim won't cooperate? If he can't remember he ever had a mother. Peter is right, though. I must talk to Jim and establish whether his background memories are sound. For a fleeting moment, I pause and reconsider, contemplating whether I could have made an awful mistake. But not for long. Teddy is noticeable by his absence and would not abandon me for anyone less worthy than his master.

"Will you ask Jim to speak with me?" I beg.

Peter nods. "If he agrees. Wait here while I fetch him."

I hunch forward, one hand on the grass, the other picking heads off daisies. My stomach squirms with a barrage of butterflies as I wait in dread for Jim to burst my fragile illusions.

Teddy arrives first, bounding towards me, his head in the air, almost wearing a smile as if all his doggy dreams had come true. Jim picks his way uncertainly behind.

"Do you mind if I sit?" he asks, lowering himself to the floor before moving a safe distance from me. Teddy fills the void between us and puts his head on his paws.

"What's troubling you?" he asks softly.

"Your name is Jim Douglass," I say.

"It's not, but let's sort out why you think it might be."

"I knew you before."

"In Hampshire?"

"No. I don't think so."

"Well, that's where I come from," says Jim. "My aunt and uncle lived in a Romany camp in Boldre. They took me in after the accident. I've only recently left them. It's been just under a year, and I only left because they were moving on to Ireland. I'll visit, of course. But the idea of joining them didn't feel quite right."

"What made you come to Ashton Keynes?" I ask.

"Have you met Samuel yet?"

I nod. Samuel is one of the Bruderhof – a man-mountain with a bushy beard and a shock of red hair. His bulky frame occupied every inch of the large chair he used by the range during lunch. Not a man easily forgotten.

"Samuel is Irish and was visiting his family in a village near our camp. We met in a pub and got talking. He told me about the Cotswold Bruderhof. I thought they'd only be interested in their own kind, but Samuel assured me they welcome anyone willing to work hard and support the community and its values. And coming from a God-fearing family, their life felt very natural."

My eyes widen. Jim has remembered something. His mother went to church regularly and always supported parish events. "Maud would be so happy to hear that."

Jim frowns. "Who's Maud?"

"Your mother."

"My mother is dead. A cart knocked her down when I was a small boy."

I chew my lip, trying to veer towards a more comfortable mode of questioning. "And your father?" I ask.

"Dad died six years ago."

"I'm sorry."

"Thank you."

"I didn't know my parents," I offer.

"Poor you." Jim offers his condolences but doesn't elaborate. I dig for more.

"What was he like?"

"Who?"

"Your father."

Jim shrugs. "I don't remember."

"Were you estranged?"

"No. At least, I don't think so."

"Do you remember your childhood?"

"What is this? An interrogation?"

Jim's face falls, and his eyes darken. I sense hostility and retreat a little in my questioning.

"Do you have brothers and sisters?"

Jim shakes his head.

"I don't either."

"You don't miss what you never had," says Jim.

"I do. I'd love to have had a sibling."

"Or another dog," he says, rubbing Teddy's belly. I seize the opportunity.

"Have you owned many dogs?"

Jim's eyes dart heavenward as he considers my question, and I know from his frown that he can't remember.

"Two or three," he says uneasily, his eyes still staring into the distance.

"What was your occupation before you came here?"

Jim faces me. "Hard labour," he says, holding out his

palms. I see evidence of manual work, but not the calloused hands of someone who has toiled their whole life.

"Farming?"

"Among other things. Whatever it takes, not to mention the time maintaining the caravans. The women in the camp vastly outnumber the chaps. So, all the hard graft falls to us. And we spend a lot of time collecting supplies if you know what I mean?"

"Poaching, scrumping?"

"A man must do whatever it takes to put food on the table."

"Gosh, Jim. I never thought I'd see you operating on the wrong side of the law."

"My name is Dougie," he snaps, and the good-tempered joshing ends abruptly.

"No. You are PC Jim Douglass of Her Majesty's finest," I retort, hoping to shock him into sudden recall.

Jim shakes his head. "A policeman?" he asks incredulously. "Do I look like a policeman? Dear God, I'd be frog-marched from the camp if the others heard that."

I reach for Jim's hand, but he snatches it away. "Don't," he says. My stomach knots as a sudden, awful thought takes root.

"Are you married?" I ask.

"That's too much," he says. "I'm trying to help you, but you have no right to know everything about my life."

I gasp involuntarily. "Then you are?"

"No, I'm not. No wife, no girlfriend, no sweetheart. Just a man and what's left of his family trying to go about his business."

Jim shakes his head as I loudly exhale, my heartbeat returning to normal.

"Just humour me for a moment," I say. "Can you remember anything from six years ago?"

Jim closes his eyes and sighs like a man who has reached the end of his tether.

"Yes, I can. Of course, I can. Perhaps not every detail, but who does? Look, Connie. I'd like to say it's been nice meeting you, and I'm sure you're a very pleasant girl when you're not in the grip of hysteria, but you're mistaken about me. I'm not who you think I am, and I don't like your insinuation that I was a copper. It's insulting; you're mistaken, and it's best we say our goodbyes."

Jim leaps to his feet and strides across the field. Teddy stands but does not follow. Instead, he turns and curls into me as my tears fall into his fur.

Chapter Twenty-Seven

FLEEING DISAPPOINTMENT

"I'M SO SORRY," says Peter for the seventh time as we drive away from Ashton Keynes and the man who once was the love of my life.

I try to speak but make a wordless sniffle, a giant frog trapped firmly in my throat. My cheeks are still wet from sobbing, my dreams shattered. If I wrung my handkerchief into a bowl, Teddy could drink from the many tears I have cried.

After Jim left, Peter came back, saw the state of me and packed me into the car. Then he returned to apologise to Kurt and the others. He was away for twenty long, painful minutes before returning, first without Teddy. And then, having realised something was missing, another twenty while he tracked Jim down and prised my dog away. Thank goodness Jim's memory loss is complete. I dread what would have happened if he'd remembered owning a dog and wanted to keep Teddy. I couldn't bear to lose my loyal companion and still suffer from the loss of my now unrequited love.

Teddy turns his back to me and stares from the rear window, whining pitifully. I turn around, trying to ignore my heartache, and for the first time in a long while, a tugging burns the back of my scalp. I foolishly tell Peter, who scowls.

"Don't be tempted to use your powers, Connie. You must leave dreamwalking well alone. I know what you're like, and you'll want to use it to make this awful situation better. But you can't change anything and mustn't interfere with Dougie. Don't think badly of the Bruderhof. They understand your position; really, they do. They know genuine emotion from troublemaking. But it's awkward and embarrassing for Dougie, and they must protect their own. They have asked us not to return."

"But Jim will never remember me if I stay away."

Peter's eyes soften as he turns and speaks. "Jim is unlikely to remember you at all, not after six years. Try to be glad that he is alive, move on, and find someone else."

"I'm not sure I can," I say, my thoughts momentarily betraying me and settling on the only other man I have ever yearned to kiss. My heart flutters as I think of Kit Maltravers, his handsome face, kind personality, and somewhat attractive solvency. I mentally compare him to Jim with his newly roughened hands, worn clothes and farmyard odour. I should want Kit by a country mile, but for all the years I have fantasised about Kit, Jim has my heart and always will.

"You must."

"But it's not all about me. What about Jim's poor mother?"

Peter turns his eyes back to the road, narrowly avoiding a collision with a cyclist. "Goodness. I must concentrate. That was close."

"Poor Maud," I murmur.

"I know. I thought of her too," says Peter.

"For all the good it did."

"No. I mean, I thought of her and acted on it."

"What do you mean?"

"Here," says Peter, passing me a piece of paper. My heart turns little somersaults as I stare at a five-line address on a dog-eared envelope penned in Jim's writing. I flip it over eagerly, but there's nothing on the other side.

"What's the point of this?" I ask.

"Prior planning," says Peter. "I asked Dougie to write down the Bruderhof address when I took Teddy."

"Why?"

"I thought you could check his writing and see if you recognise it."

"That's a good idea. It looks familiar, and I can compare it when I get home. Good plan, Peter."

"And, if you can find anything else, a picture of Maud, or the house or something that Dougie might recognise, you can always send it to him."

"I could hug you," I say, feeling a surge of affection for Peter's thoughtful act.

"And another thing. Dougie was reluctant to take it, but I insisted on giving him one of Cora's calling cards. If he ever remembers anything, he knows where to contact you."

I gulp down another sob, determined to quench the tears that threaten again. "Except I won't be there, will I? I may never go home again if everyone gets their way."

Peter opens his mouth to speak, then closes it again. And I know he has held back a waspy retort about my lack of gratitude for their protection. He must be seriously worried about my state of mind to hold back.

"We're not trying to hurt you," he says. "And you will return to Pebble Cottage. Probably sooner than you think. I understand your position better than you know. Selfishly, I can't bear the thought of losing you. Crossley is a dangerous animal, and you have already come into contact with him more than is good for you."

"So everyone keeps saying, but I am determined to do my bit, now more than ever. I honestly don't care whether I live or die, so I might as well be useful."

"But I care, so do Cora, Elys and all your friends in Porth Tregoryan. And Vera would want you to live a long, happy life too."

"Peter, that's the point. I am unhappy, and that's unlikely to improve for some time, if at all. I've no family of my own and little prospect of having one. I am well and truly on the shelf."

"Rather like me," says Peter.

"Except that you have a mother, an aunt and countless uncles and cousins. I have a dead guardian and a fading photograph of a family I don't recognise from a derelict Suffolk property. You can't compare our situations. They are not the same."

"I know," says Peter, patting my hand. "But you have so much to live for. You are a well-regarded, integral part of our community."

"And a cripple who can't walk, doesn't work and contributes nothing particular to the world. It doesn't matter what you say, I know my worth, and it's vanishingly small. Now I've nothing to look forward to. No hope at all."

"There must be something we can do to cheer you up."

"Yes. Drive me home. Let me serve my country."

"Not that. Anything but that."

I sigh. Peter is immoveable, and I am starting to feel numb. How long will it take before I don't care at all?

"Where are we going?" I ask defeated.

"Anywhere you like."

"Don't waste words. We've already established that my wishes count for nothing."

"How about Lincoln, then? Or the city of York?"

I curl my lip. There was a time when I would be excited to go anywhere a few miles north of Newquay, but those days have gone. I couldn't care less, and the thought of a long drive depresses me further still.

"Can't we stay closer to home and go further south? Dorset perhaps?" I know I'm trying my luck, but it's worth a stab.

"I don't know," says Peter, chewing his lip. "That sounds too close for comfort. It's been a few days since we've spoken to Stella's crew. I'm not entirely sure of Crossley's location."

"Let's stop somewhere and telephone Oliver Fox."

"We can't," says Peter.

"Why not?"

"I wasn't going to tell you this," he continues. "But the brigadier pulled Fox out of the field for his own good. He's writing a book and is strictly off operational service."

"Why?"

"Crossley started the nocturnal visits to his home again a few days ago."

"He's used to it."

"Not like this. The attacks have returned to the same level as those when Harold Grady was in post. And if you remember, it jolly nearly finished Fox off then. He's not strong enough to cope. Crossley will either kill him or drive him insane. And that's not the worst that could happen."

"How much worse could it be?"

"Grady says they're worried that Crossley could infiltrate his mind and use him to get to you."

"I don't believe it."

"Well, you should."

"But nothing's happened for years. The threat's been dormant."

"Not now," says Peter.

"How could you know? You've been in Cheltenham with me. Or do you know more than you've said?"

"I'm in touch with Grady. It's part of my new role."

"What are you talking about, Peter? What role? How could you keep this news from me?"

"It was confidential."

"Not the news about Fox. I mean, how could you take on a job for the organisation and not tell me about it?"

"I see. I didn't want to worry you."

"I'm in this as deeply as you are, if not more so. You should talk to me. We're supposed to be friends."

"You are a little volatile, Connie. I didn't know how you would take it."

"You mean you don't trust me?" I sit bolt upright, desperation replaced with volcanic anger.

"Of course I do. But there is so much to consider. It's easier all round if you know nothing about it."

"Well, you've let the cat out of the bag, so you'd better tell me everything. Every tiny detail, or our so-called friendship, is history. Who else is involved in this secret?"

"Swear you won't say anything. I mean it, Connie. Lives are at risk if this information sees the light of day."

"I swear on Vera's grave," I say, feeling guilty to the core, but knowing nothing less will secure Peter's trust.

"Good girl. Our pod has three trusted members: me, Mary, and Crawford. We report directly to Harold Grady. This is so secret that the brigadier doesn't know."

"My Mary?"

"Yes."

"Unbelievable. No wonder I haven't heard from her.

How can Mary be a safe pair of hands when she is intimately acquainted with Tilly Donnelly? You said I couldn't go anywhere near Bosula because of the relationship between Tilly and Crossley, yet it's alright for Mary."

"I know it seems unfair, but Mary is sound. They have checked her credentials in every conceivable way. Anyway, Grady recruited Mary before we knew about Tilly."

"That's not much of a testament to your intelligence gathering capabilities."

"It was less than desirable, I agree. But we regrouped, checked security and everything is fine. Mary is and always was utterly reliable."

"Unless you happen to be one of her close friends," I say bitterly, still reeling at the deception around me.

"She's sound because she cares for you so much," says Peter softly. "Mary will do anything to keep you safe. Besides, she has Crawford to help her."

My head snaps up as Peter's words hit home. "You don't mean…" I say.

"I do. But it's top secret. And I couldn't risk it at all, had you not already seen Crawford's hiding place. As you rightly guessed, Crawford had dallied with Calicum Aureum, realised the danger, and fled for his life. He faked his death in Salcombe Harbour before unknowingly settling in the capital not far from Crossley's den. Grady thought Crawford might be a useful ally, recruited Mary and told her where to find him. Six months ago, she visited her brother and moved him to a safehouse. They live there together while working for the psychic defence division. And that's why you haven't heard from Mary for a while. She's out of contact with everyone."

I sit silently for a few moments, seething at the thought of all the subterfuge behind my back.

"I can't believe this. Everyone I trusted is plotting against me. Does Cora know? Does Elys?"

"No and no," says Peter. "Only you."

"Right." Somehow, I feel better for his words and my heartbeat settles, only for anger to flare up again within seconds.

"So, everyone except me can contribute to the war effort?"

"If there is a war," says Peter. "The politicians may yet contain the threat."

"Regardless. Virtually everyone I know is helping the cause, except yours truly. And you are the primary reason I can't get involved. I've had enough, Peter. This control of my life must stop. Take me home or I'll walk."

"I can't."

"You won't."

"Then take me to Bosula."

"No."

I grab the door handle and open it a fraction. Startled, Peter reaches across me and slams it shut.

"Not Bosula, not home. You can go anywhere else if you just calm down," says Peter. "Just name the location and we'll drive there now."

And that's how we ended up in Polperro.

Chapter Twenty-Eight

POLPERRO

WE PULL into Polperro a little after teatime, fighting a surprising flurry of traffic passing in the other direction.

"Tourists," says Peter, as if we were any different. Polperro is beautiful, but it is not my home, and we have no more right to be there than any other holidaymaker.

"Slow down," I reply for the second time that day. Peter is zipping around the narrow streets at an alarming rate of knots. And I have yet to locate the address of Brian Sullivan's cottage, such is my apathy now that I have left Jim behind forever. We drive towards the harbour, and my heart gladdens at the sight of the sea glinting beneath a late afternoon sun. I can smell the ozone, taste the salt, and hear the seagulls chattering together in great crowds. I am home, but not home. Back in Cornwall, but far from the place I long to be. But I have made progress, and that must do for now.

I pull myself together and feel around in my handbag. After a bit of rootless fumbling, my mind distracted by thoughts of Jim, my hand closes over the notebook Charles Ince gave me. I flip it open and search for the page with the cottage address, finding it beneath a bookmarked envelope containing an advertisement for Camp Coffee. But when I remove the magazine clipping, I notice a thin sheet of paper covered with writing on both sides. I am about to read it when Peter suddenly brakes. The car catapults me forward and then back as Peter shoots out a protective arm too late to stop a sudden pain.

"I am so sorry, says Peter, glancing anxiously towards me. "Only trying to save a feline life. Are you alright?"

"Yes," I reply, running a cautious arm over the back of my neck. "But a little notice would be nice next time."

"There won't be a next time," says Peter. "Though I expect the cat has lost a good few lives pulling a stunt like that."

He nods towards a large tomcat, walking nonchalantly along the road as if it hadn't a care in the world. For a moment, I envy its casual attitude to life.

"Well done for avoiding it," I say, watching Teddy raise a flicker of interest, but not enough to jump from the open window. Since Mr Moggins has educated him in feline superiority, Teddy is a perfect gentleman around cats.

Peter and I start at the sound of a horn blast behind us. "Move along, would you," says a florid-faced man.

"Sorry." Peter doffs his hat and pulls into the side of the road.

The car passes by, and Peter looks over my shoulder at the notebook. "Well. Where are we going? Shouldn't we get a move on before all the hotels shut? Or perhaps we should secure a room before trying to find the cottage?"

"Whatever you think," I say, suddenly worried about the mission at hand. I hadn't given it much thought, having barely scanned the notebook since Ince handed it over, my mind distracted by Elys and her unfortunate accident and then Jim. I realise I don't know whether to expect an occupier or an empty property. Or, worse still, the possibility of Irene Sullivan in residence. Our presence would be tricky to explain if she opened the door.

"You decide," says Peter.

I shrug.

"Come on, Connie. You made enough fuss about coming here. Take charge. It will take your mind off things.

I grudgingly agree and examine the notebook. "There," I say, pointing to the address.

Peter squints. "Hedgey Ditches," he says, pulling a face. "What kind of name is that?"

"I think it's rather quaint."

"Any idea where to find it?"

"None at all," I reply. "Why don't I ask?"

Peter opens his mouth to disagree. He always prefers taking the lead in such matters, but I am surprisingly quick off the mark, have opened the door, and heaved myself from the car before he can say no. I stretch my stiff legs, take my cane, and wander into a nearby chemist. The doorbell clangs, and I ease my way into the empty shop, approaching the counter, where a slender man with a shock of white hair counts pills into a bottle. I wait quietly until he has finished then he looks up.

"Thank you for your patience, young lady," he says. "Tallying up is a painful job when interrupted, but you had the good sense to wait your turn, and I appreciate it. Age is a terrible thing. Nothing works quite as well as it once did, including my memory. Now, what can I do for you?"

"I'd like directions," I say.

"She'd like directions," he parrots, and for a moment, I think he is talking to himself. But then I hear a faint purr and glance at the countertop to see the same large moggy, now safely ensconced on the counter.

"Oh," I exclaim, reaching to tickle his chin. "He almost had a collision with a car."

"Then I wouldn't like the motor vehicle's chances," says the old man.

"I think the cat would have come off worse."

"She doesn't know you like I do," says the man, touching the cat's nose. It burrows into his chest, purring loudly.

"Where do you want to go?"

I am so entranced by the apparent affection between man and cat that I have almost forgotten why I'm there. But I check myself and open the notebook. "There," I say, pointing towards the address.

"Ah. Hedgey Ditches," he says. "You'll find it next door to Sunrise. There, that one." The chemist has noted what I had not – another address, a little farther down the page.

"Yes, I know the cottages well. They use them as holiday rentals. Come," he continues, beckoning me to the window. I follow and wait while he gestures left and right with a baffling array of hand movements. But I leave the chemist with a vague idea of where we are going and direct Peter accordingly.

Five minutes later, we arrive outside two little white-washed cottages on the slope of a hill. At first glance, they appear rather pretty, but the closer we get to the front doors, the more obvious the flaws. The whitewash, which, on closer inspection, is more of a grey wash, is riven with watermarks of the kind indicative of dampness. Paint flakes away from a rotten window ledge, and a smashed tile lies across the doorstep. The house looks unloved and, more importantly, empty. I turn to Peter. "Shall we take a look?"

We glance around and, seeing no evidence of nosey

neighbours, peer through the window of Hedgey Ditches. The curtains to the front room are open, revealing an unlit and sparsely furnished parlour. We see no signs of life but tiptoe through the side gate to the rear to confirm our suspicions. Once again, all appears quiet. The empty kitchen and curtained dining room indicate no one is home.

"It's a pity we don't have a key," I say.

"I wonder?" says Peter, returning through the gate. I follow as quickly as possible and find him stooped by a small stone hedgehog nestling by the front door. He picks it up, looking triumphantly beneath before realising that his cunning plan has come to nought.

"Damn," he says, tugging and pulling at stones and ornaments in his quest for a hiding place. We almost give up when I have one last idea.

"Have you tried the doormat?"

Peter clicks his fingers and peels back the heavily worn coconut matting. "Well done," he says, grasping a large iron key. He slides it in the lock, and the door opens with a rusty squeal. We bolt inside and size up the property as a curious bystander passes and watches, hands on hips. We wait until she leaves.

"I'll pull the car up the drive in a moment," says Peter. It will look less suspicious." He leaves me alone in the hallway, breathing in the odour of rising damp. I tentatively open the parlour door and perch on the couch before retrieving the letter from the envelope, marking the notebook's address page.

By the time Peter returns, I have read the document and familiarised myself with the cottage's provenance, legal status, and Brian Sullivan's mode of income generation.

"It's not his," I exclaim as Peter strolls through the door.

"What isn't?"

"The cottage. Or should I say cottages. They belong to a Mrs Mills of Aberdare Gardens. Brian only rents them."

"Does he now?" says Peter.

"Yes. He's taken them for three years at the princely sum of thirty-two pounds per annum to rent them out to holidaymakers."

"Subletting?" asks Peter.

"Something like that. No wonder he seemed hard up. Sure, he had an income, but Brian couldn't sell what didn't belong to him. I wonder how much he made?"

"Not enough to live on," says Peter. "Just look at the state of the place." He runs a hand along a strip of peeling wallpaper and wipes it on his jacket.

"Yes, it does need rather a lot of work. But one could have a nice enough holiday here if not too fussy about appearances."

"Well, the couch is comfortable," concedes Peter. "Wait here a second."

He bounds upstairs and returns moments later after a quick visit to the kitchen. "Someone has made both beds up, but there's nothing in the larder. And no sign of any incoming holidaymakers. Do you want to stay here tonight?"

"That's the sort of risk you don't normally take," I say, impressed at Peter's boldness.

"Granted. But it will save us a bob or two. You wanted to live dangerously. How about it?"

I take a moment to test the gas mantle before replying. It performs satisfactorily. "Yes, let's. We'll manage anything else as long as we have heat and light. It feels naughty, though."

"I'm tired and past caring," says Peter. "Staying here might break the odd rule, but none that risk your safety or my position. Settle yourself down, Connie, and we'll find somewhere for a bite to eat.

Peter brings in our suitcases, but we don't unpack them. There's no point, as we will leave tomorrow once we have acquainted ourselves with the cottage and asked the locals if they know Brian Sullivan. Peter is reluctant to move the car, so we settle for fish and chips from a little shop a short distance from the cottage we passed earlier. Peter offers to go alone, but now I am here, I want to be fully involved in the investigation, however brief it may be. We pull on light coats to protect ourselves from the weather and set off down the hill.

Chapter Twenty-Nine

HEDGEY DITCHES

THE GOSSIP from Polperro's smallest chip shop is enlightening. Granted, you couldn't swing a cat in the tiny front room where Peter and I queue like sardines with four others, but there's no easier way to fall into conversation than a long wait in an uncomfortable place with discontented strangers.

Peter and I enter just ahead of a teenage boy but behind two elderly men and a woman of indeterminate age wearing a permanent scowl. They had been waiting for some time and were shamelessly slandering the chip shop owner in full hearing of his harassed assistant. We wait fifteen minutes before Peter becomes concerned about my obviously flagging limbs and asks for a seat. The greasy-haired young man behind the counter briefly stops frying and lugs a narrow wooden chair into an already packed room. And to stop myself from falling over, I risk disapproval by sitting down. To my surprise, it has a unifying effect.

"You should have gone to Perkins," says Scowl Face, her lips pursed like an ageing trout.

"Who?"

"Perkins, at the top of Lansallos Street."

"Thank you," I say uncertainly. "But why?"

"He fries quicker and in a bigger room. Not that you could get there in your condition. Polio, was it?"

"I don't think so."

"Don't think so? Well, if you don't know."

The woman puffs out her chest, hands on her hips, as if personally affronted by my lack of medical knowledge. If she thinks she's frustrated, she should try growing up with no memory of her formative years.

"Leave her alone, Mabyn," says one of the men.

"Mind your own business, Margh."

"Your funeral. If you frighten off the holidaymakers, they won't come here anymore. And who will buy the tatty trinkets in your shop?"

"*Taw taves*, old man."

"Enough." The second elderly man squeezes towards me and offers his hand. "Trevor Trelawney, gentleman of this parish. Excuse my rowdy friends."

"Constance Maxwell and Peter Tremayne." I return the shake as firmly as I can.

"That's a good old Cornish name," he says, smiling at Peter.

"Quite right. I'm as Cornish as you are."

"Probably more so. My mother was Welsh."

"It's nice to meet you." Peter offers his hand, and before long, he is chatting with Trevor about life, family history, and the merits of living by the sea.

I sit quietly, my stomach rumbling, happy to let the world go by, but Scowl Face has other ideas.

"Visiting family?" she asks.

"No."

"So, you're on holiday?"

"No, we're not."

She's quiet momentarily, taken aback at this second challenge to her assumption that we are holidaymakers. But it doesn't last long. She can't contain her curiosity.

"What then?" she demands.

I marshal my thoughts, weighing up the risk of revealing our illegal occupation of the cottage against my need to know more about its owner and settle on a half-truth. "We're inspecting a holiday let," I say.

"Which one?"

"Hedgey Ditches."

"That hovel!" Her face breaks into a sneer.

"It's seen better days, but with a little work, it could be charming," I reply, feeling obliged to defend the little dwelling.

"I'd sooner live in a barn."

"I thought you did," Margh whispers under his breath, but not quietly enough. Mabyn narrows her eyes and is about to reply when the chip shop assistant yells, "Haddock's ready."

Mabyn reaches out and swipes the paper package before elbowing past and storming through the door.

"No standards," says Margh, waspishly. "Common as muck."

I resist the urge to mutter pots and kettles and return to watching the world go by.

"Did I hear you say Hedgey Ditches?" asks Trevor as Peter takes a breath.

"Yes."

"Byron Smith's place?"

I stare blankly. "Byron, who?"

"Brian Sullivan's alter ego," says Peter, one step ahead of me again.

"Yes, of course," I reply, remembering the information gleaned from Charles Ince. Quite why Brian Sullivan used an alias, he didn't say, but if the good people of Polperro are aware, he must have used it regularly.

"Yes. Byron Smith's place."

"It is a little run down," says Trevor.

"I know. But far from a hovel." I am still in defence mode.

"Isn't he Baggy's pal?" asks Margh, scratching his nose thoughtfully.

"Why yes. You're right."

Peter and I stare blankly.

"Everyone knows old Baggy," says Margh.

"We don't," Peter replies.

"Baggy Correll," says Margh, with the air of a man speaking to a pair of idiots. "Otherwise known as Captain Charles Correll. They're very matey."

"They were very matey," says Peter. "Byron is dead."

"You don't say? Does Correll know?" asks Trevor.

"Must do." Margh shakes his head. "They weren't just pals. Baggy managed the cottages for him for a small commission. Someone must have told him."

"Yes, but no one's been in Hedgey Ditches for a while," says Trevor. "It must be months since I saw life in the old place."

"No, no, no." Margh wags a finger. "Byron's mother has been there recently. Doris saw her."

"Yet she didn't mention she'd lost a son?"

"Might have done. Doris didn't tell me. But the old girl's away with the fairies half the time."

"Even so. You'd hardly forget the death of a young man. Byron wasn't old by any means." Trevor Trelawny straightens himself as he speaks.

"I'm not saying she didn't tell Doris, only that Doris didn't tell me." Margh's voice rises, and Trevor places a calming hand on his shoulder.

"Alright. Not that it matters. But the cottages are empty more often than not."

"Baggy can't be making much from this enterprise?"

"I don't suppose he is. I expect it's more of a favour to a friend. You know what he's like."

I am only vaguely listening, having drifted away as the two men gently argue. Then Margh speaks again.

"There was someone there in January," he offers.

"That was months ago. How can you be sure?"

"I saw Ronnie Enys chucking a snowball at the window while running down the street. The silly little fool didn't realise he had caught a stone inside. It fairly clattered the window, and he was lucky it didn't break. The little rat ran away, but not before some chap waved his fist at him from the window."

"A chap. Are you sure?" Peter finally raises some enthusiasm for the conversation.

"Certain."

"Was it Brian"? I ask, receiving only a puzzled look. "I mean Byron."

"Could have been," says Margh. "I only saw him fleetingly. Could have been anyone."

"Early or late January?" I ask.

"Not early," says Margh. "The snow came halfway through the month this year.

"When?"

"I don't know. What's this all about?"

"Please try to remember," I say, my heart thumping at the potential implication of this news.

" I can't be sure," says Margh, pausing for one last try. "No. No idea, I'm afraid."

"Food," says the assistant, slamming another two packets on the countertop.

"At last," says Margh. "I'll be seeing you." He grabs his packet and then leaves. Trevor follows, turning back and doffing his hat. We are now down to three: Peter, me, and the teenage boy who has shifted towards the corner and is quietly picking his nose, wrongly assuming a mantle of invisibility.

I turn away, feeling sick. "What do you make of that?" I ask Peter.

"Disgusting," he says, having also noticed the boy.

"Not him. The January visitor to Hedgey Ditches.

"It's interesting, but the timing is everything. Where are you going with this?"

"Well, if Brian hadn't died, if he wasn't in the coffin, he could have come here, couldn't he?"

"Not without someone recognising him?"

"They'd only see him if he left the house. Brian could have bedded down with enough food for his visit, parked his car somewhere, and moved around in the dark. He could have kept from sight if he'd wanted to."

"I don't know. Your idea sounds farfetched."

I dismiss Peter's concerns, sure I'm on to something. "No. A man was here. Who else could it have been?"

"A holidaymaker?"

"In the middle of January? Don't be ridiculous."

Peter sighs. "I take your point. But I'm not sure. How

about…?" But his sentence remains unfinished as our long-awaited order of cod and chips arrives. We leave the shop and are home five minutes later, where we sit on the sofa, snuggled under a blanket with fish and chips on our laps. It tastes delicious.

"I'll set the fire in a moment," says Peter, nodding towards the cold, empty grate.

I am relieved to see a bucket of coal, tinder, and spills.

"Great. Get to it. Then we can have a good poke around the house before bed. Our visit has been worthwhile already," I continue, thinking of the January occupant. Peter is not so sure and expresses himself accordingly, but I am too hungry to worry and polish off every chip before feeling uncomfortably full.

Peter finishes a few moments before I do, and by the time I have limped to the chilly kitchen, boiled a kettle, and made tea, he has set a blazing fire, and the parlour heats up nicely. With the curtains shut, a warm glow in the grate and the lingering smell of an excellent fish supper, we are soon feeling right at home.

"Well worth the risk," I say.

"So it was. A pity we must move on tomorrow."

"But where?" I ask.

"Let's think about it in the morning. I'm too comfortable to move."

I leave Peter sprawled across the sofa and open the cupboard doors on either side of the fire. Inside the left-hand cupboard is a row of dog-eared books, several packs of cards, and a chess set. The other cupboard is curiously full of odds and ends of yarn.

I exit the room feeling disappointed. I have no particular expectations of what I might find, but this is less than a worst-case scenario.

The kitchen cupboards contain nothing more than kitchenware, and the dining room is bereft of storage. So, I take my first steps upstairs, managing the twisty staircase reasonably well.

There are only two doors off the tiny landing, the first leading to a large bedroom and the other to little more than a glory hole with a single bed stuffed between muddles. How Brian managed to rent it, cluttered with standing lamps, unwanted furniture, and disorderly boxes of papers, I don't know. But clearly, some people were less fussy than I would have been. I decide to tackle the small room last, mentally allocating it to Peter, and make my way to the main bedroom.

The curtains are already closed, creating a homely air, and a large double bed with a bright counterpane enhances the welcoming feel. I park my stick and recline on the bed, hands behind my head as I examine my surroundings. Two watercolours of Polperro harbour grace the opposite wall, and beneath them stand a dressing table and mirror. I wave to my reflection from the bed, then tire of frivolity as my eyes grow heavy and my lids begin to droop. I shake my head and press my nails into my palms, knowing I had better get on with my search before sleep takes me and tomorrow sneaks up too quickly. So, I turn on my side and stretch a hand towards the bedside cupboard. The top drawer slides open easily, and I take the opportunity for a good rummage. I remove an empty journal and a tub of hair gel and pull out a sheaf of papers. I discard several racing schedules before finding a postcard marked 'Megalithic burial chamber, Zennor'. I admire the picture for a moment or two before turning it over, and my heart races as I read the carefully written script – Carn Cottage, 10.00 pm, Monday, 23rd May 1938.

I sit, bolt upright, snatch my bag and scrabble inside, finally locating my diary. Ignoring my throbbing temple, I compare the dates. Someone recently resident in this cottage has an assignation on 23rd May, less than 48 hours from now. And come hell or high water, I mean to be in Zennor to meet them.

Chapter Thirty

APPOINTMENT WITH FATE

I TAKE the card and rush downstairs, almost tumbling in my haste. Peter is lying with his legs on the couch, gently snoring as his arm brushes the floor. Teddy sits a few inches away, patiently waiting for Peter to wake.

I take my stick and prod Peter in the midriff. He grunts but does not rouse.

"Peter," I yell, leaning over and shaking his shoulder.

"What's up?" asks Peter, bleary-eyed.

"Look." I thrust the card towards him, but he pushes it away.

"Come on, Connie. I've been driving for half the day. Give me a chance to sleep it off."

"But it's important. Look."

I hold the card to Peter's face, leaving him no option but to read it.

His eyes cross as he tries to focus before snatching the card and sitting upright. "So, you've found a postcard of Zennor. What's the problem?"

"Look on the back."

Peter obliges. "I'm still none the wiser," he says.

"Oh, come on. A recent visitor to this cottage has an appointment there in a few days' time."

"Great. I hope they find it productive."

"Oh, Peter," I say, almost stamping my foot in frustration. "Whoever has the appointment stayed here recently. They must have brought the card with them as there's no postmark. What if it's Brian? What if he's still alive?"

"That's a big stretch, Connie. Especially as we know his mother recently visited the cottage."

My face falls as I consider his words. The card could belong to Irene Sullivan. "Give it back," I demand.

"Suit yourself."

I take the postcard and clutch it to my chest, closing my eyes as I try to find a connection. I haven't reacted to an item for many years, but then again, I haven't tried. Inanimate objects have channelled strong impressions in the past, most notably Annie Hearne's possessions. Though I have not always interpreted these emotions correctly, they have given me insights into their owner's thoughts and feelings. And anything could be helpful with so little to go on. If I can produce a reaction once, I can do it again. I chew my lip in concentration.

"What are you doing?" demands Peter.

"Hush. I'm trying to read it."

"You won't get very far with your eyes closed."

"Not that kind of reading."

"Please don't dabble," says Peter.

"We've been over this. Let me do something useful."

I take the card and stalk off into the kitchen. It's too narrow to sit down, and there aren't any chairs, so I turn my back to the draining board and lean against it while holding the card against my cheek. I stand like this for several minutes until my thoughts turn fuzzy, and my mind enters daydream mode. But after a while, the mists clear, and I feel a moment of clarity. In that instant, I know for sure that the card belongs to a male. I smile triumphantly, looking forward to entering the parlour to deliver the news. But Peter beats me to it, appearing in the kitchen doorway with a pair of empty mugs.

"Tea?" he asks. I am still half detached as I nod my acceptance, and just as my head bobs down, a symbol flashes across the front of the postcard. I stare, hardly believing my eyes, as the smoky outline of the image fades away. When I look again, it's gone. I trace my fingers across the standing stones of Zennor, and they burn red beneath my flesh. The symbol has vanished, but its power remains vibrant and strong, a never-ending unicursal hexagram, the emblem of Crossley's ceremonial magic. My heart thuds at the thought of Brian Sullivan in thrall to Felix Crossley. But why not? Others have succumbed to his evil charms.

Peter stares at me quizzically. "What's on your mind?" he asks.

"Nothing." I feel guilty for lying, but I cannot tell Peter what I think I have seen. I brush my fingers across the postcard again. It is cool to the touch, with no symbol or trace of heat. I wonder if I imagined it, but I know I did not.

"I'd like to go to Zennor," I say.

"Don't be silly," says Peter, setting the kettle on the stove. He lights the gas hob and stands opposite me, scrutinising my face. I turn away, then back again. I must not look suspicious. Peter cannot know that Crossley is loud in my thoughts.

"It's not silly. We shouldn't waste this opportunity."

Peter snorts as he drops teabags into a pot. "What opportunity? We can't run around southern England looking for a random stranger who happened to leave an appointment card in a holiday let."

"It's more than that," I say.

"How do you know?"

"I just do."

"And anyway, do you know how to get to Zennor?"

I shake my head.

"You should. It's in Cornwall and a long drive south. It will take the best part of two hours in that thing." Peter gestures towards the car parked in the driveway.

"Oh. Then it can't be far from Bosula."

"Correct. Zennor is about twenty minutes away. Not far at all, which is precisely why we will not be going anywhere near the place. Far too close for comfort."

"Not if Crossley's in London."

"I don't know where he is, Connie. It's been several days since I checked in. I badly need to find a telephone."

"There must be one in the village."

"I'd like to think so. I need an update as soon as possible. Anything could be happening."

"There's a phone at Gullimont House," I say, thinking of Mary's study in the artist's retreat.

"I'm tired, Connie. Don't test me."

"You really won't take me to Zennor?"

"Absolutely not. And don't keep asking. I won't change my mind."

Defeated, I retreat to the parlour, drink my tea, and make an excuse for an early night. Peter is still downstairs when Teddy and I take occupation of the large bedroom. An hour later, I hear him climb the stairs and settle into the uncomfortable spare room. Only when I hear gentle snores coming through the walls do I dare consider my next steps.

Chapter Thirty-One

TRAVELLING ALONE

SLEEPING DOESN'T COME EASILY when early morning rising becomes a necessity, especially without a means of waking up. I hadn't seen an alarm clock at Hedgey Ditches and didn't habitually carry one myself. Even if I had, I wouldn't have dared to use it. But with Peter's firm rebuttal and a burning urge to go to Zennor, there was only one course of action.

Teddy and I crept from the cottage just after five the following morning. I had waited until the small hours to decant my suitcase into a carpetbag for easier travel, taking only what was absolutely essential: a change of underwear, a little dog food, and a few toiletries. I had forgone even a single book in my bid to travel light.

I had spotted the bus stop on the way into Polperro the previous day, noting that the covered shelter was quite a hoof from the cottage. I would need some help, and I had hoped for a passing milk float or similar to give me a lift to the road. Sure enough, a kindly drayman had obliged, depositing Teddy and me at the stop where we waited for half an hour for a bus to arrive. A bus that frustratingly terminated at Liskeard, meaning a classic case of going backwards before making progress. We eventually boarded a second bus, travelling for what felt like hours until we entered the outskirts of St Ives, a well-travelled road, heart-achingly familiar to me from previous visits to my dear friend Mary.

And now, as we pull into the bus terminus, I feel a familiar pang of hunger and a sense of missing out on time with dear friends. I could take the next bus to Bosula for all the good it would do, but Mary wouldn't be there. She now lives in a safehouse with her brother, and only Peter knows the location. I still haven't forgiven him for keeping secrets, and a tiny part of me feels a sense of karma for the bewilderment he would have felt when he missed me this morning.

Teddy and I wander the streets of St Ives until we find a cafe willing to accommodate a small, well-behaved spaniel. Although I am not particularly hungry, we both eat, and I attack the plate of food with something less than wholesome relish. I have spent most of the bus journey thinking about Jim. I wish and hope that things were different, that Jim will suddenly wake one day with a burning desire to track me down. But I fear that will never happen. So, I eat to fuel my body, not for enjoyment, but to prepare for what happens next when I find my way to Zennor.

I finish my meal, pay the bill, and buy a cake to eat later if my appetite returns. Then I ask the waitress if the village has a public telephone. She is just saying that she does not know of one when a jolly middle-aged woman raises her hand and waves. She beckons me to her table, and I wait while she empties her mouth of the large cake she has just imbibed.

"There's a telephone at the manor," she says.

"Oh. Where is it?"

The woman responds with a series of curt directions and then slows down as she sees my stick. "Oh, you'll never get there," she says, her words trailing away.

"Oh dear. Never mind. Thank you for trying."

I grab Teddy's lead and walk away, but feel a hand on my shoulder, having only taken a few steps.

"Butler will drive you," the woman says. "Don't look so confused. He's my chauffeur."

My mouth hangs open as I try to comprehend what she's offering.

"Mouth shut, my dear. You'll catch flies. Wait here. I'll summon him closer," she says. This woman is bossy and authoritative. Against my better judgement, I obediently wait.

"That's Lady Joyce," whispers the waitress.

"Who?"

"The widow of a local landowner. Filthy rich. If she can't help you, nobody can."

"I only wanted to make a phone call," I say, regretting my decision. I'm already dreading this conversation, which I could well have done without. And having troubled the local landed gentry, my mission seems even less desirable.

Lady Joyce returns, striding back into the cafe, her curly hair windswept and her riding attire needing a good wash. Her complexion is florid, but a smile breaks over her round face as she regards Teddy. She drops to her knee and ruffles his coat.

"I do like a spaniel," she says. "Good working dogs, the lot of them. You know where you are with a spaniel, not like ruddy terriers. The damn things run rings around me.

"His name is Teddy," I say, suddenly short of small talk.

"Is it? Then I will call him Edward. Are you ready, whatever your name is?"

"Connie," I say.

"Hmm. You don't look like a Connie. More like a Mildred. I had a heifer called Mildred once. Damned fine milker, she was once she'd calved. Now let's get to it."

Lady Joyce strides towards a big black beast of a Bentley, and I dither by its side, not confident whether it's wise to trust myself to this strident woman. But she barks at Butler to open the door, and he ushers me in, casting a frown Teddy's way. I sit down before I can think better of it.

Ten minutes later, we have left the winding streets of St Ives and are heading south towards Carbis Bay. My heart swells as we catch glimpses of the coast, and before long, we have pulled up in the driveway of a fine country house that looks more like a mansion than a hotel.

"Bloody awful shame," says Lady Joyce as we approach the front.

"What is?"

"Giving up this lovely old house to tourism. I'd rather live in a shed than allow people into my home. It's too bad."

I don't know what to say and remain dumb, but my silence does not stop Lady Joyce from continuing her tirade.

"Things were different when Edward was alive. I'm sure he'd turn in his grave if he could see the old place now. That's what happens when you sell out to a hotel chain. Just look at it."

The car pulls up, Butler opens the door, and I emerge, blinking into the sunlight. I regard the manor and its generous grounds.

"It's super," I say.

Lady Joyce raises an eyebrow and frowns. "I daresay if you hadn't seen the place in its heyday. But Edward would have strongly disapproved. I say, Butler. You could have spent your time chauffeuring here if my mother had accepted his offer of marriage. Edward courted Mama when they were both young and foolish. He could have been my father."

"Then you wouldn't have been you, ma'am," says Butler.

"Good point," says Lady Joyce. "Now, let's get you in there before you die of sunstroke." She grabs my arm and manoeuvres me along the pathway and into a reception hall.

"Sit down," she commands, directing me to a sofa. "Fetch the girl a drink, Butler."

Butler sighs and disappears while Lady Joyce strides towards the reception desk and presses her finger on the bell. Two seconds later, she presses it again and keeps jabbing the brass button until a flustered woman appears. Tucking back her hair, the receptionist arranges her features into an unconvincing smile and then realises who she is facing.

"Lady Joyce," she stutters.

"That's my name. Who are you?"

"Emily."

"I haven't seen you before. Are you new?"

"Fairly new, my lady," says Emily, lowering her head to avoid eye contact.

"Be a good girl and fetch Margaret."

"She's upstairs and doesn't want to be disturbed."

Lady Joyce stands tall, sticking out her matronly chest. "That does not apply to yours truly," she says.

"But…"

Lady Joyce stops Emily in her tracks with a menacing glare.

"No buts."

"Very well, my lady."

"Oh, for goodness' sake. Don't fawn, girl. Call me Joyce. I don't care for titles."

Butler shimmies back, bearing a glass of water and a garibaldi biscuit.

"Cook says to eat that," says Butler. "It will help with your sunstroke."

"I haven't got sunstroke. I'm perfectly fine. Only tired and a little disorientated. Teddy is suffering more than I am."

"He shouldn't be in here," says Butler.

"Then we'll both go outside."

"No need for that," says Lady Joyce, approaching Butler from behind. "Take a break, Butler. I'm sure Cook will make you a nice cup of tea."

"Yes, ma'am." Butler disappears, and Lady Joyce throws herself onto the couch, ruffling Teddy again. He plays up to her, exposing his stomach, his tail thudding against the floor.

"Butler doesn't like dogs. Can you believe it? I wouldn't have employed him if I'd known, but they don't write these things in references. Poor form. How are you feeling?"

"Better," I say, too cowed by her personality to admit I hadn't felt ill in the first place.

"Ah. Here's Margaret. "We'll have that phone with you in no time."

In the event the phone didn't come to me. After five minutes of gossip, Margaret, hotel housekeeper and child-hood friend of Lady Joyce, showed me to the hotel office, a former study occupying almost the same position at the back of the house as the library in the Porth Tregoryan Hotel. I wait until she has gone, and Teddy has settled by my side before closing my eyes for a moment and imagining myself there, back in the old days when my only worry was what I would read that day. My eyelids flutter. I am tired, getting too comfortable, and could easily fall asleep. But I have spent much of my young life causing untold worry and have learned a lesson about running away. Though no one will ever stop me from following my own path in life, I know better than to hide. I wish I could take back all the times poor Mrs Ponsonby fretted about me, and I carried on with my plans regardless, not caring about her feelings. I won't do that to Cora or Peter. I am here where I need to be, and they can join me if they wish. But I must tell them where I am, however angry their response may be. I raise a shaky finger and dial the hotel.

"Reception. Roxanne speaking."

I nearly drop the phone as I listen to the curt tones of the last member of the Tregoryan Hotel staff I would ever wish to speak to: Roxy bloody Templeton. But time is not my friend, and I mustn't lose my nerve, so I take a deep breath and ask if she will fetch Cora. Roxy snorts in disbelief. "Where the hell are you?"

"Just get Cora, will you? Or Elys. Please, there isn't much time."

"You never learn, Connie. You are so busy playing detective you show no gratitude towards the people around you. It's a pity. We've given up a lot for you."

"I am grateful. But that's a conversation for another time. Please find Cora."

"Very well. Hold the line."

Roxy stomps off, and I picture her in my mind's eye. Her thin lips set into a stern face, attractive until she frowns. She'll be ugly now, exasperation written all over her face. Roxy's position is too high to be manning reception, so someone has already let her down today, and as much as she is my protector, she has disliked me from the moment we first met. My latest breach of protocol will not have endeared me to her. I wait and wait some more, anxiously eyeing the door, hoping I will not be disturbed and moved along before speaking to Cora. And finally, she arrives on the other end of the telephone, her voice bright and breezy.

"Ah, there you are," she says.

"Were you expecting me to call?"

"Not necessarily. But I knew you would turn up. Peter's rather cross that you've given him the slip. He's coming to find you, but you'll be a few hours ahead. My car packed in just outside Truro."

"Oh dear. Is he alright?"

"Tired and cross, my dear. But the car is in a garage, and they're taking good care of it. Peter will be with you as soon as he can."

"It's a pity he didn't take me in the first place."

"You know, Peter, always erring on the side of caution."

"I'm so grateful for your support, Cora."

"I wouldn't go that far. I'd rather know you were safe. You know who is on the move, and we need to find out where he's going. There's a danger he could be in Cornwall."

"What makes you think that?"

"Crossley's wife comes from Bosula. He'll return there sooner or later."

"Understood. I won't be silly, Cora, or take unnecessary risks. I'll observe this meeting tomorrow and come straight home."

"I wish you wouldn't go alone. Peter is extremely concerned."

"He always is."

"With reason. I wonder if I should come too?"

"No need," I say.

"I suppose not. It's as well you're not here. Dora's hanging around the hotel."

"I know. Someone saw her before I left."

"She came to the house to speak to you."

"Why? We haven't seen each other in years."

"I don't know. She tried to speak to Elys, who gave her short shrift."

"Where is Dora now?"

Cora is momentarily silent. "Camping out in your cave."

"Oh God. She's been there before and destroyed it. I had such happy times before she started using it for dark rituals."

"You haven't been there in a long time."

"Even so. It's upsetting."

"Tell me more about this postcard."

"There's not much to say. It's a black-and-white image of some megalithic stones entitled Carn Cottage, Zennor, with an appointment on the back. It's all very mysterious. Especially considering the symbol."

Seconds of silence pass before I realise I have said too much. Why did I mention the hazy emblem? It wasn't even visible except in my fraying imagination. I could bite my tongue off in frustration.

"What symbol?" asks Cora curtly.

"Nothing."

"Then what did you mean?"

"I thought I saw something, then it went. Nothing to worry about."

"What symbol, Constance."

Cora has gone full Vera Ponsonby, using my given name punctuated by silence, signalling her disapproval.

I sigh and chew my lip.

"Stop huffing. Just tell me."

"A unicursal hexagram. Just in my imagination, though. It wasn't real."

"Doesn't matter. You always could attune to Crossley. Let's not take a chance. Can I persuade you to come home?"

"I'd love to. It's all I've wanted since leaving, but I must see this through first. I'm expecting Brian Sullivan to turn up here tomorrow. Something is fishy. I know it."

"Then we will come to you."

"We?"

"Peter and I, at least."

"You're overreacting. This isn't to do with Crossley. It's about the torso killing. That's all."

"Where will you stay, Connie?"

"I don't know yet. I'll call you again."

"Right. Well…" Cora's voice trails away, and I hear a mumbling in the background. Moments later, she returns, "Elys said someone called at the hotel looking for you."

"Who?"

"I don't know. He didn't leave his name but arrived yesterday evening."

"Not helpful," I say.

"It's all I've got. I'll see you soon, Connie."

Cora rings off, and I spend a few fruitless moments wondering about the phone call before the door opens and Lady Joyce appears.

"Got what you wanted?" she asks.

"Yes, thank you."

"Well, I'm off now. I must see a man about a whippet, but that's another story. Butler will drop you off first. Where are you going?"

224

"Zennor," I say.

"You won't see much there. It's small. Where are you staying?"

"I haven't got that far yet."

"Well, you can't walk the streets, girl. Are you planning to sleep in a barn? And what about your dog?"

"I hope to find a guest house."

Lady Joyce snorts.

"In Zennor? Don't be ridiculous. It's a tiny village. There's only one thing for it. You'll have to stay with Ka."

Chapter Thirty-Two

A ROOF FOR THE NIGHT

"WHO?" I ask, momentarily baffled.

"Ka Cox. Lives up at Eagle's Nest. She's a good type, charitable and a stalwart of the community. She'll take you in, I'm sure."

"I can't ask a perfect stranger to house me."

"No, but I can."

"It's kind of you, but no. I'll manage."

"How?"

"I don't know. I haven't worked it out yet."

"Well, go ahead with your plans if you find a night under the stars appealing. I won't try to stop you. I'm only thinking about practicalities."

Lady Joyce looks momentarily crestfallen. Not for the first time today, my thoughts go to Vera Ponsonby and the many times I rejected her offers of help.

"You're right. I haven't properly thought this through, and I do have a responsibility to Teddy, if not to myself. I would greatly appreciate your help if you think that Mrs Cox won't mind."

Lady Joyce beams. "She'll love another project," she says. "Butler, about turn and take us to Eagle's Nest."

We hear a deep sigh from the driver's seat as Butler indicates, pulls over, and performs a nifty three-point turn in the road. Moments later, we are travelling in the opposite direction.

"Shake a leg," says Lady Joyce. "Don't forget I have an appointment."

"You'll never make it, ma'am," grumbles Butler.

"Then I'll be fashionably late."

I lean back on the comfortable upholstery, suddenly overwhelmed with relief. I have been a ball of worry since arriving in St Ives, not so much about where I would sleep, but how I would get to Zennor. The stone quoit featured on the postcard is clearly remote, and Lady Joyce refers to Zennor as small. How easy will it be to get to Carn Cottage if it's off the beaten track? I ask the question aloud, and Lady Joyce stares at me, momentarily silent. I can almost hear the cogs whirring in her mind.

"Why on earth would you want to go there?" she asks.

Her question has put me on high alert. I am suddenly wary and start backtracking. "I didn't say I would go, but I've heard of it and wondered where it was."

"Too far for someone in your condition to approach unaided," Lady Joyce replies. "Carn Cottage is in the middle of nowhere, which is just as well if the rumours are true."

"What rumours?"

"Don't concern yourself with them. Just stay away from the cottage and its inmates. Do you understand?"

"Not really."

"I'd rather not spell it out."

Lady Joyce regards my puzzled face. I stop speaking

momentarily, hoping my silence will encourage her to continue. She frowns, and her eyes drift across the landscape.

"Have you heard of satanism?" she asks.

My heart skips a beat.

"I think so," I offer as goosebumps shiver up my arm.

"Satanism is rife in some parts of Cornwall. It's the splendid isolation, you see. You can do anything without fear of exposure."

"Then how do you know?"

"A good question, girl. My family is rich and powerful. And as such, we hear the local doings. I know more than I'd ever wish to hear."

"But surely not about Carn Cottage? Does anyone live there?"

"Yes. Gerald Vaughan, a business manager who descended on Zennor last year and married Ellaline Norwood. They've since had a baby. The Lord only knows why they would want to bring up a child in that godforsaken place."

"And are they Satanists?"

"I wouldn't say that, though they are odd and paganistic. And Ka says strange incidents have plagued them."

"Such as?"

"Carvings of odd symbols, cairns of stones appearing around the property. It's probably the locals trying to frighten them away."

"Why would they?"

"They don't like nosey incomers who might see too much. You know what it's like. Cornwall has a rich history of underground activities."

"I see," I say, not really understanding but assuming a covert reference to smuggling. Oddly, it makes me feel more well-disposed towards Zennor. We have always been a county of free traders.

"Here we are," says Lady Joyce as Butler turns into a narrow drive off the road towards a long stone cottage perched on the edge of the moors. There is not another property in sight. If Lady Joyce thinks Carn Cottage is more isolated than this, I dread to think how far it is from human habitation.

Butler opens the door, and I clamber out, fighting with Teddy for exit rights. Lady Joyce strides ahead and hammers on the door. Presently, a slender, greying man appears, short-haired and wiry-framed. He cocks his head.

"Lady Joyce. Is Ka expecting you?"

"Not at all. I've bought her a waif and stray."

I blush to my roots, mortified by her frank introduction.

"Hello, young lady," says the man.

"Will Arnold-Forster," says Lady Joyce, gesturing an introduction. "This is Constance. Not sure of her surname, but harmless and in need of a bed for the night."

"Right," says Will, uncertainly.

"Where is she then?" barks Lady Joyce.

"In the drawing room. Please go through."

Lady Joyce barges past, and I follow in her wake, clutching Teddy's lead. He is the only thing keeping me sane in this pantomime situation. I should not have allowed Lady Joyce to take over my life this way.

Ka Arnold-Foster is reclining on a daybed when we enter the room. She looks up, bleary-eyed, and I realise we have interrupted a late afternoon nap. I clutch my face in embarrassment. This is going from bad to worse. We have intruded on this poor couple, who are about to be left with an unwanted guest. But when Lady Joyce explains the situation in a few curt sentences, Ka's face becomes wreathed in smiles.

"Of course we will help," she says. "The spare room is already made up. It's no trouble at all."

"I told her you wouldn't mind," says Lady Joyce.

"Ka is the salt of the earth," she whispers loudly in my ear. I'll be off now that it's all settled. I'm pleased to meet you, Constance," she adds, nodding to me. I hope you find what you need and keep safe." Pausing only to tickle Teddy's ears, she exits the room.

I stand there, dog lead and small carpetbag in hand, feeling horribly awkward. I chew my lip, not knowing what to say.

"Sit down," says Ka, patting the seat beside her. "You must be tired. And you're leaning dreadfully hard on that stick. It can't be good for you."

"Thank you," I say.

"Take your dog off the lead," she says. He's welcome here. I dare say he'll find Floss and Woozy if he looks hard enough?"

"Dogs?" I ask.

"Cairn terriers. They'll gang up on him for a moment or two but make friends in the end. Now, tell me about yourself."

I impart a modest amount of information, securing my welcome by revealing my Cornish roots, such as they are. Ka does not need to know that I am also, strictly speaking, an incomer. But having resided in Cornwall since the age of four or five, I feel a right to claim a Cornish heritage. Although impressed with my Cornish credentials, Ka herself hails from out of the county. Within a few moments, I discover she has spent time in bohemian London and is artistic and altruistic, not to mention a powerhouse of local affairs, immersing herself in governance and charitable endeavours. She is what Peter would have called a do-gooder. I think of Peter as I chat to Ka, wondering where he is now. And how on earth is he going to find me? Nobody but Lady Joyce knows my location, and Eagle's Nest cottage is likely too remote to contain a phone.

"Let's get you to your room," says Ka. "Then you can freshen up and take supper with us. Is that alright?"

"It's very kind of you," I say, feeling more relaxed. Though a busy woman, Ka seems genuinely pleased to be helping me. She radiates a welcoming air, and I don't mind that I have become her latest charitable endeavour. Ka guides me to the stairs and insists on carrying my bag. Teddy, has reappeared and shadows me to my room, settling by my legs as I examine my surroundings.

I drop my bag to the floor and make my way to the window overlooking a shaggy lawn. But the garden and its magnificent blooming rose bushes are nothing compared to the view beyond. The rugged moors lie ahead in a glorious blend of stark rocky outcrops, purple shades of heather and grassy scrublands. Here and there, distant sheep move like dirty clouds in the wild terrain. The May sun is dwindling, and an evening mist draws in. I glance at the unlit fire to my side and momentarily shiver. But one look at the jolly coun-terpane and a large vase of dried flowers atop a mahogany chest of drawers lifts my spirits. So, too, do the Cornish seascapes adorning two of the walls. The room, like Ka, is welcoming.

I gaze at my reflection in a large standing mirror. I look dusty, dishevelled and in need of a change of clothes. But I have forgone most of life's necessities to travel light and have nothing new to wear. I unpack the paltry items in my carpet bag and hunt for my face cloth and toothpaste. I decant water from a jug into the accompanying bowl, then use my flannel to remove the worst of the stains from my dress. I do not look perfect by any means, but I will not be a total disgrace at the supper table.

Before vacating my room, I check the postcard one last time and re-read the appointment time. 10 pm Monday 23rd May – tomorrow. My date with destiny draws closer.

Chapter Thirty-Three

EAGLES NEST

WE SIT down to a modest supper of potatoes and lamb chops, Will Arnold-Forster at one end of the table and Ka sitting opposite me to his side.

While Ka is good-natured and friendly, Will is aloof, portraying something of a superiority complex. He is quick-witted, intelligent, and able to speak authoritatively on various subjects, and I listen entranced. Will is the gardener in the family, having created the beautiful flowerbeds I saw earlier. But a shaggy lawn resulting from an injured odd job man who should have mowed it a few days ago but is otherwise indisposed, eclipses his exquisite work. I don't mention that I have noticed this flaw in an otherwise perfect land-scape as Will returns to the subject several times throughout supper. Although he must be in his fifties, Will Arnold-Forster is agile and as slim as a rake. He is perfectly capable of rolling up his shirt sleeves and cutting the grass himself. And as it means a great deal to him, I wonder why he would rather complain than get on with it. But I keep my feelings to myself as both Will and Ka have been excellent hosts to an unexpected guest, and as my stomach fills with good, hearty food, I express my gratitude.

"You're welcome, my dear," says Ka. "More than welcome. There are only two of us rattling around in this cottage. Stay as long as you like. What are your plans?" I gaze at her earnest face. Ka is not what you would call conventionally attractive, and her figure is more lumpy than svelte. But she exudes an air of friendliness, of quiet determination. I pause only for a second before deciding to trust her.

"I won't trouble you for long," I say. "But a friend of mine is visiting Carn Cottage tomorrow, and I thought I'd go along and surprise him."

Will and Ka exchange glances. "I didn't know Gerald had visitors," says Will.

"Oh, they do," Ka replies. "Ellaline asked me along, but it's one of *those* parties. And with you about to leave, I declined. Will is giving a lecture abroad," she explains. "He'll be leaving at the crack of dawn tomorrow."

"How exciting," I say.

"Routine," Will replies curtly. For all his intelligence, I have learned that Will's manner is abrupt, and I'm wondering whether it is deliberate or if he lacks self-awareness.

"Who's your friend?" asks Ka.

I risk the truth. "Brian Sullivan."

"Ellaline didn't mention him," she says. "But we know the Vaughans quite well. I'm sure their dinner party will be popular. They are keen for their friends to meet a new village resident. He only moved here a few days ago and took a cottage in Tregerthen. An unusual man. Something of an expert on pagan rites. He's very keen to explore our local history. Talking of which, have you seen our stone quoits?"

I shake my head. "Not yet, and if they are as remote as they appear, I never will."

Ka opens her mouth to speak, but I am still mulling over her previous remark, and I interrupt. "What do you mean by one of *those* dinner parties?" I ask, inflecting in the same manner.

Will frowns. "Katherine," he warns.

"Oh, she's not a child," says Ka. "Our friends are interested in esoteric matters. You know what I mean. Table turning, Ouija boards. That sort of thing. Only it's caused a few problems. Gerald is the instigator with a keen interest in the occult. Ellaline has gone along with it, but it's badly affected her, and she's become afraid of these things as if they were real. I think it's time for Gerald to put a stop to these parties and concentrate on his wife. She's not long had a baby and should involve herself in other things. At least the little one won't be there. Ellaline has arranged a babysitter."

I barely notice the removal of my dinner plate, and only when I instinctively take a spoonful of sponge pudding do I realise the Arnold-Forsters have a maid. My thoughts are elsewhere, mired in the realisation that Brian Sullivan is about to turn up in the middle of a pagan-centric dinner party in remote Cornwall. And it all makes sense. The unicursal hexagon at Tower Lodge and all the other clues indicating someone was there long after Brian should have expired. A sudden thought pops into my head. Could Brian be the man who had recently rented the cottage at Tregerthen? He already operates under the nom de plume of Byron Smith. What's to say he doesn't have a third identity as an expert on esoteric matters? Anyone can have a hobby.

"I'd like to attend the party," I say boldly.

Will Arnold-Forster shakes his head. "I wouldn't," he replies. "It's not an appropriate moment to surprise your friend."

"I know. But it's my best chance of tracking him down. I know exactly where he'll be at the appointed time. The postcard is very clear."

Will raises his fair eyebrows and regards me sternly, projecting an air of disbelief. I scrabble in my purse for the card and lay it on the tablecloth.

Will picks it up and passes it to Ka.

"Definitely one of those parties," she confirms. "Ten o'clock is far too late for supper."

I recover the card and return it to my purse. "You see my problem?" I ask.

"Yes, but wouldn't you be better off going tomorrow morning and asking the Vaughans to make a note of your friend's address?"

"He might leave the same night. I don't know his ongoing movements." I set my jaw stubbornly, signalling my intransigence on the subject.

"Very well," says Ka. "I'll write you a letter of introduction. That will get you through the door. I hope your friend appreciates it."

"Thank you so much," I reply. I had doubted the Arnold-Forsters for a moment, but despite our short acquaintance, I soon realise these people are kind enough to do anything for anyone.

"She'll need help getting there," says Will.

Ka shrugs. "I can drive you, but only so far. It's a remote spot, and you'd need to walk for a while. Will you manage?"

My heart falls, and I shake my head. My determination is no match for my disability. I can't move far at the best of times, but attempting a trek on the rugged moor late at night would be futile.

"What about Jones?" asks Ka.

"If you can raise him. I tried yesterday, and he wasn't around." Will Arnold-Forster sports a look of disappointment, once again.

"I'll ask Milly to call in on her way home," says Ka. "Jones is a local farmer with a tractor. It's not the most comfortable means of transport, but it will get you there. He will be happy to help."

"At that time of night?" asks Will.

"I think you'll find he will cooperate after what we did for his daughter," says Ka confidently. "I'm not sure your plan is wise, my dear, but if you must go to Carn Cottage tomorrow night, we'll get you there."

Chapter Thirty-Four

CARN COTTAGE

I DIDN'T SLEEP last night, my thoughts punctuated with doubt about the risks I would soon be taking. Of all the foolish things I have done to date, descending on Carn Cottage is by far the most stupid. I am about to embark on a trip after dark to a remote building in the presence of an occult expert who may be the murderer of Captain Butt and who is sufficiently cold-hearted to hack Butt's body to pieces and drop it over a bridge.

I tried to get ahead of myself before the event, straining in vain to leave my body while waiting for sleep to come. Had things gone well, I might have managed a nocturnal reconnoitre of Carn Cottage ahead of my visit. But nothing happened despite my best efforts, and my soul stayed pinned to my body as if weighted by a block of stone. It wasn't stone but mortal terror that inhibited any prospect of astral travel.

The unholy dread was still with me when I woke and met a pale-faced Ka at the breakfast table. We'd exchanged a few words, most of which revolved around

Will's departure that morning. I'd spent the rest of the day alone until dusk fell and when we heard a tractor pulling into the drive, Ka took me outside. I slipped a leash on Teddy and handed him to Ka to look after for the night. She waited until I was about to board the chunky vehicle before handing me a warm woollen coat and insisting I wear it. That was fifteen minutes ago. And I am now pulling it across my chest as we drive deeper into the moorland, the stuttering engine loudly announcing our presence.

Jones is a swarthy-faced, sullen man with no small talk. We drive silently, watching the faded light while stones splinter beneath the tyres as we make our way along ancient tracks. The sunny day has turned into a cloudy evening, fading to foggy darkness. Mists swirl over the moor, and as we dip down a track, it is so dark that, for a moment, I can't see my hand in front of my face. The moor is desolate, lacking in cover. It feels several degrees colder than outside Eagle's Nest.

"Straight ahead," grunts Jones, pointing at a pale light in the distance. I squint but cannot see anything identifiable. But as we draw nearer, the rugged stone cottage nestled beneath a slate roof, appears in view. My heart thuds as we draw closer.

"You'll have to walk the last bit alone," says Jones, pointing to a dip by the cottage. It doesn't look far, but the terrain is uneven.

I take a deep breath, make a brave face, and hope to manage the walk without falling over. Jones sees the look of uncertainty and speaks.

"I can't get the tractor down there," he says. "But you can hold my arm if you like."

I thank him but refuse, buoyed by his offer, which

creates unexpected fortitude. "Can you wait five minutes in case they turn me away?"

"I can. But only five minutes."

I toss my stick from the tractor and clamber down, collecting it from the ground before negotiating a grassy slope. I don't attempt it with dignity but sit and slither until my feet hit the stone pathway beyond – not my finest moment, but a good, safe decision.

Now, closer, I can see a welcome glow in the cottage windows. They must have switched on every light in the place, and the jolly strains of music escape through an unlatched window. I glance at my watch. It is a quarter to ten. I am early yet wonder if all the guests are inside. I draw a deep breath and rap on the door.

They don't keep me waiting for long. A short-haired young woman with pale features and bags under her eyes opens the door. She frowns as she sees me and stumbles on her words.

"Oh, hello. So pleased you could come," she says uncertainly, and I realise she thinks she ought to know me and feels embarrassed by her lack of recognition. I seize the opportunity.

"Lovely to see you too, Ellaline," I reply. My hand closes over the letter of introduction as I prepare to use it, but Ellaline ushers me inside. "Why don't you introduce yourself to the others?" she asks, abrogating the awkward task. "But let me get you a drink first. What would you like?"

"A gin would be nice," I say.

"I'll fetch it in a moment. The others are through there."

I enter the room to see six people already in conversation, all armed with alcoholic drinks. The chatter stops as I enter, and nerves almost get the better of me. But I take advantage of Ellaline's absence and announce myself. "Elys

Clark," I say, taking my long-suffering housekeeper's name in vain. "Ellaline asked me." I cross my fingers at the little white lie. Ellaline had asked me to introduce myself. What did it matter if I omitted a word or two to imply I was her guest?

"I'm jolly glad to have you. My wife didn't say you were coming, but the more, the merrier. I'm Gerald; this is Philip, Clara, and Vincent. And the lovely Marlene is chatting to the captain over there. I glance at a pretty blonde-haired woman in earnest conversation with a man standing with his back to me before I concentrate my attention on my host.

"I'm so happy to be here. I find it all fascinating."

I have said the right thing, and my host beams. "It's early days for us," he says. My wife and I are still learning the ropes, but we've managed some successful invocations and are becoming more proficient with every new attempt. I'm glad Ellaline has brought you along. She's lost some enthusiasm lately, but involving a friend bodes well for future gatherings."

Ellaline enters the room, her drawn face more pinched than before. She hands me a drink, and I thank her before purposely engaging her in conversation to keep her away from her husband.

"Are there any more guests?" I ask.

"Well, yes. We are waiting for our new resident." Ellaline does not name her outstanding guest but speaks of him reverently with an undercurrent of fear. I chew my lip as I consider her reaction. If I am correct, then Brian Sullivan is her guest. But though he has contrived to commit terrible acts, I have seen several photographs of him, and his appearance is benign, more like a bespectacled school-master than a killer. However grim my suspicions may be, I could never find him frightening. Have I jumped to the wrong conclusion?

"Would you like a seat while we wait?" asks Ellaline, her eyes drawn to my stick.

"Yes, please," I say. I look less like a cripple sitting down, not that it matters. Nobody, including Brian Sullivan, knows who I am. I should conserve my energy in case I need to stand later, so I take advantage of her suggestion.

Ellaline guides me to a sofa at the other end of the room and sits beside me, so I am not alone. We chat briefly before she spots a guest with an empty glass. And only then, in her absence, do I gaze around the room. My view is clearer now that I am sitting in a different vantage point. I can no longer see the pretty blonde, but I have a perfect view of the captain, who has faced away from me until now. His face blurs in a rush of recognition. I know him from a photograph I saw on my astral travels from our cottage in Old Bath Road. The identity of the Cheltenham torso is still a mystery, but one thing is certain. It wasn't the remains of Captain Butt, who now stands before me as if he hadn't a care in the world.

Chapter Thirty-Five

A SHOCKING DISCOVERY

GOOSEBUMPS CRAWL ACROSS MY SKIN. If I am in the presence of Captain Butt, then I can't reasonably expect to see Brian Sullivan tonight. The postcard cannot have been intended for him and Butt must have been the man using the cottage at Polperro. So, Brian is dead after all. And if Brian really had killed himself, then who ended his days in pieces by Haw Bridge? I slowly get to my feet, determined to speak to Captain Butt, despite my revulsion. Perhaps it isn't him. Perhaps he has a doppelgänger. I stand unsteadily and walk across the room. The blonde frowns but Butt flashes a sharklike smile and makes the introductions. "Marlene Cooper," he says. "And I am Captain Cedric Parker."

I keep my cool, through my conviction is wavering at the unexpected name. "I'm Elys, I say. And I'm terribly excited to meet our guest tonight. Such fun, don't you think?"

The captain fixes me with a stare. "It's a very serious matter," he says. "Which you will know if you've attended an incantation before."

"I have," I say, trying to recover his good opinion. "But not for some time."

"Then I hope you are prepared. We are dealing with ceremonial magic at the highest level."

"Should she be here?" asks Marlene, gently touching the captain's arm.

"I'm not frightened," I say. "I may not have your level of experience, but I am not a stranger to the dark arts."

The captain nods. "Good," he says. "Because this is no place for beginners and the wrong reaction might risk all our lives."

My heart plummets as he speaks. While Gerald and Ellaline are treating this like enthusiastic spaniels, the captain is serious. And I wonder how deeply involved he is in black magic and whether I have wandered into a practising coven. My spine tingles and fear snakes through my body as I realise, I am hopelessly out of my depth.

I try to refocus on my original intention to draw out details that might identify this man as Captain Butt. I ask about his military history, but his replies are vague. Marlene tries to change the subject, but I steer it back again, this time to a familiar location.

"I've just had a lovely holiday in Cheltenham," I say.

"That's nice," replies Marlene, her eyes wandering elsewhere, with no effort to disguise her boredom.

"Do you know it?" I direct the question to Marlene, as asking the captain would be too obvious.

"Not at all. I don't care much for cities," she says.

"It's not a city," says Captain Butt.

"Have you been there?" I ask.

He shakes his head. "I've passed through it once or twice."

"Well, it's a lovely place with a stunning Winter Garden in Pittville Park."

"I don't think so," snaps the captain.

"It is. I've been inside."

"Not in Pittville Park, you haven't."

"I'm sure it's Pittville Park."

"I think you'll find the Winter Gardens lie in Imperial Park."

I tut. "Of course they do," I say. "Silly me."

Marlene smirks as if in agreement.

"Excuse me," I say, "my leg is hurting, and I must sit down."

The captain doffs his forelock and Marlene immediately ignores me and continues her game of flirtation. But I have heard enough. It is nowhere near an admission, but the captain clearly knows Cheltenham like a man with more than a passing acquaintance. I am sure Cedric Parker is William Butt. But if Captain Butt is here and Brian is dead, who is the special guest and master of the esoteric rites? I sit uneasily as a horrible thought takes root. But it doesn't nest there long. A series of loud knocks startle me, and I am not alone in my surprise. The guests stop talking and turn to face the door as Gerald bustles through. Ellaline joins me on the couch, wrapping her arms around her shoulders and looking like a little girl lost. The door opens and we see Gerald welcome his guest. And as I stare at the door, I am filled with a terrible sense of foreboding. Time stops as I catch a momentary glimpse of the last man in the world, I should be anywhere near. A man who I dreamwalked into only a few short weeks ago. Bald headed, jowly, and dressed in the robes of Calicum Aureum, Felix Crossley authoritively enters the room while something inside me dies.

Chapter Thirty-Six

THE GUEST OF HONOUR

THE GUESTS RUSH TOWARDS HIM, clustering like fans around a Hollywood starlet. Only Ellaline and I remain where we are, both frozen in fear. Ellaline looks as if she is about to cry, holding her head in her hands with trembling fingers. Her visible terror is enough to motivate me. Grabbing my stick, I slink through the door to my right. I clutch my chest, half expecting it to slam open again as someone spots me and follows, but nothing happens. They are all too busy greeting Crossley.

I wait momentarily for the panic to subside, then drop to my haunches and peer through the keyhole. I can't see much because of an inconveniently positioned sofa, so I rise and search the room, finding an old, unused serving hatch half covered by a row of books. I move the hefty tomes one at a time, so quietly that I can hear my jagged breath as I struggle to keep my fear under control. Mission accomplished. I gently pull the sliding panel. It is stiff and unwieldy and in any other circumstance, I would give it a good tug. But I must remain silent or they will discover my hiding place. I pick, prise, and mither at the panel, breaking a nail and collecting a splinter before it finally eases open to an inch-long gap, allowing an excellent view of the area while keeping my cover intact. I press my face to the hole and peer into the room. The lighting is low, and the occupants have changed into purple robes, worn over very little else. Far from being a bunch of casual satanic worshippers, I am in the heart of a group with clear associations to Calicum Aureum. My heart beats faster. I am in grave danger if anyone finds me. I pull my face away, eyes darting anxiously around the room for a means of escape if they discover my presence. My leg does not allow me to move far or fast, but there is, at least, a low window in the wall. I calculate how long it would take to get there, should the need arise. But first, I will discover Crossley's intentions. I must have something tangible to report to The Order when I finally escape.

Having a plan gives me purpose and calms me. I resume my position by the sliding panel, watching and listening as Crossley speaks. He stands in the dim light, illuminated by recently erected candleholders, while the other participants lounge below, robes askew. I close my eyes, repulsed by the flesh on show and hope I won't have to witness the depravities of a satanic orgy. I am all for gaining intelligence, but that would be beyond the pale.

Crossley smiles beneficently, then speaks, his voice low and controlled. "Greetings, adepts. You are here to learn, as I am here to impart knowledge gained from decades of study. You all wish to pass through the abyss, and I will help you in time. But first, I will demonstrate what it is to control one's soul and detach from your mortal being. The ability to astral travel is rare, and you may not have witnessed bodily separation before. Now is your chance. Watch and learn."

Crossley sits in a high-backed chair and focuses on a candle. Within seconds, I see what his adepts cannot. Crossley's spirit rises from his torpid carcass and hangs in the air while he decides on a direction of travel. He glances towards me, and I hold my breath, willing my heartbeat to still. Crossley's nose flares as his bodily chest rises and falls as if in sleep. But his spirit eyes dart this way and that as if he suspects something is amiss. I chew my lip, ready to flee towards the window at a moment's notice, but Crossley's spirit moves in the opposite direction, exiting the room momentarily before returning and reuniting with his body. His heavily lidded eyes flutter open, and he rouses himself and stretches before standing in front of his silent adepts, still seated quietly on the floor.

Crossley crooks his finger towards Gerald Vaughan. "What is in your study?" he demands.

"A desk, a chair," stutters Gerald.

"What is on the desk, fool?" Crossley treats his host with contempt, asserting his authority over the household. A look of humiliation passes over Gerald Vaughan's face, but he is in too deep to complain.

"A letter."

"Correct. A letter. An uninspiring missive from your butcher in Lelant asking you to settle his account. Dated yesterday, from Tyringham Road, with a large thumbmark on the bottom right-hand corner. Tell me, what's wrong with the butcher in St Ives?"

"N-nothing," stutters Vaughan. "J-just a matter of personal choice."

Crossley lunges forward until they are nearly face-to-face, hushing him with a finger over his lips. "I don't care," he hisses. "I'm merely making a point, dear boy. Did you or did you not escort me directly from your front door into this room?"

"I did," says Gerald, more confidently.

"You cannot see me cross into the astral realm, but now you can vouch that I have. "

"It's true. He couldn't have known about the letter any other way." Gerald enthusiastically nods his head, reaching for Ellaline's hand. She snatches it away, recoiling from his touch, and pulls both parts of her robe tightly together, her face marble white.

"Do you aspire to this skill?" asks Crossley, gazing eagle-eyed at the group.

They reply in the affirmative, except Ellaline, who is still visibly trembling.

"And you want to know how?"

"We do." The words tumble from their lips in a chorus.

"To progress, you must show single-minded devotion to the cause, and sheer selfishness of mind. You must do as you wish regardless of others to spend every waking moment in pursuit of knowledge. Leave your family, place your daily toil at the bottom of the list, and indulge not your children. The route through the abyss is for you and you alone. Are you resolute, rapacious? Do you have the steely resolve to succeed?"

"We do."

"Then tell me about it." Crossley returns to his chair, pulls it across the floor and sits before the group, crossing one leg carelessly over the other.

"You," he says, pointing to Gerald Vaughan. "Your one supreme act of selfishness this year. Something to show me your disregard for the human race carried out entirely for your own ends."

Vaughan stares, blinking as his mind whirrs, opening,

and closing his mouth while considering his recent behaviour. "I didn't buy a dog licence," he says finally. "I told them Bracken was dead. She isn't." He points to a little wire-haired terrier cowering beneath the sofa.

"Get it out of here," says Crossley. "I despise dogs. Dreadful creatures. Stupidly loyal. Kick it, and you'll see what I mean."

I place my hand over my mouth to still a gasp, knowing I could not sit by and see an animal suffer. But to Gerald's credit, neither can he. He takes the little dog and gently puts it outside. It does not whine or scratch to get back in, no doubt preferring the discomfort of the brisk May night to the volatile atmosphere in the cottage.

"A dog licence," spits Crossley. "Is that the best you can do?"

Vaughan nods, and Crossley raises his eyes heavenward. "And you?" he asks, pointing to Ellaline. She shakes her head mutely.

"I appreciate you are our hosts for the night, but you're very disappointing. Are you sure you wouldn't rather take an evening walk with your animal?"

"No. I'm game for anything," says Gerald brazenly. Ellaline stays silent, mute with fear.

"Anyone else?" Crossley's mood has darkened. Philip raises his hand. "Vincent and I performed incantations on the moor before last month's full moon."

"Commendable," says Crossley. "But what is self-centred about that?"

"We were naked," says Vincent. "Tackle out and standing by the quoit in the early evening with people in sight."

"In front of hikers," continues Philip. "It caused the devil of a fuss and made the papers, but they put it down to bohemian excesses. Artistic types can get away with murder."

"Good," says Crossley. "And you, young lady?" He points to Marlene, sprawled across the captain in continued flirtation.

"I went dancing," she says. "It was back in March when mother was particularly poorly. She needed me, and I left her alone to fend for herself overnight. Mother tried the usual emotional blackmail, but I reminded her that everyone should be able to do what they want whenever they want. Caring for others is a choice, and duty is a bore. My choice is to care for myself."

"That's the spirit," says Crossley. "Now, you." He clicks his fingers by Clara's head. She narrows her eyes. "I stole the charity box in the local cafe. I didn't need the money, but I thought, why not? So, I did it to see if I could."

"Better. Much better. Now, Captain, it's no secret that our paths have crossed before. I know what you did, my friend. Why don't you tell the others?" Crossley beams, casting a benevolent eye over the captain as if he were a long-lost child.

The captain stands, towering over Crossley like an equal. Crossley scowls at the challenge to his authority and waves him to one side. The captain remains standing, hands on hips, his pallid white legs contrasting with the purple robe settling over a slight bulge in his stomach.

"I killed a man," says Captain Butt. Marlene gasps, shrinking away from him momentarily before regaining her composure.

"By accident?" she gasps.

"In that instance, yes."

The room falls quiet, all waiting for the captain to fill the unsettling silence.

"What do you mean, Parker?" asks Vincent.

"Butt, actually," says the captain. "William Butt, Bill to my friends."

Philip sits up, stroking his chin. "You're supposed to be dead."

"I know. And you are very privileged to know my secret. Thanks to my dear friend Felix, I'll be across the channel by the end of next week."

Crossley smirks. "Tell them everything, Butt. We haven't got all night."

The captain crosses his arms. "It started in January, just after Christmas. Bloody awful weather, holiday plans ruined and a half-mad wife to boot. Things were not going my way. I went out one night for a snifter and had more than I'd intended. I jumped in the car and hit a chap walking along the road late at night, making a fine mess of him. Long story short, I threw him in the car and took him to a friend at Tower Lodge. The man was dead by the time I got there, and judging by his ill-fitting, ragged clothes, he must have been a tramp. But I didn't want a scandal, so I called on Brian Sullivan, an acquaintance of mine. Sullivan and I cleaned up the car, cut up the body and rolled the pieces into an old piece of carpet. I mulled over the matter for a day, then put the car in the garage to hide it away. I slipped Brian and his friend a few pounds to dispose of the corpse and laid low at Tower Lodge until they had finished."

"That sounds like an accident," says Clara. "No intent at all."

"Yes, not sure that qualifies," says Philip, equally put out.

Crossley grins. "Carry on," he says.

"All went well at first," says Butt. "Sullivan's friend Keith Newman took his share of the payoff and returned to London. He was a minor crook who disliked the police, and

I knew he was sound. But Sullivan was a different kettle of fish, naïve and with an insatiable conscience. He dwelt on his part in the affair for a day or two before saying he couldn't live with the lie and would hand himself in at the police station the following day. It was time for me to act. I could have legged it over to France there and then, but I needed more time. And they'd already missed me at home. I knew the corpse would make an appearance eventually, and if I was gone with no one around who knew my where-abouts, they might think it was mine. After all, the dead man was of similar height and weight. The idea appealed enormously. I could leave my miserable life and make a new one. So, I dropped something extra in Brian's evening drink, and while he was asleep, I opened the gas taps in his bedroom. Then I forged a suicide note to his dear old mum and decamped to Ashton Keynes to hide in a religious colony until the press became bored with the story."

"Selfish to the core," says Crossley, proudly clapping Butt on the back.

"Kneel," he demands.

Butt drops to his knees and lowers his head. Crossley walks over to the fireplace and returns to Butt, daubing a sooty print on his forehead.

"Congratulations," says Crossley. "You have earned the black mark."

I retreat to take a moment to myself. Butt murdered Brian Sullivan. Who would have thought it? I knew some-thing was wrong, but until arriving here tonight, I hadn't considered Butt for a moment. Poor Irene Sullivan. She's tortured herself for months, unaware of the circumstances of her son's death. If I get out of this hellhole, I'll make it my mission to find her and tell her the truth. I shift position to make myself more comfortable before returning to my vantage point. Ellaline has also moved in the few moments I was away and is now standing before Captain Butt, pale-faced and shaking. She advances closer still, her hands tightly clenched.

"I won't have a killer in my house," she says, in a wobbling voice.

Crossley raises an eyebrow and moves forward in his chair. "What did you say?" he growls.

"I want you out. All of you. This should have been a fun evening. And here you are, paying homage to a murderer. I won't have it."

"Sit down and shut up."

"I say, old chap." Gerald Vaughan moves to stand, but Crossley stares disdainfully, and he silently resumes his seat.

"Get your woman under control," barks Crossley.

"Calm down, Ellaline," says Gerald.

"You coward." Ellaline is so frightened her teeth are chattering, but she won't back down.

Crossley sighs, puts his hands together, and chants a few Latin words. Then, he slowly opens his cupped hands to reveal a dark mass. Glaring at Ellaline, he whispers, "Run, my beauty," and throws the object towards her.

Ellaline screams as the black mass unfurls into a fist-sized, hairy-legged spider. It bounces from her shoulder, falls to the floor, and skitters under the couch. It is too much for Ellaline. She rushes from the room straight towards me, leaving no time to hide.

Chapter Thirty-Seven

BLACK MASS

ELLALINE RUNS SCREAMING through the door. I confront the problem head-on, moving towards her with my finger on my lips. Her eyes widen in surprise. Out of sight, out of mind, she had forgotten I was in her house. I catch Ellaline's wrist, asking for quiet before pulling her towards my hiding place at the end of the room. She crouches, trembling, beside me.

"Did you see what happened?" she whispers.

I nod.

"Are you frightened too? Is that why you're hiding?"

I glance nervously through the peephole, hoping Crossley is too preoccupied to hear Ellaline's frantic questions. And sure enough, the narcissistic magician is concentrating so hard on his ritual that he doesn't care what happens to Ellaline. He has raised himself to a standing position and is lording it over the others, addressing them in a language I don't understand. The room darkens as Crossley speaks, his incantation growing louder and more intense. I turn to Ellaline.

"Of course I am afraid, but please whisper. Felix Crossley must not find me."

"Is that his name? He introduced himself with another."

"I'm not surprised."

"Do you know him?"

"In a manner of speaking. Hush now. It's too difficult to explain."

A gust of wind swirls through the opening, making me blink. By the time I refocus, the candles are out, snuffed by the unexpected blast of air. I can still see faces bathed in the glow of two wall-mounted gas lamps, but the room has taken on a sinister turn without the extra light. Crossley stops chanting, claps his hands, and points to Marlene. She stands, drops her robe, and walks forward unclothed.

"Tonight, you will be my scarlet woman," purrs Crossley, directing Marlene to the vacant chair. She sits seductively, glowing with importance and undisguised ambition. Philip, Vincent, and Clara weave provocatively from side to side with their eyes closed, looking almost entranced. But Gerald Vaughan is clearly uncomfortable, and even from a distance with little light, I see beads of sweat forming on his forehead. Crossley also notices and frowns.

"Don't you want to be here?" he asks. "On this most fortuitous night. Look at the skies." He points a finger towards an open window to the front of the cottage. "A clear path to the moon, not a cloud in sight. It's the perfect night to try something important, something I have never succeeded in before. I want to take advantage of the experience in this room and the magnificent determination of those who wish to learn. If you don't want to be a part of it, join your wife, wherever she is."

"You want me to leave my own home?" asks Gerald.

"You are either in or out, no middle ground." Crossley tosses more indeterminate objects towards Gerald, and this time, a dozen tiny spiders emerge from a smoky mass, swarming together before disbanding into the corners of the room.

Gerald flinches. "That's enough," he says, wiping his forehead.

"Then leave."

Gerald stoops, grabs a pile of clothes, and stomps off in the opposite direction. I sigh, hugely relieved that he did not try to follow Ellaline. She is pressing against me, watching proceedings through the sliding panel, now wide enough for us both to see. She wipes her face and sniffs while trying to stifle a sob. "How could he?" she whimpers.

I put my arm around her and whisper in her ear. "He's frightened, too."

"Then why didn't he come for me?"

I cannot answer without risking offence, so I pat her shoulder and shake my head. Ellaline blinks away tears, and we resume our watch over the room.

"Shall we begin?" asks Crossley.

"Yes, master," says Philip. Vincent displays more curiosity. "What are you planning?"

"A good question," says Crossley. "Something you won't have seen before. The way of mastery breaks all rules."

"To what end?"

"Tonight, we will perform an incantation to generate a manifestation of evil."

"You'd better watch your step, Captain Butt," says Philip. "In terms of wicked deeds, you're the winner by a country mile."

"This is a serious matter," snarls Crossley. "Nobody has

succeeded to any degree. Even I have managed little more than a ghostly image lasting barely thirty seconds."

"Why us? Why tonight?" asks Clara.

"Because you are in the presence of a man who has truly demonstrated his disdain for humanity. Selfishness is powerful, and I must harness the energy while I can. Do you object?" Crossley lowers his head towards Clara. She calmly crosses her hands.

"Not in the least," she says.

"Then off with your robes, all of you."

I silently thank God that the lights are low as I watch through the gap. Ellaline is still sobbing silently and leans into me as if searching for reassurance.

Another chant, another babble of the unknown language, and Crossley is in full swing, pacing the floor, his paunch on full display. He holds his hands aloft, appealing to a dark God somewhere in the sky. The adepts sway, touching, clinging to one other but curiously restrained. If Crossley intended a demonic orgy, the very British reticence of the participants falls far short of his expectations. But for all the lack of action, Crossley continues spraying words across the room, his face contorted, a passionate inflexion to his words. He roars a final incantation before the room falls silent. Crossley waits, hands still held up, palms open before him. I hold my breath, waiting. Then, the floor seems to heave and sway as tiny spiders swarm into the room, covering the floorboards in a carpet of writhing menace. Ellaline whimpers. I hush her, but she is trembling from head to toe.

Crossley raises his hand yet higher and fires off a click of his fingers that echoes in the silent room. More spiders follow, this time the size of small rodents. It is too much. Ellaline screams.

I freeze as Crossley's head jerks up. "You may not interfere, woman," he roars. "Bring her through and silence
her."

Vincent breaks his reverie and looks up at Crossley. "You
won't hurt her?" he asks.

"Of course not. But she must not interrupt. Let the
stupid woman sit in here where we can keep an eye on her."

The danger I feared is now upon us. I cannot react, so
Ellaline must. "Run," I demand, pushing Ellaline forward.
She sits blinking on her haunches, paralysed with fear.

"Run! Fetch help. Get Ka. She's only across the moor."

Ellaline shakes her head, breaking the spell. "I'll go at
once."

She runs across the room, flinging open the window as
Philip and Vincent enter. They lunge for her, but she wrig-
gles free, flopping onto the ground below.

"She's gone," shouts Philip.

"Good. Then come back through, and let's get on with
it," snaps Crossley.

"Shall I bring the other one?" Vincent has seen me
cowering behind the bureau. My heart thumps in my chest
as I hear Crossley bark a reply.

"What other one?"

"Ellaline's friend."

I have only a few seconds to think before inevitably
coming face-to-face with my mortal enemy. He may not
know me in person, but he has seen me on the astral plane
and will doubtless recognise his old nemesis. Crossley is
stronger than me, both physically and in spirit. But I would
gain a head start if I could snap into a dreamwalk before he
realises. Though astral travel no longer comes naturally, it
might separate me from my body and buy a few seconds'
grace. I stare Philip full in the face, using the light reflecting

from his eyes to fix my gaze. Then, concentrating like never before, I will myself in two as my spirit gently pulls away from my mortal form.

"The bloody woman fainted," says Philip as I dart through the wall and begin my search for Ellaline.

Chapter Thirty-Eight

LOST ON THE WILD AND WINDY MOOR

I HEAR Ellaline before I see her. She is only a few yards ahead, running for dear life, clad only in the thinnest of robes. She darts across the moor, weaving through gorse and bracken, her unshod feet gashed and bloody from stones and thorns. But if she feels any pain, it does not slow her. She pushes on as if pursued by the devil himself. I catch up and run beside her, a silent companion in her hour of need.

Ellaline runs for almost ten minutes before slowing down. She leans over, deeply heaving as she tries to recover her breath. Her breathing calms, and she turns full circle, her face anxious and tear marked. I know what she is thinking. She has lost her sense of direction.

I leave her momentarily as I run ahead, taking a false turn before seeing Ka's cottage before me. I know where to go, but how do I communicate directions to Ellaline? I could never influence the living. They cannot see or feel me.

I return to Ellaline, still moving aimlessly in small circles, trying her best to find a sensible direction to take across the moor. She is so close to Eagle's Nest, albeit unaware. Finally, she takes the plunge and moves away. But she is heading ninety degrees in the wrong direction.

I clasp my astral hands on my cheeks, internally yelling in sheer frustration. Nobody hears. Nobody can. I dart towards Ellaline and lunge for her, hurling my body through hers. I might as well have whispered into the wind for all the good it does. Ellaline continues unperturbed. I cannot make my presence felt and try another tack, running forward beyond her to find anything that might provide a means to turn her back. I am about to give up in despair when I run into a ewe and her half-grown lamb, separated from the herd. I have occasionally succeeded in attracting the attention of domestic animals. Could I influence the behaviour of this sheep?

I gently pat its head, whispering in its ear. My hand passes through the rough-fleeced animal. It barely moves, now quietly settled for the night. I try again with the lamb, which cocks its head slightly. I squeal into its ear, and it jumps to one side. The mother sheep emits a concerned bleat and moves towards her offspring. I try again and move a few yards behind the lamb before running towards it, clapping my hands above my head, and screaming like a banshee. It leaps ahead, and I dart behind it, screeching for all I am worth. The lamb takes fright and darts off, hooves pounding on the ground. The mother lowers her head and charges behind it, eyes wide in panic. They hurtle down the narrow track and towards Ellaline. She hears them before she sees them, moving her head as her eyes try to catch up with the information coming from her ears. As the two sheep pound towards her like ghostly clouds, Ellaline gasps, gathers her robe and runs for dear life toward Eagle's Nest cottage.

I run behind her, only stopping when she crosses the drive and pounds her fists on Ka Arnold-Forster's door, tears rolling down her face. She doesn't stop, slamming one palm after another against the wood until she slides to the floor, overcome with tiredness and fear. I pace, watching while a light flickers in Ka's room above. She heaves the window open and leans out, calling aloud.

"Is somebody there?"

"Me," sobs Ellaline.

"Who?"

"It's Ellaline. I'm in terrible trouble."

"Wait. I'll come down."

Moments later, the door swings open. Ka stands in her nightdress, candle aloft.

"Oh, my dear. Whatever is wrong?" she asks.

"They've taken over my cottage," sobs Ellaline. "It's too much. The house is full of fornication and devilry."

"Calm down," says Ka. "Have you had another one of your seances?"

"No. Far worse. Gerald left me alone with the spiders. They said they'll summon worse. And they've captured a young woman."

"Oh God. Not Connie?"

"I can't remember. She uses a stick and can't get out alone. I said I'd run for help."

Ka's mouth sets in a thin line. "I feel terribly responsible for this. I wish I'd never agreed to it. Wait inside. I'll be ready in five minutes."

Ellaline collapses on the chaise longue while Ka takes the stairs two at a time. I prepare to join her when I feel a sharp pain against my cheek. I instinctively raise my hand before feeling the same sensation on the other side. My mind whirrs with possibilities, and I settle on the obvious. I am close enough to Carn Cottage to feel mild sensations from my body. And the tugging at the back of my head proves my point. Logic tells me that Crossley has found and recognised me and is slapping my cheeks to rouse my slumbering body. Thank goodness he is too preoccupied to travel astrally. I wouldn't stand a chance.

I wait with bated breath while Ellaline slumps in a heap, her chest rising and falling as she struggles to regain her composure. Eventually, she tips her head backwards and loudly sighs. Then, she stands, leaning against the fireplace while she waits for Ka's return. It doesn't take long.

"One moment," says Ka, striding through the door in a knee-length tweed skirt and jacket. She exits to the rear, and moments later, I hear a swoosh and watch as a red comet zips vertically into the sky.

"What was that?" asks Ellaline, repeating the question as Ka re-enters the room.

"Just a flare," says Ka. "We always keep a few around the premises. Better safe than sorry when living in this isolated environment. Someone will come to check on me." Ka gestures to the door, flings it open and ushers Ellaline through before slamming it into my face. I don't take offence to the unintended slight given my invisibility and pass through to see Ka fixing a note to the door with a metal tack. "Carn Cottage. Come Quick," it says.

"Right. Best not hang around," says Ka. The two ladies stride into the night, and I run on ahead, my stomach knotted with nerves, knowing Crossley has my mortal body in his evil grasp. And as if on cue, a tight pain crushes my wrists, making me pause for breath. Steeling myself, I move on to face my greatest fear.

Chapter Thirty-Nine

RISE OF THE UNDEAD

I ARRIVE FIRST, slinking through the door and hoping Crossley will not notice me. But he is standing behind my body with his arms draped across my shoulders, waiting for my return. He spies me and smirks triumphantly. "Well, well, well. Who have we here?" he asks.

I stand uncertainly, not knowing what to do. Crossley will easily overcome me now, no matter what form I take. I consider my options and conclude that they are all as bad as each other. Crossley clicks his fingers. "In you jump," he says. I acquiesce, feeling a world of pain as my parts rejoin. Crossley has weaved a vicious rope around my wrists, biting into my flesh. And I suspect the marks around my cheeks were of the variety made by a clenched fist. One of my eyes is almost closed, the other unfocused. I raise my head and peer around the room. The five adepts before me remain seated, gazing entranced towards Crossley without the slightest sympathy for my condition.

Crossley takes a handful of hair and yanks up my head. I wince at the sudden sharp pain. "A change of plan," he says. "I can now perform a magnificent event long denied to me. If you only knew how long I have waited for this moment and a chance to attempt my greatest feat ever."

"What was wrong with raising evil?" scowls Philip.

"Nothing," booms Crossley. "But now, we will up the ante by raising the dead."

Clara glances to her right, and I detect a flicker of fear. But I am too subsumed with my terror to care about hers. My teeth chatter, and I try to clench them shut, hoping my apparent dread will not fuel Crossley. But he grins wolfishly.

"This girl," he says. "Is the daughter of a vicar, a man of God, if you will. I attempted a similar ritual two decades ago to raise Satan himself, but the incantation failed because her father stole my sacrifices. He took two godly children away from me at the worst possible time. I had groomed them for months to be suitable sacrifices. Well, she might be older, and her father long gone, but this woman is still the child of a man of God. And that will make up for everything I have lost. Tonight, I will raise Satan from below, summon the undead, and sacrifice this creature before me for the good of Calicum Aureum. And you, my adepts, will assist. So, too, will my loyal acolytes, those who have followed me for years from one end of this world to the other. One more ritual before we begin, and I will summon them tonight to join us in my masterpiece."

Crossley turns his back and rummages in his robe pocket, pulling out a coin before placing it in his mouth. He tilts my chin again, head lowered, his rancid breath close to mine. Then he opens his mouth and I see the gold disc glistening with saliva. He smears the coin down my cheek before replacing it on his reptilian tongue. Crossley turns, holds his hands aloft, and chants frenziedly.

The door slams open, followed by a horde of bats, who

speed towards Crossley before abruptly stopping mid-flight before him. He whispers something high-pitched, and the bats turn tail before swooping through the door straight into the path of Ka Arnold-Forster.

"Stop," she says, holding up her hand. Crossley's nose twitches as he regards her with disdain.

"Do be quiet," he hisses.

"I will not. Stop this nonsense at once and leave Ella-line's house."

"Or what?"

"I will call the police."

Crossley croaks a hollow laugh. But the other guests fidget awkwardly. Many know Ka and find the behaviour of their host embarrassing – all except Captain Butt, who sticks his chest out. "Do as he says," Butt booms.

Crossley nods in satisfaction and moves to one side.

"And you can untie Constance immediately," says Ka, spying me behind his portly frame. She advances towards me. Crossley scowls, and striking like a serpent, he grasps her wrist.

"Hands off me, you coward," says Ka.

Crossley's nails dig into her hand, and he points a finger, muttering a silent chant while Ka struggles to free herself. I feel a sudden chill as the temperature drops again. Crossley moves towards the captain, still dragging Ka by the other arm.

"Hold her still," Crossley lisps, the coin rattling around his mouth. He repositions it, waves again, and his jowly face breaks out in relief as a large shadow looms by the door. Ellaline sees it first – a trembling, glistening dark tube covered in bristling hair follicles. It pushes blindly through the door, skittering this way and that until it reaches Ellaline and taps her feet. Ellaline's eyes widen, then close as she passes out in a dead faint. Crossley stops chanting, and the room falls silent as a pair of slavering fangs follow behind the leg.

The hairs on my neck stand to attention, and a familiar dread hangs like a pall. I've heard this monster many times, but the sheer size of Crossley's giant arachnid sets my pulse racing, thumping through my neck like a throbbing generator.

Clara gasps, Marlene too. Neither one as bold as they imagined before encountering Crossley's beast. Ka struggles from the captain's grasp, stepping forward towards the spider. She wrenches a candleholder from the floor and holds it aloft, waving it towards the creature. Crossley laughs maniacally. "Do something with her," he tells the captain, as the spider drools only yards away.

Ka lunges again, pushing forward and nearly sending Crossley flying in her attempt to get to the spider.

"I said, sort her out. This beast is my means to sacrifice," he snarls. "It must remain intact."

Butt steps up and strides towards Ka. She swings the candle towards him and knocks him out of the way before flinging herself at the spider, hitting it in the mouth with a hefty clunk. The spider hisses and rears on its legs, spitting blood and a large chunk of damaged tooth. It screams aloud, long black legs flailing ahead. Then it stops, quietly composing itself, jaws open and sticky with saliva. It slowly advances, recalibrated and ready. Ka spins around looking for help, but they have trussed me up like a turkey, and Ella-line is out cold. Ka is alone. She waits until the spider is almost upon her, the candle brandished in front. Confident enough in his beast to let it prey alone, Crossley allows it free rein. And just as the spider lowers its head, gaping mouth open and preparing to bite, Ka reaches behind, pulling at Captain Butt, who is lounging arrogantly against the wall. Butt is unprepared and quickly dragged forward by the more resourceful Ka. The spider's maw opens, Butt's head disappears from sight and with one terrible scream, he is gone, head yanked from his neck by the predator before him. His body drops to the floor, and Marlene screams.

"Shut up," yells Crossley, whipping a roughly hewn wand from his robe pocket. He jabs it in the air and makes a quick incantation before thrusting it into the captain's body, which crumbles into dust.

"I want to leave," screams Marlene, but the words barely leave her mouth before another dark shape looms against the door. I blink, hardly believing my eyes as a sightless goat, rotting skin hanging from a skeletal frame, blunders into the room. It darts towards the spider, now sated and slow, butting it twice as it panics to escape its unexpected resurrection.

Crossley strokes his chin, torn between pride and annoyance. He takes his wand again, jabbing it repeatedly while muttering incantations. All the while, Marlene screams, Clara beside her, stroking her hair with visibly trembling fingers. Amid the chaos, Ka Arnold-Forster has crouched beside me and is busy loosening my bonds.

After muttering several expletives, Crossley finds the right ritualistic words while waving his wand at the goat. It stops dead in its tracks and almost comically falls over before crumbling into a pile of bones. The spider is next, and Crossley shows off his skills, reluctant to kill his favoured creation. Instead, he splits it into thousands of smaller spiders that disperse through the cracks in the floorboards. But Crossley's evil magic has only just begun. Small decaying animals arrive one after the other, a crow here, a weasel there. I watch Ka tiptoeing towards the window, following her trajectory of vision. I see her stand stock still, eyes widening, then witness her hand claw at her chest before she drops to the floor. She lies without moving, no rise or fall to her chest. She has witnessed something so horrifying it has stopped her heart. And moments later, I see it too.

Chapter Forty

DARK SATANIC FORCES

IT LOOKS like a goat standing upright in the moonlight, but the half-formed, dark-skinned, red-eyed creature bristles with undisguised confusion. It doesn't move but stands writhing, pinned to the earth, its cloven hooves tight to the ground. Marlene is now hysterical, and Clara violently shakes her, trying to make her shut up. But Marlene has damaged Crossley's concentration. He strides towards her and knocks her to the ground with one hammer blow to her jaw. Clara steps back, hugs into the wall and makes herself small, while Crossley follows my eye line to the window and stares triumphantly at his creation.

"Magnificent," he declares. Philip pales, and Vincent looks as if he might bolt from the room. Crossley sneers. "Call yourself men," he says. It's just as well reinforcements are on the way."

And I know he is right. I can feel them coming, pods of evil acolytes in close proximity. They will arrive any moment. Clenching my fists around the untied ropes Crossley hasn't spotted, I wait for the worst.

Crossley watches his land-tied creation through the window, scratching his head and muttering under his breath.

"What's wrong with it?" braves Philip, his voice trembling.

"I don't know. Nobody has ever performed this feat. But the creature should be strong and powerful, not insubstantial. The girl is here. Perhaps that's the problem. She's still alive, and I must offer her to the great beast. You two, take her." Crossley gestures to Philip and Vincent, who advance towards me.

"Oh no, you don't," says a familiar voice as Cora Pennington strides through the door.

"Who do you think you are?" asks Crossley, half amused.

Peter Tremayne and Roxanne Templeton are moments behind. "It just gets better," says Crossley.

Cora reaches into her pocket and brandishes a handgun. "Step back," she says coldly.

"Don't be ridiculous." Crossley looks irritated now.

"Then sit down and shut up."

"You have no idea what you are dealing with." Crossley's eyes narrow in concentration.

"Stop him," I say. "He's going astral."

Cora slaps Crossley in the face, interrupting his focus.

"You'll regret that when the others arrive."

"Who?"

"Calicum Aureum. Every man of them. The whole damned lot. They'll be here any moment now, and I will be unstoppable."

Roxy Templeton pushes through. "Is that thing yours?" she asks, wrinkling her nose in disgust at the creature outside.

"My masterpiece," breathes Crossley.

"I'd be more impressed if it weren't welded to the earth," says Roxy.

"Something went wrong," Vincent offers. He has removed his hands from my arm and moved away, seemingly undecided over which side to take.

"Yes. The girl must die," muses Crossley. "That's all it needs. The dead child of a godly man."

"You fool," spits Cora as Peter kneels beside me.

"Are you alright," he whispers.

"Not for long," says Crossley. "Get out of my way." He pushes Peter aside and yanks me off the chair, holding me against his portly body. I tremble with fear and disgust.

"Try shooting me now," says Crossley.

"I called you a fool for a reason," says Cora. "Connie bears no genetic relationship to Michael Farrow."

My blood runs cold. "What do you mean?" I ask.

"I'm sorry you must find out this way," says Cora, her face softening momentarily. "But Aurora was with child before she married Michael."

"You're lying," says Crossley, his arm sliding from my waist to my neck. He pushes harder, and I feel my throat constricting. But I almost welcome the physical pain; such is my despair at the words I fear to hear. It is too late. They arrive.

"Connie is your daughter," says Cora. She was born because you forced yourself on her mother, who later fell in love with a good man. Your magic has failed because you are missing your most desired ingredient. There is no child of a godly man. There never was."

Crossley howls, a deep, despairing yowl of rage. "It isn't true. I don't believe you."

"Please say you're wrong," I beg.

Cora shakes her head dumbly. Peter approaches as Crossley pulls me back. "It's no use," says Peter. "She's no good to you."

"You knew," I cry, devastated all over again at his betrayal.

"No," says Peter. "Not until tonight. Until we saw that thing outside, God help us, Connie. Its eyes are as red as the flare that brought us here."

"And it will walk this earth," yells Crossley. "I don't care what I have to do. And if I must sacrifice my own child, then so be it. I have another to take her place."

Cora points the gun. "I'll kill you first," she says.

"Too late," says Crossley as a hazy apparition forms in the room. I see it before Cora and Roxy. Peter doesn't spot it at all, but he has never been able to detect astral forms. One of Crossley's acolytes appears, soon joined by another.

"They're coming," hisses Cora. "We're hopelessly outnumbered."

Roxy Templeton raises her hand above her head, clicks her finger and generates a pulsing purple light. She nods to Peter, who drags me away from an unsuspecting Crossley.

He grabs his wand, watching his acolytes appear, waiting for them to overpower us.

Roxy shoves me back into the chair, and I watch as the purple light settles over me.

"I'm not strong," she whispers. "I need help. Get Stella. I'll protect your body for as long as I can. But for God's sake, go now."

Fear floods through me but I know what I must do, and ignoring Crossley, I will myself into the black, concentrating like never before, wishing and hoping for an exit point in the Shining Path headquarters. But like all my recent plans,

it fails. And I find myself standing outside directly in front
of Crossley's satanic beast.

Chapter Forty-One

SEARCH FOR HELP

AT CLOSE SIGHT, the hairy hide covering a gelatinous, unformed body strikes repulsion and curiosity into my heart. I feel like a witness to a dreadful accident who tries and fails to look away. The creature strains against its land-bound rear hooves, the unfettered front feet pawing at the air. It senses I am close though it cannot see me, and its eyes blaze like rubies in candlelight. Yet I sense they don't function properly. It is a creature born before its time.

But I have work to do and cannot afford to linger on earth. I must find my way into the astral realm if I am to save my loved ones and return safely to my body. I remember what to do when travelling is hard, and I rapidly head towards Eagle's Nest, where I dart into Ka's potting shed. The darkness swallows me as I hoped it would, and I find myself floating upwards onto the astral plane. But the dreamscape is not my friend. Swirling vortexes of purple robes replace the sparkling stars, each one a member of Calicum Aureum rushing towards Crossley. The once peaceful realm is alive with spiders and bats.

I push on, hoping I will not stand out in this hostile plane, but it is futile. The acolytes press relentlessly onward while the spiders turn tail. I stream forth in the outer black, single-mindedly aiming for London, feeling spiders nipping at my feet and a trail of bats in my tail stream. I must concentrate like never before. The closer I get to Queens-borough Terrace, the safer I will be.

I empty my mind and think of nothing but Stella McGregor, prising open old memories of successful psychic defence and imagining metal doors slamming shut over my enemies. Moments later, I find myself at the top of the road with the Shining Path headquarters only fifty yards away. But I am not alone. Thousands of furry bodies ripple before me, and the sky is black with beating wings. Worse still, two purple-robed adepts stand between me and my goal. They spot me and push forward.

They are strong, but I am desperate. I wait until they are almost upon me, then spring forward, swooping to one side before darting up the road. I have gained fifty yards, but they are catching me. I feel a chill astral hand grab my shoulder. It pulls me up sharply. I fall to the ground, trembling, a jellied heap of fear. But somewhere in my head, I hear Roxy's voice. "Hurry. I can't hold them for much longer."

I roll over, squeezing past the broader of the two figures. He rushes to catch me, and fear spikes through my core, great snaky tendrils of horror, momentarily slowing me down. I slam a guillotine over the quivering spikes, freeing them from my mind. The men might be physically stronger, but my psychic defence skills are more honed and effective than I deserve. I am almost at the door when the two bear down on me again, their astral bodies pinning me to the wall as I flail against their grip. My heart is too far away to feel the thud of nerves, but fear holds me still in their grasp. I am preparing for the end when the door bursts open, and half a dozen members of the Shining Path jostle into the fight. And when the bats turn tail, I know Stella has triumphed again.

Chapter Forty-Two

RESCUE MISSION

I BARELY HAVE time to splutter a garbled explanation before Stella commands our immediate return to Carn Cottage. She has long feared this moment, and her intense dislike of the psychic operations division has spurred her onwards, watching, training, and recruiting on the rare occasions she finds an astral talent. Within five minutes of my arrival, all the Shining Path headquarter incumbents have convened, licking their wounds in some cases.

"Stand down, Marjorie," says Stella, noting a large, bloody gouge on the young woman's cheek.

"Absolutely not. You said all hands to the deck."

Stella opens her mouth to argue but realises there is no time.

"We must go," I yell. "They can't hold on."

Stella strides towards a grandfather clock and yanks it open, sending a hinge pinging to the floor. Her hand disappears into a starry black mass, and I hear the echo of a klaxon.

"Wait," says Stella.

"No. I'm going back even if I'm alone."

Stella nods to two of her men, who lunge at me and grab both my arms. I stare at Stella, stomach sinking, appalled at the betrayal.

"Don't look at me like that. I need you to wait. Only for a moment or two, but it could be the difference between life and death."

And a minute later, when Oliver Fox and Harold Grady apparate moments before another twenty psychic defenders, I know she is right.

"Go," commands Stella, gripping my hand in hers. This time, we materialise outside Carn Cottage, watching with horror as dozens of Calicum Aureum-robed figures surround the building, lingering in the night air side by side to guard Crossley with military precision. Flanked by Grady and Fox, Stella rushes towards a lone robed figure, grounded and facing the door. I cower by an outhouse, mostly hidden from sight.

"Turn around," Stella commands.

The figure stops, takes a breath, and punches the air. "Attack," he shouts.

"Coward," snarls Stella, darting to one side to steal a look at his cloaked face. "It is you," she says.

Grady is already in the air, Fox close by his side as they dodge astral missiles raining from above. Stella flinches as debris falls around her, but she is determined to expose the hooded man. Releasing a shower of energy, Stella knocks the cloak from his head to reveal Brigadier Hetherington-Shipley, who leers triumphantly towards her.

"It's no surprise," says Stella. "We knew something was off."

"But there are more of us than you." The brigadier

stands, eyes glinting in the moonlight. The two behave as if they were unaware of the growing battle around them.

"Get inside," snaps Stella, remembering why she is there.

Fox and Grady hurl themselves towards the brigadier, clearing the way for my entry. The last thing I see as I pass through the door is a dozen robed acolytes hurtling towards Stella.

Chapter Forty-Three

THE FINAL CONFRONTATION

I ARRIVE inside the cottage to the terrifying sight of Felix Crossley standing before my body, wielding a knife. Roxy Templeton is lying on the floor, her face a bloody mess. A single tooth sits in a pool of bloody saliva an inch from her face. She blinks as she sees me, urging my spirit away with her eyes. But I am too close to my body, and it draws me towards it, inch by painful inch. I pass Peter, now bound to a chair by two heavily-built henchmen, both stoutly paunched and bald headed, as if their appearance is a homage to Crossley. Cora is hog-tied and helpless before me. She looks up and pleads with her eyes. But fate has other ideas and I move towards my destiny.

Crossley smiles as my soul joins my body. "It's about time," he snarls. "I thought I might have to start without you."

I say nothing but stare at the man who gave me life, wishing I could drain his genes from my body.

Crossley presses his face towards me, cocking his head to one side. "You look just like your mother," he says.

"You killed her," I snarl, reacting despite my best intentions.

Crossley brandishes the knife, waving it near my face. "Aurora deserved to die. She was my scarlet woman, and she left me. I blew her up with gelignite, and very satisfying it was too. I wish I had destroyed you too, not just your leg."

"I hate you," I spit, tears of rage rolling down my face as Crossley brags about his attack on my mother. "And what kind of father gloats about maiming his child?"

"Killing you will make things easier for both of us," says Crossley. "I have no feelings for you, and your dislike of me is evident." Crossley's gaping smile reminds me of a hungry crocodile, but my heart is so bruised at the mention of my mother that my fear has evaporated.

"Do your worst," I challenge.

"You'll regret those fine words when I feed you to my beast," he says.

My heart quickens. So that is his plan. I am defenceless in this cottage and can only hope the Shining Path members are faring better outside. As if on cue, the door opens, and Brigadier Hetherington-Shipley appears.

"Get outside," says Crossley. "You must protect the beast at all costs."

"It's going well. We are ahead," says the brigadier. He turns to look at Cora, and I notice an extra emblem on the back of his robe, with four arms bending sharply at right angles. I recognise it as a swastika, a symbol of the Nazi party in Germany. They have infiltrated our forces to the highest level, not only our army but our psychic defence division. No wonder official psychic operations had slowed to a halt. Harold Grady must have suspected, creating his ultra-secret cells, of which Peter and Mary were one. But it is no comfort now as I contemplate the carnage outside.

"Good. Then it is time," says Crossley. Escort me to the beast." Crossley nods to his burly henchmen, who seize my arms and drag me towards the door. I try to regain my feet, but they don't let me. Not allowing me to walk is intentional. They are flaunting their power.

"Connie," calls Cora, her face anguished.

"Get away if you can," I say, hoping my friends will not die tonight.

"Think only good thoughts," whispers a voice as they drag me through the door. I turn my head to see Roxy Templeton, flexing her fingers, eyes hazy with pain. She is alive, which is something, and I wonder what she means. But not for long.

The outside door opens to the dreadful sight of fallen comrades lying crumpled on the ground. Both sides have taken a pounding, and as many purple robes lie twitching on the ground as my friends in the Shining Path. A battle-weary Stella McGregor sits propped up against an ancient tree ringed by a group of purple-cloaked guards. Harold Grady lies face down in the grass. I cry out as I see him and drop to my knees. Rough hands pull me up again, but not before Harold mouths, "Oliver escaped."

I wish I could feel relieved, but destiny pulls me towards evil, and I am dragged bodily towards the great beast, still swaying in abject misery in front of the cottage. Rage surges through it as we approach, and the creature twists, tail thrashing, straining at its fettered hooves. Its maw heaves open, spittle flying through the air. And I should be terrified, but I recognise suffering. No matter how inhuman, nothing deserves the existential pain suffered by this great beast.

Crossley kneels before it. "I offer you a sacrifice," he says. "My child is yours. Take her."

The men push me roughly forward, and I fall at the

creature's feet, feeling the warmth of its breath as it lowers its head. Two slanted nostrils sniff ominously, and its prickly-haired beard tickles my face. I sense that it cannot see me, and it does nothing to harm me. Perhaps I am not to its taste.

Crossley stands with hands on hips. I sneak a look at his perplexed features, inching my body away from the demonic beast.

"It can't smell her," he declares. "The beast needs blood."

He nods towards his henchmen, who grasp my wrists and yank me to my feet. Crossley whips out a knife and slashes my arm, holding it over a bowl. He stops when the sticky red liquid covers the bottom. I am shaking, shocked at the pain and sudden blood loss. But Crossley is busy chanting an incantation. He finishes it with a flourish and several words which turn the brigadier's face pale.

"You shouldn't have done that," he says.

"Raising more of the dead will fix this mess," Crossley replies, pointing to the rooted cloven hooves. Felix Crossley strides towards the creature, pushing me to my previous spot on the ground. Then, he takes the bowl and offers it to the beast. The creature blindly flails, ignoring the offering. Crossley shakes his head in desperation, then pushes his hand into the bowl and smears the creature's flank with my blood. The beast screeches into the night air as if touched by acid, piteously howling, and trying to move away from its burning flesh. Crossley jumps backwards, uncertain. I stand, suddenly fuelled by an inner confidence, and limp towards Crossley, sensing a diminished power.

Wings beat against the silent night, and I look up expecting bats. Instead, I see owls swooping down and plucking at the clothes of the fallen. Injured colleagues start moving again. And I notice the owls look different, insubstantial pale imitations of their former selves. There are missing wings, damaged beaks, and feather loss. These birds have returned from the dead. Crossley's plan has worked. Yet the owls are helping, urging movement from the fallen. I see a fox in the moonlight, its flank torn and jagged. Yet it steals towards Stella, nudging her with its nose. She rises and strikes her guards with one fell swoop, and they crumple before her as if she is wielding a scythe.

Crossley watches in bemusement as long-dead woodland creatures swarm towards the beast. His eyes narrow in confusion at the sight of hornless deer, sightless sheep, and animals who should be resting in peace. He has summoned the meek and mild, missing the mark completely. And all the while, his creature strains at its earthly bonds.

The cottage door slams open. Cora and Peter push through, holding an injured Roxy Templeton, who must have recovered sufficiently to free them. They watch in wonder as the animals surround the beast. It calms, sensing a benign presence. But I am distracted by a shimmering light ahead. I see a familiar form, and my heart swells. I look around, waiting for the others to react. But they cannot see what I can. I walk towards the light, a lone living figure among the dead, and find myself standing before the ghostly image of Vera Ponsonby. Crossley has miscalculated. In attempting to kill the opposite of a godly man's child, he has raised good in place of evil. And Vera Ponsonby is the very best, kind, loyal and self-sacrificing. I reach to touch her, but my hand passes through. I chew my lip and start to cry.

"Connie. You are better than that," she says.

"But I miss you."

"We will meet again one day."

"Soon?"

"No. Your place is with the living."

"Crossley is my father."

"I know. But you must forgive him."

"I hate him. He killed my mother. And though I can't remember him, I will always love the man who brought me up."

"As you should. His name is Michael Farrow. He is a good man."

"I want to kill Crossley."

"No. Forgiveness triumphs evil."

"I cannot forgive him. I will not."

"Connie, you must."

Vera's ghostly shape begins to fade. I reach out again, trying in vain to stop her. And in the last few moments, before she disappears, Vera speaks again. "Forgive him," she says.

Tears stream down my face as I limp back into the fray. Crossley stands incandescent with rage before his injured creature. "Kill her," he demands. His henchmen exchange glances.

"Do it."

They approach me and manhandle me towards Crossley until I am kneeling at his feet. He takes the knife, looms over me, and raises it high above his head, ready to plunge. I reach out my arms and hug his hips, nestling my face against his abdomen. "Father, I forgive you," I say.

Crossley jumps back as the knife falls from his hand. "How dare you offer forgiveness," he says. "Who do you think you are?" But even as he speaks, the creature stops writhing, and a peaceful expression settles over its face as it falls to the earth and crumbles to dust. The long-dead animals skitter away, and as dawn breaks through the night sky, the fallen souls of either side vanish from sight. Philip and Victor unpin their robes and walk away as if nothing has happened while Crossley's henchmen stare in disgust before apparating back to their bodies. Crossley stands before me, and I know something has changed. His eyes close in concentration.

"Let him go," says Cora, holding my hand.

But I see what she doesn't. Crossley looks thin, insubstantial and a decade older. "He can't," I say. "Something has changed."

"Don't be ridiculous." Crossley tries again, straining to reach the astral plane, but it is no use.

"He's lost his powers," says Roxy.

"How?" Peter looks puzzled.

"His entire plan backfired. His incantation depended on hatred, but Vera showed him the power of love. I share Crossley's blood, but I am different in every way, and my forgiveness destroyed something deep in his rotten soul, as Vera knew it would. Now Crossley is just a man."

Crossley's jaw slackens as the truth of my words hits home. His face pales as he runs his hands up and down his body. His eyes flutter closed in one last attempt to prove me wrong. But he can't move. His powers are lost. Crossley hurls his staff across the room and stalks back to his holiday rental.

Ellaline Vaughan emerges from the cottage. "Ka is dead," she says, as if the rest of the night's events had never happened.

"Clean up," says Cora. "Then call the doctor and tell him she had a heart attack. It's probably wise not to mention anything else."

Epilogue

MY RETURN to Pebble Cottage was bittersweet. Moggins and Teddy greeted me along with Elys, now of whale-like proportions. But despite the relief of knowing Crossley was forever powerless, I could not settle. I missed Vera and longed for the simplicity of our old life. Peter looked after me, taking me out socially once or twice, during which time Kit Maltravers confessed his undying love. But I had changed too much for his advances to tempt me. Then, one day, everything changed. I had been upstairs looking through Vera's possessions and pondering the significance of the Mount Athos postcard in her trunk when Elys answered the door, shouting for me to come down. I initially ignored her, too consumed with my introspections to care about visitors. But after the fourth irritated yell, I went downstairs and straight into the path of Jim Douglas. Jim stepped forward and placed an arm around my waist, lowering his head towards me.

"I remember," he said.

That was six months ago, and the sun beats down on us through cobalt skies as we round the coast towards Xenophontos Monastery on the Athos peninsula. When Jim asked me where I would like to go on honeymoon, I couldn't answer. I had barely left Cornwall before, much less the British shores. With the world my oyster, I was paralysed with indecision. But after much thought, I decided on Greece. Vera's postcard had always looked so appealing. Jim agreed, and we flew out a few days ago, hiring a boat and a captain to take us to the peninsula.

Jim squeezes my hand as I contemplate the shore, knowing disembarkation will be a trial. Like Crossley, I too, have lost my powers. A quid pro quo, I suppose. I will never feel the thrill of running along the sand or standing on top of the Cornish cliffs under the light of the silvery moon. I am stuck with my injuries, yet more well-travelled than ever before. My life will be different but better. And I will never be defined by Crossley's attack on me and my family.

The boat drifts to the shore, and I gaze in awe at the stone walls of the monastery before me. It is a vast building hundreds of years old. I wonder how many souls have lived within its walls. The boat shudders to a halt, and the captain leaps ashore, mooring his vessel before handing me a veil. I nervously finger the ruby half-moon brooch I found in Vera's trunk. It is always with me now – my talisman.

I lean on Jim as we walk towards the building, my head covered in respect to the monks. Women are not allowed in the monastery, and I don't know how Jim pulled the strings that have allowed me unfettered access into an exclusively male domain. The abbot, who speaks a few words of broken English, greets us before introducing us to our guide. I am relieved to be inside and away from the relentless

Mediterranean heat. The white walls are cool, and I can walk a little better, although we pause often on our tour. I sit for a while beneath the mosaic of St Demetrius before lighting a candle and whispering a prayer for Vera. Then I say another for my loyal friends and family at home, Cora, Peter, dear Elys, now a mother of two and my new husband, Jim. Life is good.

The tour is almost at an end when our guide asks if we want to see the library. My mind flashes back to my little book cave and the good times I enjoyed in the Porth Tregoryan Hotel library when Peter would pass me the best of the week's new books. I can't resist, and we enter to the smell of ancient paper. It is like balm to my soul. We reluctantly leave after half an hour of book bliss. Though they are almost all written in Greek, handling the precious tomes as we sit by the window overlooking china blue seas, makes me glad to be alive. But time is pressing, and our boat will soon leave.

The guide warns us that we will pass the cell of an elderly English monk who took a vow of silence decades before, asking us not to speak as we go by. We tiptoe past, and I can't help glancing at the open door. The old monk sits reading at a desk, his brow furrowed in concentration. He looks up at me and stares, mouth agape, and I follow the line of his gaze to the brooch on my chest, with which he appears transfixed. The guide whispers "Leave brother Michael in peace," but I limp into the room, casting an eye to the only item on the whitewashed cell wall, an old, faded photograph of a family of three, standing close together on a garden lawn. This picture is familiar. I have seen it before hanging on the nursery wall at Netherwood.

The monk stands, his face ashen, cloudy blue eyes filling

with tears. He reaches an unsteady arm towards me, and his mouth moves noiselessly before uttering his first word in over two decades.

"My darling girl," he says.

And I embrace the only father I have ever loved.

Also by Jacqueline Beard

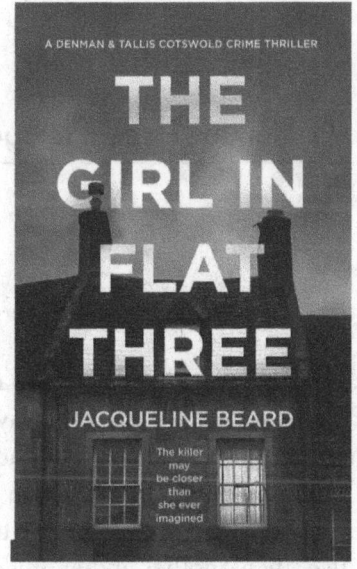

vinci-books.com/flat-three

A missing girl, an unsolved murder, and a neighbor with something to hide.

Unemployed and alone, Sass Denman's life takes an unsettling turn when a chance conversation leads her to Sean Tallis, an unconventional private investigator with a penchant for lizards. As they delve into a seemingly routine case, they uncover a missing girl with ties to a cold case from a decade ago. Could the notorious Skin Thief be back?

Turn the page for a free preview…

The Girl in Flat Three: Prologue

PALE FACE, bulging eyes, head lolling backwards. How had
it come to this? I'd let myself get carried away in a moment
of weakness, made a split decision, a poor choice – years of
restraint down the drain. A careless reaction I should have
been able to rise above. But the fear, the certainty that one
would become two, then another and another, led to a self-
fulfilling prophecy. Once an addict, always an addict, no
matter how much time has passed.

Oh, but it was magnificent. There was no better feeling,
no more satisfying way to calm the urge. How could I have
forgotten? Why did I resist when it was so much easier to
give in? Risky, but worthwhile. And all the little tricks I had
used to keep my desires at bay were no longer enough. Part
of the experience wouldn't do. I wanted all of it.

She came back. Silly girl. Left and then returned with a
feeble excuse, I didn't believe. Too friendly by half that one.
Annoyingly accommodating, endlessly helpful. Wasn't she
ever told to mind her own bloody business? Perhaps she was
and ignored the advice. The girl wasn't too bright, that's for

sure, or she'd have realised who she was dealing with. No, not an intellectual by any means, but someone with a fierce sense of right and wrong. And something else — street smarts. Whatever it was, it gave her a window into something that no one else saw. An inherent feeling that things were not as they seemed. Somehow, she suspected, and just when I thought she'd left forever, she returned.

I'd gone to the shops and might have been out longer if I'd remembered my card. I had opened and closed a bag and fumbled in my pockets, a hot flush of embarrassment mottling my neck. Leaving the basket on the counter, I had asked the shopkeeper to put it by — I'd be back in a moment. He had glowered, eyes heavenward, while the woman behind tutted loudly, and I'd left feeling stupid, just as I had back in the day. In those formative years when personalities were shaped, and consciences moulded. Detentions, slaps, rules, pain. *Shut up. Stop thinking about it.*

Thank God for that little slip. Five more minutes, and it would have been too late. The girl had only suspected something was wrong, but if I'd taken any longer, she'd have known for sure. So close to catastrophe. But as it was, I'd returned and found her interfering in my life, checking her suspicions but not quite finding the evidence she sought. A good thing — she wouldn't have stomached it. I found her kneeling, ready to check, about to unwrap, unbind, and reveal the truth she thought she wanted to know. She heard me arrive and cast an anxious glance my way but had no solid reason to fear me. So, I smiled with a forced friendliness light-years away from my true feelings.

She tried to stand, and I could have, should have, let her leave. Taken the chance that she didn't recognise what I was. But old habits die hard. I made small talk about the weather, spotted a cord on the counter, and reached for it, snapping the corner of my nail down to the quick. Searing pain made me wince, but I didn't care. The game was afoot. An equal match – I wasn't strong, but with the benefit of foresight, I was quicker.

Twisting the cord around her neck while she faced away, I missed the pleasure of seeing her bulging eyes as I dodged, turned, and manoeuvred past her thrashing limbs. She writhed and moaned, and I forced her to the floor, face down, with my foot on her back, riding her like a horse as I tugged on the reins, the cord biting deeply into her tender neck. A rattle, a gurgle, and it was over. I relaxed my stranglehold, and she flopped to the floor with a gasp like a dying fish. I stood, exhausted, my hands ridged with rope burns, fingers shaking. Now another problem. Where to put her?

I kicked her over with a shaking foot. Bloody froth speckled her lips, and bloodshot eyes stared from her head. She'd wet herself, and the stench of ammonia from the urine-covered floor made my eyes water. Not tears. Oh no. She had it coming. Too nosy for her own good. A sudden urge gripped me with fearsome force. And once I'd acknowledged it, I couldn't contain myself. My hands clenched as I tried to fight it. Better not here, if at all. But it was too late. I walked to the drawer as if in a dream. Seizing a knife and steel, I swiped it, metal grinding against metal, to a sharp, lethal edge. Then, kneeling in front of the dead girl, I drew the blade lovingly from knee to ankle, expertly paring a thin layer of skin.

Blood prickled the surface but did not bleed out as I'd kept a layer intact. An excitement rose inside me, a longing, a need for more, and I sliced more urgently, slapping the peeled flesh onto the floor, frenzied, careless now – blood splattering the tiles, the knife, my thighs. I'd need to clean the mess away, and soon. But not right now. It could wait.

Fear battled triumph with heart-stopping shivers of uncertainty. Or was it pleasure? I wasn't sure anymore. But I knew how to put it right – at least in the short term. It had been a long time, but if memory served, there was a bottle of wine at the back of the kitchen cupboard. I uncorked it and raised a glass to the only living witness of my crime.

The Girl in Flat Three: Chapter One

THE SICKLY SMELL was back again – a pungent aroma drifting around my kitchen like a malodorous wraith, its origin leaving me baffled. I had torn the place apart, emptying cupboards and drawers, trying to find the source of the problem. It didn't take long to look. Most of my possessions lay unpacked in supermarket boxes in what the letting agent laughingly referred to as the second bedroom. Boxroom, more like. I could probably wedge a bed in there if my life depended on it, but not much else. And why would I bother? I was unlikely to have steady streams of visitors to my flat, being new in town and unemployed. Thankfully, the letting agent had already taken up references before the unfortunate incident a fortnight previously that saw me marched out of Froggatt and Co by the Managing Director's PA. I can still feel the ghost of her hand on my shoulder and remember the triumphant sneer on her face as I shook it away. She didn't believe my story. Nobody did. But that son of a bitch in the sales department tried to touch me up, and nobody gets to put their hands on me unless I want them to. Certainly not a creep like Curtis Newton.

I flexed my hand, balling it into a fist as I had when I punched him in the nose, remembering the satisfying crack as it snapped. I hadn't meant for it to happen, but my well-honed military instincts had kicked in automatically. Forgetting where I was, I had reacted as if I was still a Royal Air Force policewoman, keeping the base safe. Act quickly, think clearly, and don't let them get to you – my mantra then and now. Unfortunately, the acting bit was always a few steps ahead of the thinking. And I was quick to anger. Had I calmed down and used my brain, I might still have a job and not be fretting about how to make the rent this month. But my fist was out and in Curtis Newton's face long before I'd considered the benefits of going to the HR department and reporting him for the misogynistic pig he was. So, Curtis bloody Newton got away with it while I got the sack.

I ruminated about the unfairness, which was still raw, as I scrabbled on my hands and knees in front of kitchen cupboards which had seen better days. But no matter how hard I tried, the smell was as elusive as my prospects of getting an employment reference suitable to secure another job. Ten minutes of fruitless searching passed, and I gave up. I got to my feet and opened the window, setting it on the widest latch. The window frames were ancient, like the building. My apartment wasn't awful by any means, but previous upgrades had relied on painting over or repairing existing structures rather than replacing them with new ones. So, my kitchen resembled something from the 1950s with a Belfast sink and blue painted units. It only needed a gingham tablecloth and an old-fashioned transistor radio for the full effect. But I knew the flat was a fortunate find, becoming re-available suddenly when the scheduled new occupant pulled out. The rent was cheaper than most. I hadn't much money for a holding deposit, and things could have been far worse.

I was lucky to find something close to the centre of Truscombe without it being on the High Street. A light sleeper at the best of times, my idea of hell was settling down after the pubs closed with all the drunken banter that followed. So, the flat suited me well, apart from the smell which still turned my stomach. I couldn't take it any longer and decided to shop for an air freshener.

Grabbing my jacket and bag, I opened the door to a compact landing opposite Flat Number Four, apparently occupied by a middle-aged couple I hadn't yet met. And judging by their raised voices the previous night, making their acquaintance wasn't a priority. But now was not the time to consider meeting the neighbours. It was lunchtime, and all was peaceful. The occupants were out, probably working if that's what they did to generate an income.

I clattered down the stairs, wondering when the management company would finish much-needed work on the stairwell. Bereft of a carpet, which must have been there at one time as a couple of clunky brackets were still in place, the rail also needed substantial sprucing up. I glanced at the shabby hallway, remembering the splinter I'd picked up from the banister the previous day, and rubbed the inflamed lump on my thumb. I reached the bottom just as the door of Flat One opened, and an affable-looking man I had first seen yesterday appeared.

"Hello," he beamed. "How are you getting on?"

"Well," I said. "The unpacking is coming along nicely." It wasn't true. I'd hardly started and had spent my time pointlessly searching for an elusive, noxious smell. But people don't want the truth when they ask how you are. Life is all about niceties, and a banal response keeps everyone happy. So, I smiled and continued my fictional account of how well I was settling in.

"Good for you," he said, and I was about to sail past when I heard a mewl and felt soft fur around my bare legs as a black cat weaved between them. I leaned down to tickle its ears.

"Sinbad," said the man.

"I'm sorry?"

"The cat, he's called Sinbad. And I'm Frank." He extended his hand, uncertainly smiling as if he wasn't sure whether I would return the handshake. "Saskia Denman," I said, grasping it firmly. He'd made an effort, and so would I. Frank turned around and picked up a small pot plant, which he balanced on an insubstantial plastic tray containing several others. And when he stooped to pick it up with both hands, it bowed and wobbled.

"Can I help?" I asked, imagining the mess if half a dozen pots came crashing onto the tiled hallway.

"I'll manage," he said, negotiating his way past the cat. I moved towards the front door to hold it open for him, and as I glanced at the entrance to his flat, I saw a small grey-haired woman sitting in a wheelchair at the end of the passageway.

"Thank you," he said as he passed through the open door. I followed him out, and he placed the tray beside a newly dug flower bed at the front of the house. The rear garden, which I could see from my bedroom, was large and a significant draw in choosing the property. But the front garden was only a few feet deep, with two lawned areas on either side of a path leading to the road.

"It's good of you to bother," I said, appreciating his efforts at keeping the property tidy for everyone. After ten years in the military, mess and muddles bothered me, even though my flat currently looked like a bomb had gone off inside it. But I knew it wouldn't be like that for long. I just needed time.

"We all muck in," said Frank, withdrawing a trowel from his jacket pocket. He glanced at the front window of his flat, smiled, and nodded.

"That's my mother," he said, and I followed his gaze, seeing that the grey-haired woman had wheeled herself into a position where she could watch him. I followed suit, waved, and smiled, but she did not respond.

"She can't walk or talk," said Frank sadly. "Age is a terrible thing."

His ironic remark belied the fact that Frank was no spring chicken himself. But on closer inspection, he was more likely in his sixties than seventies, as I had initially thought. Like me, Frank was slim, but his hair was sparse, and a comb-over effect did him no favours. Still, aside from a brief hello to one of the young men in Flat Two, I hadn't exchanged so much as a word with the other residents, and finding a friendly face, however old, was a good start. I wasn't a people person, but anyone, no matter how insular, needs some form of human contact.

"I'll be off then," I said, making towards the path. Frank grunted something I couldn't hear, and I left him to it.

———

I RETURNED to Bosworth House with a pair of cheap air fresheners from Truscombe's newest pound shop and placed them strategically in the kitchen, where they battled with the pre-existing smell. The open window had little effect, and I searched through the food cupboard I'd stocked yesterday for something to force down, despite my queasiness. I settled on a tin of Bombay potatoes and heated them in a saucepan with a wobbly handle before tipping the cooked mess into a bowl. Sitting on a saggy couch in the living room overlooking Mortimer Road, I watched the passers-by as I finished my evening meal. The Bombay potatoes tasted good with the additional benefit of overpowering the kitchen smell. One lit candle later, I felt relaxed and ready to re-organise my life.

Emptying one box, then another, I eventually found the dregs of my military career beneath an old, dog-eared rug. I shoved my discharge paperwork into a drawer and hung a framed picture of my passing out parade on the wall. I stood in front of it, looking at the fresh-faced girl I was back in the day – young, hopeful and a world away from the jaded cynic I became.

I straightened the picture, creating an even more lopsided effect, and almost returned it to the box. It was more trouble than it was worth, reminding me of happier times and a life filled with promise. Then, I felt a familiar shortness of breath and reached in my pocket for my inhaler, sucking it back for immediate relief. Damn that little blue bottle and its counterparts in my medicine cabinet. But for my barely controllable asthma, I'd still be in Cyprus, living in the Sergeants' mess at RAF Kyrenia just down the corridor from Greg Sanders. I wondered how he was doing. The last I'd heard, he was chancing a career-ending relationship with Chloe Singh, the unfaithful bastard.

I sat down, momentarily overwhelmed by an unusual bout of self-pity, and let it wash over me. I allowed it to fester for a few minutes, rehearsing everything I wish I had said to Greg but didn't, before letting it go. Then I popped a tin of gin and tonic and knocked it back in a few gulps. It did the trick and settled me long enough to vegetate in front of the television in a low-lit room for a few hours without paying much attention to the programme.

I must have fallen asleep and woke with a start in the small hours. It was July, and the weather had been warm and dry, but the flat felt freezing, making me shiver. I picked up the remote control and switched off the television, bringing silence to the room. The side table lamp cast a woefully inadequate pall of light over the middle part of the small square lounge. It was my third night in the new flat, and I should have been getting used to it, but the deafening silence cast tendrils of fear into my overactive brain. My loneliness rose to the surface in a bubble of despair. I had no nearby family, no partner, and barely any friends. I wondered what I was doing with my life. And why a building containing six flats was as quiet as a mausoleum? Idle thoughts turned to fear, and dread slithered through me as it did back in my childhood when I climbed the steep steps of my grandmother's house, waiting for the bogeyman to plunge his razor-sharp knife into my back. Summoning courage that came more naturally during the day, I rolled off the couch and crept towards my bedroom, dimly lit by the pale moonlight. I closed the curtains, turned on the closest sidelight, and slipped fully clothed under the duvet. But I had made a mistake. The door was still ajar, and patchy moonlight shadowed the view from my bed towards the living room, making monsters from furnishings and demons from doors. Sleep would be impossible if I didn't close it, so I gave myself a pep talk and got out of bed. But as I reached the door, lighting my way using the torch on my mobile phone, I stopped dead in my tracks at a sound in the distance – the faint keening of someone moaning in pain. It was coming from one of the flats.

The Girl in Flat Three: Chapter Two

I WOKE late Saturday morning looking like death warmed up. The blood-curdling sound had only lasted a few short minutes, but it had been enough to tickle my fevered imagination into a night of insomnia and worry. I had tried to stick with the sidelight but gave up in the early hours of the morning, switching on the main bedroom light and one in the hallway, which made sleep near impossible. After three hours of tossing and turning, I plugged an earbud headset into my mobile and listened to a podcast which bored me into oblivion. But at least it got me through the night.

The sun was high by the time I finished showering, and I donned a pair of leggings and trainers before taking them off again. For a fleeting moment, I considered going for a run, but I was tired, apathetic, and unprepared to set myself up for failure. Instead, I ventured into the kitchen and popped a crumpet in the toaster before slathering it with butter. The so-called furnished flat hadn't come with a dining table, so I reclined on the couch and scrolled through TikTok while I ate. Then I put my plate in the sink and leaned across the windowsill to see what was happening outside. The rising sun had spread over the lawn, across a bench and onto a small, paved terrace, casting a warm glow that made the garden look inviting. Having nothing better to do on a weekend morning, I picked up the latest Lawrence Harpham mystery and headed outside. The weather wasn't as warm as it looked, and I regretted my decision not to bring a light coat, but I was out now and too lazy to take the flight of stairs to my flat, so I made the best of it. I settled down and opened my book, where a receipt doubling as a bookmark held my place and started reading. Half an hour flew by. The garden warmed up, and the ragged early morning clouds drifted away, leaving clear blue skies. I tipped my head back, closed my eyes, glorying in the sun's warmth on my face, and was about to resume reading when I heard someone clearing their throat.

My eyes snapped open to see the young dark-haired man from Flat Two, who also carried a book. "Mind if I join you?" he asked.

"Er, no," I muttered. I did mind, and I'd been enjoying solitary tranquillity unlikely to be improved by an awkward, stilted conversation with a stranger. But it wasn't socially acceptable to say so, and I didn't. "Go ahead," I said, in what I hoped was a friendly tone.

"Dhruv Patel," he said, offering his hand. "What are you reading?"

I showed him the cover of my book, and he nodded as if he was familiar with the author. "Good one," he said. "But I prefer thrillers. You should try this."

Dhruv gestured, and I nodded approvingly, but not so much that he felt obliged to give me further details.

"You're new," he said. "I saw you arrive on Wednesday. It's about time they filled your flat."

"Was it empty for long?"

"Three or four months. Milligan and I looked around to see if it was worth swapping, but we decided not to in the end. I mean, there's nothing wrong with it," he added as if trying not to offend. "But it wouldn't have given us any more room."

"Are the flats different sizes?"

"Apparently. The ground floor flats are slightly bigger than the first floor, but I didn't know that until I saw yours. It's the first time we've been in one of the mid-level flats."

"Are the other residents friendly?" I asked.

"Sure," said Dhruv. "But we rarely go in for coffee or anything. Well, Mill and I don't. Perhaps the others do. For all I know, they are having dinner parties every night and don't invite us. It's not like we'd ever find out. Anyway, I'm talking too much. Would you rather read?"

"No," I said. Dhruv could talk for England, but I found his enthusiasm and desire for conversation both endearing and exhausting. He was the sort of guy you could chat to for hours without having to try too hard – a perfect foil for an introvert.

"Tell me about the others," I said. "Who else lives here?"

"Well," said Dhruv, leaning back and stretching out with his book balancing on his belly. He crossed one tanned ankle over another as his tailored shorts perfectly accentuated slim, athletic legs. "There are six flats, two on each level."

"So, two at the top as well? I wasn't sure. It's hard to tell how it all works from the front."

"Yes. The second-floor flats are studios. You know the type of thing – a bedroom and living room in one. It's alright if you're single, although I couldn't do it. I'd rather room share. And above that is an attic."

"Across the entire house?" My mind drew mental floor plans.

Dhruv shrugged. "Could be. I don't know. It's always locked."

"Doesn't matter. I was just curious."

"Anyhow, Frank and Veronica Lewis live at Number One."

"I know, I've met them. Well, I've met Frank. And Sinbad too."

Dhruv laughed. "Frank's nuts about that cat. I caught him hand feeding slices of beef to Sinbad in the hallway last week. The poor thing is getting fat."

"Sinbad didn't seem phased about the size of his waistline when I saw him," I said. "I waved to Veronica while helping Frank outside, but she didn't wave back."

"She's not all there," said Dhruv. "I don't mean that disrespectfully, but I don't know the latest politically correct term for dementia or whatever it is she has. Frank's a nice chap, though, and very handy. If you want a shelf putting up, he's your man."

"And you live opposite?"

"Yes. Mill and I share a flat and a bed. Sorry if that's blunt, but it saves you wondering. We've been together for four years and finally got engaged last month. He's going to make an honest man of me." A platinum band inset with a diamond sparkled on Dhruv's ring finger.

"Congratulations," I said.

"Well, thank you. It hasn't been an easy ride, what with our differing backgrounds. Perhaps I'll tell you about it over a glass of wine sometime. Now, where was I?"

Dhruv made a show of trying to remember, and I couldn't help smiling at his earnest face. Deep brown eyes sparkled beneath a floppy fringe, and his mouth turned naturally upward. Dhruv bubbled with good humour, and I couldn't help wondering why he wasn't on friendlier terms with the other occupants. I had only known him a matter of minutes and already felt inclined to ask him back for coffee. He seemed like a man I could trust in a crisis.

"Now, your immediate neighbours are the Fosters," he continued. "You must take them as you find them, and I won't say too much. But good luck trying to work them out."

"Why?"

"They're out more than they're in, and neither is particularly chatty."

"That suits me. I like it quiet."

"Quiet? Ah. As I say, you must make up your own mind."

"Actually, can I ask you something?"

"Go ahead."

"Did you hear anything last night?"

"Over Milligan's snoring? I wish."

"Seriously. I couldn't sleep, and I thought I heard a cry, well, more like moaning – someone in pain, perhaps."

"Sorry. I slept like a baby. A dozen burglars could have broken in, and I'd have been none the wiser."

"No matter."

"I'll ask Mill if you like?"

"It's okay."

"So, Brendan Marshall is in Number Five and Velda Ribeira in Six. Both are single, as far as I know. Brendan shares the odd chat. Velda, not so much. And now you know almost as much as I do."

"Thank you," I said, beginning to feel more orientated. Six flats, three couples, three singles. Nine people, including me. I could cope with that. "Very helpful."

"Now it's your turn." Dhruv shifted in his seat, crossed his leg over his knee, and turned to face me.

"My turn?"

"Yes. Who are you, and where are you from? Don't spare the gory details."

He smiled perceptively, knowing there must be a tale to tell. After all, most women in their mid-thirties are up to their knees in nappies and schoolwork or at least partnered up. I was neither. I gave him a short, sanitized version of my life, including my RAF police career, which satisfied him up to a point. And then he asked a further question and hit pay dirt.

"Where do you work now?"

I sighed. The question was inevitable, but I had no intention of telling Dhruv or anyone else that I'd lost my job, let alone the events leading up to it.

"I don't," I say.

"Oh?"

"I'm in between jobs."

"Ah. I see."

"And you?" I shot the question out more to head him off than because I was in any way interested.

"Oh, insurance," he said vaguely. "Not very interesting, but it pays well."

"Any vacancies going?" I quipped.

"Not at my company," he said. "But I'm glad you asked. I know where there's a job going, and he's been looking for a while."

Grab your copy...
vinci-books.com/flat-three